Praise for
VALERIE WOLZIEN
and her novels

"Valerie Wolzien is a consummate crime writer. Her heroines sparkle as they sift through clues and stir up evidence in the darker, deadly side of suburbia."

—MARY DAHEIM

"Wit is Wolzien's strong suit. . . . Her portrayal of small-town life will prompt those of us in similar situations to agree that we too have been there and done that."

—The Mystery Review

By Valerie Wolzien
Published by Fawcett Books:

THE
STUDENT
BODY

VALERIE WOLZIEN

FAWCETT GOLD MEDAL • NEW YORK

A Fawcett Gold Medal Book
Published by The Ballantine Publishing Group
Copyright © 1999 by Valerie Wolzien

www.randomhouse.com/BB/

Library of Congress Catalog Card Number: 99-94296

ISBN 0-449-15037-2

Manufactured in the United States of America

First Edition: August 1999

10 9 8 7 6 5 4 3 2

For Chuck and Sharon
Best wishes for a grand future together

PART I

STUDENT ORIENTATION

ONE

THE FIRST TIME SUSAN HENSHAW WENT TO SCHOOL, SHE wore a red plaid dress with a white piqué collar. Dark green anklets and heavy brown oxfords covered feet callused from a summer spent barefoot. By the time she left the house, the black velveteen bow her mother had tied in her hair was sliding southward. In her Dale Evans lunch box (her newest and proudest possession) there was a pimento cheese sandwich wrapped in wax paper, a banana, a bag containing three Fig Newtons, and a thermos of milk. At lunchtime she threw up after finishing the third Newton.

Forty-five years later, on the first day of her return to school, Susan wore jeans and a red silk shirt. Soft Italian leather loafers covered a recent pedicure. Heavy earrings of gold and amber hung from her ears. She wore a black leather backpack (bought on a recent vacation in Spain); inside was a bottle of French spring water, an Anjou pear, a Mont Blanc pen, two pencils, three blank notebooks, a makeup bag, and a Gucci wallet.

"And, I swear, I spent most of the day trying not to throw up," Susan announced to Kathleen Gordon, her closest friend, as she slung the backpack onto the bench in a booth at the Hancock Inn and slid in beside it.

"What happened?" Kathleen sat down across from her and pushed her blond hair up off her shoulders as she spoke.

"Well, in the first place, I was seriously underdressed." Susan twisted around, looking for their waitress.

"Susan, that's not possible! I see college kids all over the place. Half of them look like they're homeless, for heaven's sake. My kids' sitter goes to that college and all I ever see her

3

in is torn jeans and horrible seventies polyester shirts that she buys at a thrift shop. How could you possibly have been underdressed?"

"Not enough holes," Susan muttered, waving at their waitress.

"In your jeans? Well, I certainly wouldn't consider that underdressed."

"In my body. I only have my ears pierced once—each ear once, I mean. I guess that's twice."

"Oh, yes, I've seen those young women with earrings all the way up to the top of their ears. . . ."

"And in their eyebrows, and lips, and noses, and . . . and places I couldn't see. In one of my classes there were two young men in the front row comparing the rings in their tongues! And studs! Do you know that it's chic to put big studs in your body? These kids will have those holes forever. Of course, they think nothing of getting tattoos, so I guess permanent alterations don't matter. And you wouldn't believe those tattoos—"

"Susan, our waitress is here." Kathleen interrupted the diatribe. "Would you like a glass of wine or something?"

"I'd like a margarita. A large one. Salt. Rocks. Very, very large."

"I could ask the bartender to make you a double," the waitress offered. "Although our margaritas are pretty big, and I'm not sure we have any glasses that a double would fit in. Why don't I just bring you two drinks at the same time?" she suggested brightly.

Susan was exhausted but not so exhausted that she didn't care whether or not her friends and neighbors might see her drinking from two glasses at once. "Don't bother. I'll just order a second. And maybe a third. And I'll have a bottle of wine with dinner."

"I'll have a glass of merlot now," Kathleen ordered before Susan could claim the contents of both the bar and the wine cellar.

"And maybe you could bring us one of those big platters of antipasto, with extra olive oil. And some bread, please."

"I'll just get this part of your order in to the kitchen. Then I'll be right back with those drinks." The waitress dashed off.

"Wonder why she's hurrying so," Susan said.

"She probably thought we look as though we could use those drinks," Kathleen suggested diplomatically.

"You mean I look as though I could use a drink," Susan corrected her. "And if she thinks that, she's right. I do. Oh, Kathleen, it wasn't anything like I thought it would be."

Kathleen, who had spent much of the summer listening to Susan's hopes and fears regarding her return to school, waited quietly to hear the entire story.

"In the first place, you won't believe what I'm taking."

"Your classes? I thought you'd already made that decision. Introduction to Public Relations, Child Psychology, Introduction to Speech Therapy, and, for fun, some literature class that fit into your schedule."

"Introduction to Speech Pathology, not Speech Therapy. Not that it makes any difference. It was filled. All the classes I wanted to take were filled by the time I got to registration. All except my lit class. And I think I understand why that class was still open."

"Why?"

"The professor is a slave driver. It's my first class on Wednesday morning. Between now and then I'm supposed to have read a seven-hundred-page novel. *Wives and Daughters* by Elizabeth Gaskell." She looked at the large frosty glass their waitress had just placed on the table in front of her. "I shouldn't drink this. I should be home studying." Then she leaned back in her seat and started to laugh. "I can't believe the words coming out of my own mouth! Do you have any idea how many years it's been since I said that?"

Kathleen laughed, too. "Feels good, doesn't it?"

"I guess so." Susan picked up the glass and licked a bit of the salty rim before sipping the cool liquid. "In fact, it feels wonderful. I've thought for so long that everyone around me is doing something—going back to work, still raising kids, or just passionately involved with a hobby or craft. Now I can see my own life moving along. Of course, I don't know what

I'm going to tell my kids if I flunk the entire first semester of my long-awaited return to college."

"You're not going to flunk anything." Kathleen picked up her goblet. "What classes did you end up taking?"

"Creative Writing, Astronomy, Minor Victorian Women Writers, and Italian."

Kathleen laughed. "I thought you were going to take practical courses, courses that might lead to a career."

Susan grimaced. "I know. But last night I couldn't sleep and I got up to go through the catalogue one last time. I noticed the course on Victorian writers and I've always wanted to study Elizabeth Gaskell. And then the writing class sounded interesting. I suppose it could lead to a career in writing," she added quickly. "And Italian is practical. It's a skill."

"Italian literature?"

"No, the language. It's supposed to be easy. Conversational rather than written. Or something." She grimaced. "I hope that doesn't mean I'm going to have to speak in front of the entire class."

"Speaking is what conversational usually means," Kathleen said gently. "But maybe they have one of those language labs where each student talks into a recorder of some sort."

"Maybe. I didn't mean to take it, but there was a cancellation and everyone was so anxious to grab the opening. I was the first in that line—by mistake—so I thought I should take advantage of it. Well," she said, shrugging, "I just signed up. It's probably the only class I'll actually use, if I live long enough to go to Italy again."

"It certainly would be useful to speak the language the next time you're there."

"Yes. I guess. And it might not be a terribly hard course."

"Maybe that's why it's such a popular class," Kathleen suggested.

"No, I think it's popular because the professor is absolutely adorable."

"Susan, do you realize you're grinning?"

"Just remembering my Italian professor. He really is one of the best-looking men I've ever met. He was helping out at registration this morning and introduced himself to me when

I signed up. He said his classes were informal and fun and all his students call him Paolo. To stop by his office as much as I need to . . . That he's always there to help. . . ." She frowned. "He was the only bright spot in an otherwise difficult day."

"The only cute teacher?" Kathleen asked.

"I don't actually know about that. I didn't meet any other teachers. I spent most of the day registering for classes. And picking up books at the college bookstore. And finding the auditorium. And looking for the ladies' room. I've never been in a place where they hide the ladies' rooms the way they do at that school."

"So how do you know you have homework for your Victorian women writers class?"

"After my registration went through, the computer printed out a list of books required for my courses. For that particular class, the book list included our first homework assignment."

"Wow. Homework before class starts. What's all this we keep hearing about standards slipping in colleges?"

"I just hope they've slipped enough to keep me from disgracing myself. Kathleen, do you think I was nuts to do this? I can hardly remember the names of old friends sometimes. How the hell am I going to memorize a foreign language, write anything even vaguely creative, memorize the shapes of the constellations, and say something—anything—intelligent about women writers in Victorian England?"

"Well . . ."

"I could have kept taking classes at the art center downtown," Susan muttered, draining her glass. "There's a whole new series starting on faux finishes."

"Didn't you tell me that Jed thought there were more than enough stenciled walls in your house?"

"Yes, but faux finishes are different." She frowned. "Aren't they?"

"Susan, you're doing exactly what you wanted to do. And you don't know how much I admire you for making this decision. It takes a lot of courage to start going to college again when you're fifty. But . . ."

"But what? You don't think I can do it, right?"

"But I thought you were going to take easy classes and . . . and classes that lead somewhere. Like toward a job."

"I know. I seem to be doing exactly the same thing I did when I was eighteen, taking classes that interest me rather than ones designed to help me enter the job market. Which is how I ended up being an English lit major. And then I got married and had kids and never did work." The huge platter of antipasto had been placed on the table; she speared a small slice of marinated eggplant and put it in her mouth. She chewed thoughtfully.

"Susan, we've been through this before. You could have done a lot of things. Heavens, half the people we know would have been happy to hire you as a party planner after Chrissy's wedding. And you could have gone into catering or possibly decorating. But you didn't want to do any of those things."

"They're things I love to do, but for myself. It's different when someone is paying you. You have to do what they want you to do. Of course, now I have to do what my professors want me to do—like all that reading in two days."

"The girl who sits for me says she only takes classes if she knows she can watch the main assignments on videotape."

Susan frowned. "Sounds like cheating to me. Besides, I love to read."

"She sure does." A deep voice interrupted their conversation. "It's my personal opinion that my wife is going back to college so she can read twenty-four hours a day, and since she has to do her homework, I won't be able to complain about it."

Susan returned her husband's kiss, then moved her backpack and slid over so he could sit down next to her. "You never complain about my reading. And don't think I don't appreciate it."

"You're home early, aren't you?" Kathleen asked Jed Henshaw, glancing over his shoulder.

"If you're looking for your husband, he's taking a later train," Jed explained. "I promised we'd order for him. He wants a steak, rare, a baked potato with butter, creamed spinach, and a mixed salad with blue cheese dressing."

"He'll have the grilled chicken breast with grilled vegetables and the mesclun salad with oil and vinegar," Kathleen insisted. She had married a man almost twenty years her senior and was busy taking care of him and their small two children.

"That's what he said you'd say."

"The doctor is worried about his cholesterol."

"So he told me. But this dinner is to celebrate my wife's return to college. Let's not talk about cholesterol. We should be discussing grade point averages and . . . and what?" Jed turned to Susan. "What are the kids talking about these days?"

Susan remembered the young men with their tongue jewelry. "You don't want to hear about that right before you eat."

"Susan, what could be worse than all the dead bodies we've talked about during meals over the years? And many of those discussions took place in this restaurant."

"True. And that's all going to end," Susan assured them. "I'm going to be too busy doing homework to investigate any murders."

She drained her glass and didn't notice the skeptical expressions on Jed's and Kathleen's faces.

TWO

TUESDAYS WERE GOING TO BE EASY, SUSAN DECIDED, lounging on the patio behind her house. The leaves were beginning to turn on the large split-leaf Japanese maple directly in front of her, and mounds of chrysanthemums and asters dominated the perennial border. A mug of coffee was on a nearby table. *Victorian Poetry and Poetics* lay on her lap, open to the poems of Christina Rossetti. She had only one class on her schedule today. Creative writing at noon. She had stayed up late last night finishing *Wives and Daughters* and had enjoyed it immensely. She'd be done with these poems before she left home today. Tonight she would review her class notes for Astronomy while stirring the wild mushroom risotto she was planning for dinner. Tuesdays were definitely going to be easy. She gave her textbook a fond pat and, leaning back, closed her eyes.

When she woke up, she realized that if she took the time to do her hair and put on makeup, she would be late for her first creative writing class. She got up and started to run.

"And I don't think I stopped running until about an hour ago. I swear, this is the first break I've had since Tuesday morning." Susan tucked a lock of hair in need of a shampoo behind her ear.

"You call this a break?" Kathleen yanked on the leash she held in a futile attempt to convince the little fur ball at the other end that barking at a pair of Dobermans was poor manners as well as an extremely foolish act for a six-month-old Scottish terrier. The two women had met in front of Wash and Dri Puppy Parlor, the most popular dog-grooming salon in Hancock. Clue, finished with her morning's ordeal, was looking her best, the sun gleaming on her silky golden coat. Licorice, the dog Alex and Alice Gordon had convinced their parents to buy, was on her way to her first appointment. Kathleen looked worried.

"I sure do," Susan said. "T.G.I.F. It's Friday and I'm going to take the night off! No textbooks. No homework."

"Maybe you should find a bar and go out and drink beer. That's what we did when I was in college," Kathleen suggested.

"I'm planning something much more interesting. Jed and I are going to go to dinner at that wonderful little French place in Greenwich and then I'm going to go home and take a long, hot bubble bath. And then early to bed. I can't wait." She yawned.

Kathleen looked at her carefully. "You do look a little tired. But not unhappy."

"Oh, my ego has taken a beating, but I'll survive."

"Let me get Licorice in for her appointment and then we can chat," Kathleen told her.

"Okay. I'm going to put Clue in the car and then pick up some things next door. Do you want to meet me there?"

"Great, see you in a few."

It really did take just a few minutes for Kathleen to place her puppy in the capable hands of the groomer. But those few minutes were enough for Susan to fill an entire basket with bottles and pots of potions, herbs, and vitamins.

"Susan, I didn't know you shopped in health food stores."

"Usually I don't, but I keep hearing about how these things can help your memory and I need all the help I can get."

Kathleen reached into the basket and pulled out a bottle of capsules. "Gingko biloba I've heard of, but some of these things are pretty weird. How do you know they won't make you ill?"

Susan shrugged. "As far as I can tell, the kids at school are living on this stuff. They all claim it improves their memory and gives them energy."

Kathleen read from the label of the bottle in her hand. " 'Cleans out the urinary tract as well,' according to this. Impressive."

Susan grabbed the bottle from her friend. "That's just a side benefit. I've been thinking about running again. You know, get the blood circulating and all . . . Why are you grinning? Are you laughing at me?"

"No, I'm appreciating you. I think it's wonderful how you're taking this so seriously. I'll bet you get straight A's."

"Don't mention grades. I'll be thrilled if I pass my first test."

"When is it?"

"Not for a few weeks. But every day in Italian seems like a test. The professor calls on each student to speak. And my astronomy teacher keeps threatening a spot quiz. We only have two tests in Minor Victorian Women Writers. A midterm and a final—but if I don't keep up with my reading, both will be impossible. I should at least start thinking about a topic for my term paper for that class. And I'm worried to death about my big assignment for creative writing. We have to write something each week—an essay, a poem, a character sketch. You know the type of thing. Some of them are read in front of the class during what is known as critique time . . . to the professor. The other students call it 'the misery moment.' "

"That's clever."

"Yes. Needless to say, I didn't think it up. I haven't had a clever thought since I signed up for the class. And that's strange," Susan continued. "Over the years I've had lots of ideas that seemed like they would be good short stories . . . or editorials on the op-ed page of the *Times* . . . or even novels. But once I walked in the door of that class, my brain seemed to turn itself off. And I can't imagine how I'm going to complete my big assignment."

"What is it?"

"A short story—six thousand words or more—or the first three chapters of a novel in progress. The assignment is to use an interesting event from our own lives, make enough changes so that it is unrecognizable, and turn it into a cohesive work of fiction. Then . . . What are you doing?"

"Adding some ginseng to your basket. It's supposed to increase your energy—and I think you're going to need it."

Jed and Susan had the best seats in the house, a small table in an intimate alcove. Candlelight bounced off heavy silver and Baccarat crystal. Their wineglasses were filled. A basket of fragrant rolls sat next to a tiny plate piled with butter roses. Jed was enjoying a lobster bisque so good that he was having to restrain himself not to pick up the bowl and drain it. Susan was falling asleep over her pâté de foie gras, the crisp crust of baguette slipping from her hand onto the floor.

"Madam has had a hard week," their waiter announced, dashing to their table with a dustpan and a hand broom.

"Yes, she has," Jed agreed, waiting until they were alone again to reach across the table and nudge his sleeping wife. "Susan, would you like to go home?"

She blinked a few times and looked down at her plate. "Go home? Of course not! I haven't even started my appetizer!" And she picked up her fork and knife and dug in. "You know, I think maybe those pills I'm taking are beginning to work. I know they say it takes months for herbal remedies to take effect, but I feel a whole lot more alert in just a few hours."

"Almost as if you'd had a short nap?" Jed mumbled the question.

"What?" Susan looked up from her food.

"Nothing." He smiled at her. "I'm really proud of you for going back to school like this, Susan. A lot of people wouldn't have had the courage to make such a big change. Especially at your age. Not that fifty is old," he added quickly, reaching for his wineglass.

"Sure feels that way sometimes," Susan said. It was becoming obvious to her that both her husband and her best friend were amazed that she had gone back to school. What she wondered was whether this indicated a certain lack of faith in her mental capabilities. She picked up her wineglass and looked up at Jed.

And then over his shoulder at the couple sharing a table across the room. They seemed familiar. She frowned, hoping to put names to their faces, but gingko biloba aside, it didn't happen. The couple was well dressed, the man in a dark suit of European cut and the woman wearing a black slip dress, possibly a bit light for this chilly time of the year, but looking fabulous on her healthy, lean body. Perhaps they were members of the Hancock Field Club? The woman looked much too young to have children the same age as Susan's kids, so a PTA connection was out. Ditto one of the innumerable sports teams Chad had played on in the local schools. Susan stared at the fabulous earrings the woman was wearing; she seemed to recognize the style. Perhaps the woman had been one of Chrissy's art teachers. Somehow Susan could see her in an academic setting . . .

She glanced back at the man and the answer came to her. And it came as a surprise. "Jed, how much is this dinner going to cost?"

He picked up a roll, buttered it, and considered her question. "A lot, and we sure didn't order anything like the most expensive wine on the list. I'd guess about one twenty—maybe more. Depends on whether you want dessert. I remember when we moved to Connecticut, there wasn't a single restaurant in the state that would dare to charge New York City prices. Now, more and more do. But I'm not worried—

you're going to get another degree, find a fabulous job, and support me in my old age, right?"

"One thing at a time. I have to pass my first quiz in astronomy first. But, Jed, do you think a professor could afford to eat here?"

"Why? Are you thinking of becoming an academic?"

"No. But one of my professors is at a table on the other side of the room. Don't turn and look!"

"I thought I might get a peek at this Italian guy you're so nuts about."

"It's not Paolo. It's Professor Hoyer. My creative writing teacher. I told you about him."

"He's the one who scares you."

"It's not just me. The entire class is terrified of him. He gives such strange assignments and keeps talking about the creativity within. I hope I'm not the only person who is worried that there just might not be any creativity within. Besides, I overheard some older—well, they're younger, of course, but they've been around campus longer—students talking and he's known to have a rotten temper. But guess who he's with?"

"Who?"

"My lab partner! From astronomy!"

"So?"

"So they're not married to each other!"

"Susan, this is a very expensive, very romantic restaurant. I'll bet more than a few of the couples here aren't married."

"But he's married. His wife is a writer. A real one. She's been published in *The New Yorker*. He mentioned her on the first day of class. What is he doing here with a student?"

"Maybe that's why he's willing to spend the big bucks," Jed said, kidding her. Their main courses were arriving and they both stopped to admire the food. Jed had chosen salmon with sorrel sauce. Susan was having free-range lamb chops (she couldn't help imagining those little pieces of meat hopping about a green meadow). An elegant assortment of immature vegetables was fanned out around each selection.

"Looks delicious." Susan speared a baby carrot and, reaching across the table, dipped it in the puddle of sauce on her husband's plate before putting it in her mouth. "It's delicious," she told him.

"Would you like to trade with me?" he offered as usual.

"No, I just wanted a taste. Do you want some lamb?"

"No, thanks." He ate a few bites of his fish before they continued the conversation. "Why are you so interested in the private lives of your professor and your lab partner? They could be friends or they could be in the middle of a torrid affair. You've known that to happen before, right? Why the sudden interest?"

Susan rolled her eyes. "Maybe because it's familiar. There's been so much new this week. Which has been great," she added quickly. "It was what I wanted. But . . . but it's nice to have something to think about that isn't so . . . so different. I mean, let's face it, a professor having an affair with a student has been going on for as long as there have been universities. When I was in college, my freshman-year roommate was determined to sleep with every male professor she had."

Jed looked up from his salmon. "And did she?"

"Nope. She fell in love with a player on the hockey team. I don't know how she had the time to meet him; she was taking extra courses. Anyway, they got married over Christmas vacation and I never heard from her again. I never even got a thank-you note for the wedding present I sent her." She glanced back at the couple as she spoke. "Things have changed. A male professor having a sexual relationship with a female student is considered sexual harassment by a lot of people these days."

"Funny, you hear a lot more about female teachers and male students. In the news and all."

"That's because it's rarer. You know, there are fewer women who are professors and probably even fewer interested in young men. Don't you think?"

"Susan, like Freud, I would never even think of suggesting that I know what women want."

"I wonder if he really said that."

"Well, next semester you can take a psychology class and find out. Or we could ask your professor—just because it isn't his field, doesn't mean he won't know."

"Jed! I'm hoping he doesn't see me. If he is having an affair with a student, I sure don't want him to think I know about it."

"Why not? Maybe you could blackmail him into giving you a good grade."

She was right. He had no faith at all in her abilities. She opened her mouth to protest and decided instead to finish her meal. She was thinking about ordering the crème caramel, one of her favorite desserts. She figured she had burned about a million extra calories that week making her way around campus. "You know, I'm not the only person on campus who's . . . ah, around fifty. Some of the students are retired people."

"I understand that's a trend all over the country. Colleges and universities expanded in the sixties to accommodate the baby boomers and now they're trying to fill those classrooms with nontraditional students."

"Yes. I think it makes for a nice mix." What she really thought was that the kids were fresh, fast, and, so far, completely lacking in any interest in a "voice of experience"—at least not when it was her voice. But both her children were in their early twenties; she was accustomed to being ignored.

"There is actually a support group for older students. I keep seeing notices about it on bulletin boards around campus. I'm thinking of going to the first meeting."

"Might be fun." Jed seemed more interested in his food than in what his wife was saying.

"You know, I took a class at night when I was in college," Susan mused, rearranging the vegetables on her plate with her fork. "I think the subject was actually women's roles in nineteenth-century American literature. I remember struggling through *The Last of the Mohicans*, *Uncle Tom's Cabin*, something by Edith Wharton, and more than one Henry James novel."

"Interesting," Jed said in a manner that made Susan think that, as a European history major, he didn't care about any of these works.

"But what I remember most about that class was that it was held in the evening. And that about a half-dozen middle-aged women were taking it. Because the class was at night, I suppose."

"And?"

"And they were awful students. At least that's what I thought at the time. They kept saying things like, well, When you get to my age, you'll understand. Blah, blah, blah. I thought they were just awful," she repeated.

"So you won't be like that. Right?"

Susan looked up at her husband. "Jed, I hate to admit it, but I'm afraid I'm going to be exactly like that. Today I found myself using that exact same phrase in my Victorian lit class. In my head though."

"You mean you didn't say it out loud."

"No, I haven't started speaking up in any of my classes—except Italian. But, Jed, I've become one of those women I looked down on thirty years ago."

Jed, who had lived through many phases, from "Do you think I'm getting fat?" to "Do you think I'm beginning to look like my mother?" by using the same adequate phrase, used it again now. "Don't worry, hon. When I look at you, I always see the bride I married."

It didn't work this time.

"Bull," she muttered under her breath.

"Excuse me?" Their attentive waiter dashed to their table. "Does madam need something?"

"Just a new brain and a new body," she answered.

"Pardon?"

"Never mind. Just bring me a crème caramel for dessert."

THREE

"I DROP A COURSE OR TWO AFTER THE THIRD WEEK OF classes—at the latest date possible. It's easy to find a reason. Too heavy a course load. The professor has it in for me. A bad case of the flu the second week of class and I'm too far behind to catch up. You know the type of thing."

The attractive young man speaking was the center of attention. He ran his hand through his shoulder-length blond hair, favored one of the four young women crowded around him with a smile, and continued. "My parents don't really give a damn whether or not I take a full load as long as I pass. And one semester they didn't even realize I'd gotten a tuition refund. That year I flew to Cancún for spring break."

Susan, sitting at the next table in the Student Union, nursed her cup of awful coffee and wondered if the smiles on the female audience's faces indicated appreciation of the young man's appearance or approval of the way he was scamming his parents. She resisted the urge to break into the group with a lecture.

"Ah, Signora Henshaw. Susan, yes? You are sitting alone and looking so . . . so thoughtful."

"Not thoughtful. Old." She looked up into the attractive face of her Italian professor.

"You feel old? But a beautiful woman is never old. And you know why? Because we Italians know how to appreciate the mature beauty."

"I . . ." She didn't know what to say. Was he flirting with her?

"May I sit down?" An elegant sweep of his hand indicated a chair at her table. "I prefer, not unnaturally, to spend my free time with beautiful women."

"Of course!" He was flirting with her! Susan could hardly believe it. Not that men didn't flirt with her sometimes. But usually it was a party or some sort of country-club function when they had had just a tad too much to drink.

"I haven't seen you on campus before this year, have I?" He looked around and Susan wondered if he was expecting a waiter to appear with a cappuccino and a selection of pastries. In this room, which reeked of decades of French fries and greasy burgers, it was an unlikely scenario.

"No, I just started taking classes this semester. I've been out of school for . . . for over two decades." That sounded better than "slightly less than three decades."

"And how are you enjoying your classes?" His dark eyes peered into hers as though he expected to be enthralled by her answer.

"Frankly, I feel stupid a lot of the time," she admitted.

"Like a child."

"Well, sort of." A very, very old child.

"*Bene!* Good!" He waved his arms in the air in some sort of gesture of appreciation for her. "You see, when we are children, we learn new things all the time. All the world is new. And when we get . . . ah, older . . . learning is a more novel experience and it makes us feel like children again. Sometimes foolish children, to be sure. But it is good. You should embrace this feeling and go on. I think," he added, leaning closer, "that you may turn out to be one of my star pupils. I think you have an Italian soul."

"Well, I make pretty good pasta."

"As do I. Perhaps we can compare recipes some evening. I know a small trattoria in the city. It is owned by a friend. We could have dinner there and talk."

"I'm awfully busy these days."

"Of course. But we could, of course, order in Italian. It would be like homework. Extra credit." He was too sophisticated to leer, but Susan got the general idea.

"That might be fun," she admitted. "I . . . I have to get to my next class."

"*Sì. Ciao, bella* Susan."

Susan left the Student Union feeling less like a child than an adolescent who had no idea of how to act on her first date. She mused on the situation all the way across campus and up the flight of worn granite steps to the front door of the old Connecticut Science Building, where her astronomy class was located. The science department had moved twice. Once in the sixties when an ultramodern laboratory complex had been built on the other side of the campus and then again ten years ago when another science building and laboratory had joined the second one. But the need for space had always been too profound to tear down the original. Now the classes that were held there were for students trying to fulfill their science requirement as painlessly as possible—and for those like Susan, who had stupidly thought astronomy sounded exotic, interesting, and fun, almost like one of those learning vacations some people always seemed to be taking. In fact, astronomy was turning out to be difficult and incredibly boring.

Who would have guessed, she thought, pushing open the classroom door, that astronomy was basically math and physics?

Professor Madeline Forbes-Robertson was sitting on a stool by the window. She turned and glared at Susan. Susan smiled weakly and hurried past the front row of empty chairs toward the only seat available in the back of the room. When she sat down, she discovered why. The chair wobbled dangerously.

"I'm afraid you will have to observe the class from a spot closer to me, Mrs. Henshaw." Professor Forbes-Robertson pronounced each syllable. "Be assured, I don't assault my students."

There was a nervous tittering as Susan, bumping into more things than she would have thought possible, made her way to a seat directly under her professor's nose.

When Professor Forbes-Robertson introduced herself on the first day of class, she had mentioned (proudly) that she had received her doctorate during the same month her third child entered college. From this Susan had assumed that the professor would feel some sympathy for a woman returning to school after more than twenty-five years at home. Her assumption had been wrong. If anything, Susan got the impression that Professor Forbes-Robertson, as the young man in the Student Union had phrased it, "had it in" for her.

"Now let's start on our next chapter's work. As you know if you've been keeping track of our progress in the class syllabus, you will be quizzed on the first section next Monday, but since we've gone over that material once, I see no reason we shouldn't continue onward before then."

Susan could think of about a million reasons why she, at least, could use another review, but she kept quiet and flipped her notebook open.

For the next forty minutes she was so busy taking notes and trying to follow the flowing diagrams on the chalkboard that there was no time to think about the quiz. Okay, that's the way it should have been. The reality, Susan had to admit to herself, was that the more confusing the material became, the more likely she was to drift off into thoughts of what to have for dinner and whether or not she needed a new winter coat.

The buzzer announcing the end of the class was ignored by the professor, and students wrote furiously, trying to get her final thoughts on paper. "And, remember, Thursday night we'll be taking our first look at the stars in the college planetarium. I hope you're all familiar with the way our old telescope works and what you have to accomplish. It was on that handout I passed out last week. Each team has very little time to complete their appointed task. I'm sure you'll all want to show up for the entire time. Watching the mistakes of others can be a valid learning experience." Without further explanation, Professor Forbes-Robertson swept from the room as gracefully as was possible while wearing Birkenstocks.

"I don't know about you, but I sure wish we weren't the second pair at the telescope."

Susan turned and discovered that her lab partner, garbed in jeans and a black T-shirt instead of the silky dress she had worn at dinner on Friday night, had slipped into the chair next to her. She wished she could remember her name. "The second pair?"

"Yeah, it's on the last sheet of that handout. The one we're supposed to have memorized by tomorrow night, apparently. The list of who looks when. You and I are up second. I don't know about you, but I sure as hell hope the first pair knows what they're doing—or maybe that they don't. Then good old Forbes-Robertson will have to spend lots of time explaining and we won't look stupid." She stared at Susan. "Or maybe you know the material already and you're not worried about looking like a fool?"

"I don't know anything," Susan admitted, still puzzled about what to call this young woman. Her named started with an M. Maggie? Marion? Mary? That was it! Mary. "I haven't even glanced at that handout, Mary. I thought the papers she gave us the first day of class were the schedules for tests and quizzes."

"The first three pages were. Then six pages about the telescope and an explanation of our first viewing opportunity. At least, I think that's what she called it. Say, do you want to get a cup of coffee and do a quick review of everything?"

"Yes, but not now. I have a scheduled meeting with my creative writing professor. We're supposed to discuss ideas for my short story." Susan gathered up her books as she spoke. Her short story? She couldn't believe she was talking about her short story. Of course, all she had right now was a short list of ideas to write about. She grinned, remembering her favorite idea, and then saw the serious expression on her partner's face.

"Oh, who are you taking it from?"

The question had been asked in an overly careful manner and Susan answered it in the same way. "Professor Hoyer." *The man you were eating with on Friday night,* she reminded her silently.

"I hear he's pretty good," the young woman said. "What do you think?"

Susan assumed she was asking for an opinion of the professor, not of her ability to lie convincingly. "He seems interesting." She was, in fact, telling the truth. In class he was almost weird, but there were things about his personal life—including his relationship with this woman—that could turn out to be fascinating. "So when do you want to meet?" she asked when there was no response to her comment.

"Later this afternoon?"

The room was filling up with people, probably students taking the next class, and Susan dumped the last of her papers in the backpack at her feet.

She'd finally gotten her schedule down pat. "Great. How about three o'clock at the Student Union?" She was still getting a kick out of casually mentioning the Student Union.

Apparently, it held no such appeal for her partner. "Not there. All those young kids. The place makes me feel like I'm about a hundred years old." (Susan guessed that she wasn't even thirty.) "I know a spot near campus." She mentioned a coffeehouse Susan had passed a few times. "Three-thirty?"

"I'll be there." Susan stood and, turning quickly, ran into an exceptionally good-looking student. "I . . ." She looked up and felt herself begin to blush. "I'm sorry. I . . . I have to go!" And grabbing the pack at her feet and flinging it over her shoulder, she dashed out of the room, angry with herself.

She had gone back to school, but she didn't have to act like a silly schoolgirl!

Susan sat alone in the coffee shop. Fearing she might have difficulties finding a parking place in the university vicinity, she had left her car in the lot for commuting students and walked there. (When Susan had gone to college in the sixties, it was a rare student who drove his or her own car to class. These days cars were as common on campus as peace signs had been in her day.)

She had arrived at Professor Hoyer's office on time for her conference, but he had been on the phone. To be more precise, he had been yelling into the phone, cursing like a sailor at the person on the other end of the line. His mood hadn't improved a bit when Susan nervously dumped the contents of her backpack on the floor in his office, trying to find her notebook.

Having stuffed everything back into her pack without looking at it, Susan had returned to the hallway. "Don't worry," the department secretary, whose desk happened to be located right outside his door, said to her. "After he vents a bit, he calms right down."

Susan had decided not to wait around to discover if this

was true. The professor had liberal office hours. She could meet with him another time.

The clock on the wall of the coffee shop declared it to be four o'clock, and Susan, deciding she would wait fifteen more minutes, ordered another espresso and reached into her backpack. She might as well get back to Rossetti.

Except that her hand, scrounging for the heaviest book in the pack, came up with *Theoretical Diagnoses of Psychopathic Personalities in Deviant Populations*, not *Victorian Poetry and Poetics*. For a moment, she wondered if she had forgotten one of the classes she was taking. Just for a moment. Then she yanked the pack off the back of her chair, plopped it on the table, and discovered that it wasn't her backpack at all.

During the weekend, Susan had replaced her new leather pack with the old L.L.Bean one Chad had used in junior high. (After she spent more than an hour removing embroidered patches bearing the logos of now-defunct heavy metal bands.) She wouldn't have admitted it publicly, but that aging, ripped-up pack made her feel more like a regular student—and much less like an upper-middle-class housewife.

While this pack was the same brand and color as Chad's, it certainly didn't contain any of the same things. The texts were from different courses. There was no bottle of water. No fruit. No bottle of gingko biloba. No makeup bag. No hairbrush . . . Well, she corrected herself, pulling a pink plastic object from the bottom of the pile, there was a hairbrush. But it sure wasn't hers—not a gray hair among the entire mix. She leaned back in her chair and stared at the unfamiliar items. She might have left a book on the floor of Professor Hoyer's office. She might have picked up a stray pen or two. But she couldn't possibly have completely exchanged the contents of her pack in such a short time. This was someone else's pack. No doubt about it.

She continued to scrounge. If there was a wallet or some kind of identification, she could find the person she had taken this pack from—and maybe the same person had hers. Realizing she needed her books to do her homework tonight, she stood, dumped the contents of the pack on the table, and sorted through the mess. She put textbooks in one pile, notebooks in another, the rest in a third pile. Two key rings, pens and pencils, two combs, the hairbrush, three tubes of Chap Stick, a single amber and silver earring, and a Swatch with a broken band offered no indication of their owner's identity.

Susan went through the books, hoping to find their owner's name, but the hardbacks had been bought used and many different names had been written on the inside covers. The paperbacks weren't marked. She frowned and started opening the notebooks. All she was positive about when she had finished was that the owner of this pack was taking an incredibly heavy course load. Two advanced psychology courses, statistics, social psychology, and astronomy. And, Susan decided, this pack's owner was probably even more desperate to get it back than she was to see her own again.

Her pack, she realized, would reveal its ownership. Not only was her wallet inside, but each and every one of her texts and notebooks was carefully identified with her name, address, and phone number. All she had to do, she thought, was head home and wait for a phone call. As she pulled her keys from her jacket pocket, she realized that if she had put them in her pack, she might have discovered her mistake sooner.

There were no messages on her answering machine. Susan decided a little exercise might be in order. Clue, her large golden retriever, seemed to agree. Leash held between her teeth, the dog's eyes were pleading.

"Give me a break," Susan muttered, attaching the lead to the dog's collar. "I happen to know that you had an extra long walk this morning. I was the one on the other end of the leash, remember?"

Clue stretched toward the doorway, giving the impression that she had been locked in the cellar for at least a decade.

"Okay. Let's go. But if I don't get my work done on time, you'd better be prepared to swear you ate my homework!" Susan warned, as the dog pulled her out of the house.

It was a gorgeous day. A few leaves were just beginning to fall and Clue pounced on them eagerly. Susan, unable to do any homework for the first time all week, allowed her mind to wander on to other, more frivolous subjects. By the time she arrived home, tired but relaxed, she had decided to treat herself to a new pair of black boots this year. Clue dashed in the door as eagerly as she'd left it a while ago. Susan noticed the flashing light on the answering machine when she hung up the leash. She pressed the play button, expecting to hear the breathless voice of a young female student announcing the discovery of Susan's backpack. Instead a familiar male voice came on.

"Susan, I think we have a problem," Brett Fortesque, Hancock's chief of police, announced without a preliminary greeting. "I just got a call from a colleague in another department. It seems your backpack was just found. It was lying on the floor next to a dead body. Susan, you'd better call me as soon as you get this message."

FOUR

SHE WAS TRYING TO REWIND THE TAPE SO THAT SHE COULD listen to Brett's message again when the doorbell pealed. Clue, remembering her self-imposed position as official greeter of the Henshaw family, was instantly alert, tail wagging, tongue dripping drool on the carpet. Susan answered the door.

"Hi, Brett, come on in."

He glanced at the answering machine as he passed the hall table. "You got my message?"

"Yes. Who is it?"

"We haven't got a positive ID yet, but we're assuming she's Meredith Kenny. At least that's the name of the young woman who rents the apartment where she was found."

"I don't think I know anyone named Meredith. What does she look like?"

"I haven't seen her. I was called by the local police when she was discovered. Only because your bag was found nearby. The police thought you were dead until an observant young officer noticed the age on the driver's license. Apparently, the dead woman looked closer to thirty than fifty."

"Oh." For just a moment Susan envied the dead woman; she sure would like someone to say the same about her. "You said her name was Meredith?"

"They think so. Do you know her?"

"Maybe. My lab partner is named Mary. At least that's what I thought she told me. But she might have said Merry and that might be short for Meredith."

"Your lab partner?"

"Yes, in my astronomy class," she explained. "It would make sense. She's a junior . . ." Susan stopped speaking, remembering the textbooks she'd discovered in the backpack now sitting nearby on a Hitchcock chair. "On the other hand . . ."

"What?"

"Well, there was an astronomy text in the pack I picked up."

"You have someone else's backpack?" Brett asked, looking confused.

"Yes. It looked a lot like mine. Probably a case of mistaken identity. They may have been sitting close together and either I picked up the wrong one or the person who has mine did and then the other person just assumed the wrong one was hers. If you know what I mean."

"Only because I'm used to the way you think. Of course it might not have been an accident."

"Why not?"

"Susan, the young woman didn't die naturally. She was murdered."

"You're sure?"

"Yes. She was strangled."

"With what?"

Brett bent down to pet Clue before he answered. "With the strap of your backpack."

"I . . . Oh." The idea of her personal property being used to kill someone was shocking. She took a deep breath and then continued. "So that's why the police looked in it right away."

"Possibly. Or maybe they didn't have to open it. The contents could have been spilled during the murder."

"I suppose." Susan frowned. "You know, I don't want to sound self-centered, but I need my books and notebooks to do my homework."

"I doubt if you're going to get them back anytime soon. This didn't happen in Hancock. The police over there don't know you. Those guys are going to be playing by the book."

"You mean I won't be getting any special attention."

"Exactly."

Susan frowned again. She could buy more books, but how was she going to replace her notes and the class handouts? She needed a dose of caffeine. "Do you want a cup of coffee?"

"Excellent idea. Just let me call in first. And why don't we look through that backpack you brought home?"

"Fine with me. Come on, Clue. Time for a cookie." The dog was crashing through the swinging door to the kitchen before Brett had dialed the phone.

Susan headed straight for her coffeemaker. It was her usual route, and she wouldn't have been surprised to discover a path worn in the ceramic tile floor. Clue had other ideas, prancing back and forth in front of the large white ceramic container labeled Fromage, which, years ago, Susan had hand-carried home from her first Paris vacation. Found to be too large to fit on even the biggest refrigerator shelf, it had been relegated to a cupboard in the basement until Clue's arrival. It was exactly the right size for the supply of Milk-Bone biscuits to which the dog was addicted.

Susan tossed a cookie to the animal and grabbed the bag of coffee beans. By the time Brett entered the room, backpack in hand, the kitchen smelled like fresh coffee and Clue was begging again.

"I thought you promised her a dog biscuit," he commented, heaving the pack onto the kitchen table.

"She's had three," Susan answered. She placed a steaming mug in front of him and turned back to the counter to slice a loaf of pumpkin bread studded with dates and pecans. After she'd cut an ample supply, she returned to the table with the bread and a second mug of coffee. "I already went through that," she said as he began to empty the pack.

"So you know who it belongs to."

"No. There weren't any names that I could find. Well, actually, there were too many names," she added, and explained about the used books whose flyleafs bore evidence of their previous owners. "But it certainly could belong to Merry."

Brett took a sip of coffee and reached for a thick slice of pumpkin bread. "Hmm." He was opening his mouth to speak when his beeper began to do its thing. "Damn." He glanced down at the message. "Mind if I use your phone?" he asked, moving toward it with the assurance of a man who knows what the answer will be before he's even finished asking the question.

"Sure." Susan, reluctant to eavesdrop, headed toward the basement stairs. She might as well use the time to figure out what she and Jed were going to have for dinner. She was walking back to the kitchen, Tupperware bowl of frozen chicken noodle soup in one hand and frozen loaf of garlic bread in the other, when she caught Brett's last words.

". . . I'll bring her in, but I think you're making a big mistake." He hung up the phone and turned to Susan.

"You look angry. Anything wrong?"

"They want me to bring you in."

Susan started to laugh. "You're kid—" She looked more closely at her friend. "You're not kidding, are you?"

"Susan—"

"You're not kidding? You're going to arrest me?" She could feel her heart beating and her face flushing.

"Susan—"

"Brett, you know me." She grabbed his hand. "You know I—"

"Susan, there's no reason to overreact here."

"Brett, it's not overreacting to get upset when you're under arrest."

"Susan, you're not—"

"It's stupid. It's really stupid."

"Susan." He grabbed her shoulders and shook her gently.

"I know how upset you must be and I know you didn't kill anyone. Of course you're not under arrest. They just want to see you. Probably for questioning. And if I don't bring you in, someone you don't know will. I'm going to give you time to finish your coffee and call a lawyer. Then we'll drive very slowly to the police station, and, I hope, by the time we arrive, you will have told me everything you did this morning, so we will have an alibi and you'll be back home for dinner. Okay?"

She frowned and pulled herself from his grasp. "Couldn't I run away? You know, just vanish until this is all over?"

"You could. But it would probably make things a lot more difficult—for me as well as for you. Besides, you didn't kill anyone. It's a mistake that your backpack is there. All we have to do is prove it."

"Well, today I—"

"First call a lawyer. In fact, first call this guy." He grabbed a piece of paper from the pad near the phone and wrote down a name and number. "Call now and insist on talking to him. Don't take no for an answer."

"Who is he?"

"The best criminal lawyer in the state. You wouldn't believe the guilty people who are walking the street right now because of this guy."

"But I'm not guilty of anything!"

"Of course not, but it never hurts to have the best on your side. Call."

She called, but the man responsible for so many guilty people walking the streets was out of the office. His secretary assured Susan that the message would be passed along as soon as possible. She hung up and explained the situation to Brett.

"Okay. Do you want to call Jed before we leave?"

"No. If I'm going to be home as soon as all this is cleared up, there's no reason to worry him."

"Fine. I can always call if there . . . if you're going to be late for dinner."

"Just let me get washed and put on some fresh makeup and then I'll be ready to go." She tugged at her earlobes. "And I want to put on some earrings."

"You don't need—"

"It will make me feel better."

"Fine," he repeated.

Susan hurried upstairs to her bedroom. She really did want to wash and put on fresh makeup—and change her clothes for that matter, but she kept wondering what else she should do. She wasn't so naïve as to believe that her innocence would protect her from being arrested. And if that happened, Brett would take care of telling Jed. And she could, she supposed, assume that the lawyer he had recommended would protect her rights. But if these were her last moments of freedom, there must be things she should be doing. She looked around her large bedroom as though expecting to find the answer to her dilemma stenciled on the walls.

And found nothing. Shrugging, she headed into the bathroom to clean up. Ten minutes later she was back in her bedroom, rummaging in the bottom drawer of her nightstand, when Brett yelled up to her.

"Susan! If we don't get going, those guys are going to think something is up."

"I'm coming. I'm coming." She was staring in the mirror when Brett appeared in the doorway. "I was just on my way," she insisted, turning and walking past him and out the door.

"What about your earrings?"

Susan touched her naked earlobes. "I . . . I just decided there was no reason to wear a lot of jewelry."

"That's probably smart," Brett agreed, following her down the stairs. "Why don't you grab a pad and pencil? You can write down everything you've done since . . . well, since you last had your backpack and who can testify that you were doing what you say you were. Then we'll have something to give these guys."

"I have my Filofax . . . No, I don't. It was in my pack."

"Any notebook will do."

"Yes, but that means the police have my Filofax. They won't look in it, will they?"

"If it was in your backpack, I'm sure they already have."

"Brett, that's invasion of privacy. My privacy."

"Susan, it's a murder investigation. You know what happens to privacy during a murder investigation."

She frowned and opened the drawer in the hall table. "I think I saw a notepad in here the other day . . . Yup, here it is."

"Well, bring it along and let's hit the road. The sooner we get there, the sooner we can get this thing settled. Then you'll be free to get back to your schoolwork."

"Yes. Sure."

FIVE

SUSAN HAD THE FEELING THAT SHE WAS GOING TO MISS THE Hancock Police Department.

It wasn't as though these three policemen were beating her with rubber hoses; it was just that they looked as if they would have enjoyed doing so. Instead they asked her question after question, frowning as if dissatisfied with each and every answer her lawyer (who had appeared at the police station only a few minutes after her arrival) allowed her to give. But, in the end, the police had to let her go. She and Brett had worked hard in the car on the way over, so she could account for every minute since she'd arrived at school that morning. And Merry had already been killed by the time she got home.

"I don't think those guys like me too much," Susan commented as she walked out of the police station between Brett and her lawyer.

"They hate you," the lawyer stated flatly. "You ruined their plans."

"What plans?" she asked.

"They were going to arrest you. Then this evening they planned to call a press conference to announce the murder and their quick arrest, after which they would go out and celebrate their collective cleverness."

"Sounds like you've worked with this department before," Susan stated.

"More than once. They have a basic problem: The college lies within their jurisdiction. On the other hand, the college has its own security department. The town guys are always convinced that the college guys are covering up. And in some cases they are. But generally, with a serious crime, the campus cops are glad to have the town force take over. That way Mommy and Daddy will have someone else to complain to when their little darling is put in jail for something they consider small—like a drunk-and-disorderly or even a rape."

"Oh."

"It's a difficult position to be in," Brett added.

"It's going to be difficult for me if they don't find the person who killed Merry." Susan tried to bring the conversation back to what she considered to be the most important point. "I suppose they will all be investigating? Will the campus police want to talk to me?"

"No. I suspect they'll take a hands-off approach to the murder. It took place off campus, after all."

"As far as we know now," Brett added cautiously.

"You think she was killed on campus? Strangled with my backpack and then carried back to her apartment—in the middle of the day?" Susan was incredulous.

"I know it's not likely, but we really don't have many facts at this point. You knew her . . ."

"Not really," Susan protested. "I mean, she was my lab partner, but that isn't the same as knowing someone personally. At least, not for me, because I don't spend a whole lot of time chatting during class." Partially because she had to concentrate so hard just to figure out what was going on. And partially because she hadn't even heard of most of the movies, music groups, and clubs her fellow students discussed.

The lawyer looked as though he believed her. "Well, I'd better be getting back to the office. Big trial tomorrow and I want to be prepared. Call me as soon as you hear anything . . . anything at all . . . from anyone official."

Susan nodded and got into Brett's car as the other man walked down the street to where he had parked his vehicle. "Do you think he thinks I'm innocent?" she asked as Brett slid into the driver's seat and put his key in the ignition.

"It really doesn't matter what he thinks."

"Doesn't matter? Brett, what if I'm arrested? How is he going to defend me unless he believes in my innocence?"

"Susan, the man spends his life defending the guilty. He gets them off, too. He's good."

"Brett, you don't think I killed anybody?"

"Of course not, Susan. But you know it looks strange that something you owned was used as the weapon."

"But that's just because Merry and I accidentally exchanged packs at school. It was an accident."

"On your part, yes." Brett glanced over his shoulder before turning out into traffic. Susan suspected that driving a car that announced his position as chief of police made him rather casual about such things. Certainly the drivers sharing the road had slammed on their brakes at his approach.

"You think Merry might have taken my pack intentionally? Why?"

"I have no idea if she did or why. It's just a thought."

So Susan thought. If only she could come up with an answer . . .

"I still don't have any idea how I'm going to get my homework done tonight," she muttered, returning to her original worry.

"Maybe your professors will give you extensions."

"Maybe." She yawned. "Frankly, I'm too tired to worry about it right now. It's been a long day; I'm too tired to microwave dinner."

"Why don't you both come over to my apartment tonight? I'm doing my last cookout of the year. I've got six nice fillets sitting in the refrigerator and Erika's bringing salad. Knowing her, she'll bring enough for an army."

"Six fillets?"

"We were going to have company, but they canceled last night." He looked down at his watch. "Erika's coming at six-thirty. We can have a glass of wine or a beer while I cook the meat. Eat at seven or so. You and Jed will be home by eight-thirty. You can study then."

Susan thought for a minute. Jed would enjoy the company and she wouldn't have to cook or clean up. "Sounds good to me. What can I bring?"

"You don't have to bring anything, but if you want, you can stop on your way over and get some ice cream for dessert."

"Fine." Jed could pick up a quart of nutmeg ice cream at the specialty shop in town on his drive home from the train station. It would go nicely with the blueberry pie waiting in her freezer. And maybe she should bring along a loaf or two of garlic herb bread. It would be fun spending the evening out with old friends like they used to, before she started school. Susan was enjoying her plans so much that she didn't hear Brett's words. "I'm sorry. Excuse me?"

"I was just wondering what you knew about the dead woman."

"Not much, except that she was having an affair with my creative writing professor."

"Susan . . ."

"Well, I don't really know that, but why else would they be together at the most romantic restaurant in town?" She mentioned its name.

"Also the most expensive," Brett added.

"Yes, I guess it is. And I know what you're going to say," she added as he opened his mouth. "The fact that they were eating there doesn't necessarily mean they were romantically involved."

"Well, not many men would spend that kind of money on a casual acquaintance," Brett suggested.

"She might have been paying half."

"It would still come close to a hundred dollars apiece if they had wine and dessert." He looked at Susan and grinned. "Erika and I went there a few months ago. It was a special celebration. My credit-card company almost went into shock."

Susan wondered what they had been celebrating. A born matchmaker, she was firmly convinced that Brett and Erika should get married. She had hoped that Chrissy's wedding might inspire them, but here they were, months later, still dating and, as far as she knew, not even engaged. But Brett was still talking.

"You must have spoken to this woman about more than your schoolwork."

"Not really. Astronomy meets twice a week for class and there's a night laboratory once a week. We've only met four times. The night viewing is on Thursdays, but there was none scheduled for the first week of classes—tomorrow is the first one. During class I was busy working—taking notes and trying to figure out what the professor was writing on the board—and Merry was busy flirting with one of the young men who sits across from us. In fact, if I hadn't seen her with my creative writing professor, I would have assumed they were involved. You know, that's interesting, isn't it?"

"Not particularly. Unless you're considering investigating this murder, and I sincerely hope your thinking is heading in a different direction."

"Brett, this is the first time something I own has been used as a murder weapon."

"And the last, I sincerely hope. So why don't you just back off and let the police look for the killer? Believe me, it's the smart thing to do. There are two police departments involved—let them do their work and you can return to your studies. You don't want to get behind this early in the semester."

"No, of course not." Susan watched the side of the road flash by. The leaves on the trees were just beginning to turn, and Connecticut, beautiful in most seasons, was promising to be spectacular this autumn. She usually took long drives in the fall, visiting faraway orchards more for the ambience than the apples. She bought gourds and placed large bowls of them around the house for decoration. She lined the bay windows in the living room with rust-colored chrysanthemums and flanked the front door with more of the same in antique Italian urns, which were stored in the dark recesses of the garage during the rest of the year. She baked, oh, how she baked. Apple pies with sweet crumb topping, gingerbread with lemon sauce, plum kuchen, Swiss pear bread, doughnuts . . .

But not this year, she reminded herself firmly. This year she was going to be busy with school.

"Susan? Are you listening to me?"

"Sorry. Just thinking about how beautiful the leaves will be this year. The rain this summer and all."

"You won't see them from a jail cell."

He had her full attention now. "Brett, no one is going to arrest me. I'm innocent."

"Well, you do have an alibi for the presumed time of the murder."

"Exactly! I have an alibi!"

"There are people who say a good alibi is just meant to be broken."

"But I wasn't anywhere near Merry when she was killed. I don't even know where her apartment is! Besides, if you think I might be arrested, why don't you think I should look into the murder?"

"The men who were questioning you. Do you remember the blond?"

"The older man?"

"Thanks. We went through the police academy together. I hadn't thought of him as old, but I guess he is a senior member of his department." Brett frowned. "His name is Michael. Michael O'Reilly."

"An Irish cop?"

"Don't imagine Michael as the friendly guy on the corner helping little old ladies cross the street. Michael is tough. He had to be. He worked the streets in New Haven for over fifteen years. He left because he was injured during a big drug bust in ninety-one. He could have taken his disability and sat at home watching TV, but he's not that kind of guy. He likes the challenge of police work. So now he works on a suburban force—and he's the liaison with the campus police. And . . ."

"And?" she prompted when Brett stopped talking.

"And he's not very fond of upper-middle-class women who don't have to work."

"One of those prejudices he picked up on the mean streets of the big city?" Susan asked sarcastically.

"No. Something he picked up when one of them dumped him on the day they were supposed to be married."

"Isn't that rather stupid?"

"I don't know the whole story. I just know you're not going to find him on your side. And if the police don't arrest someone for Meredith's murder, they'll be looking at old suspects again. And my guess is that Michael will be directing his attention at you."

"Unless I find the real murderer," Susan declared as they arrived at her driveway.

"Look, I've got to get home and start dinner. I'll see you in half an hour or so and then we'll talk. But believe me, Susan, I'm bound and determined to convince you to stay out of this."

"I'll think about it over dinner," she promised, slamming the car door and starting up the sidewalk to her house.

Susan had filled Jed in on the details of the murder during the drive over to Brett's home. And Brett must have used the same time to get Erika up to speed because it was the main topic of conversation before they were even seated on Brett's small balcony.

"I agree with Susan," Erika said, picking up a raw mushroom, dipping it in the tamari-yogurt sauce, and popping it in her mouth. "She should take charge of her life, and that includes making sure that someone with a bunch of baggage doesn't try to ruin it."

"Exactly!" Susan, who had been admiring Erika's slim, olive corduroy slacks and gold hand-knit tunic, agreed enthusiastically.

"On the other hand, you went back to school to change your life, and investigating a murder is sort of the same old, same old, isn't it?" Brett suggested.

"Well, that's true . . ." She had to agree with him with perhaps a bit less enthusiasm.

"And you have been saying that what you liked about your kids being gone and going back to school was that you could live your life without being swayed by the priorities and needs of those around you," Jed said, ignoring the healthful appetizer and grabbing a handful of barbecued sweet potato chips.

"Of course, I did mean that at the time. . . ." She fell silent.

"Susan?"

"What do you think?"

"What are you going to do?"

"I haven't the foggiest what I'm going to do," Susan answered. "And I was just thinking a course in logic might have been more useful than Italian and an in-depth study of Victorian women writers."

SIX

"IT SAID TEA AND SYMPATHY FROM FOUR-THIRTY UNTIL SIX."

"Maybe we're in the wrong place."

"Wouldn't surprise me. Since classes started, I've been in the wrong place more times than I like to think about."

"Join the crowd. Apparently, I'm the only person on campus who didn't know that the old library is called the Carn and the new one the Darn. When my political science professor said he had books on reserve in the Darn, I thought he was making a joke. Finally one of the librarians took pity on me and explained. Andrew Carnegie donated the money to build the original library. Then the Darningher family donated a large part of the fortune it cost to build the new building. The Carn. The Darn. It all makes sense . . . if you know."

"If you know. But when you don't know, you end up feeling like a fool."

"They want us to feel like fools. Old fools."

Susan, who had been leaning against the doorjamb, eavesdropping on the conversation of the dozen or so women seated around a large metal table in the conference room, was gently bumped from behind.

"Excuse me. I thought you were walking into the room."

"Sorry." Susan moved out of the path of the cart that was

bearing the evidence that tea would, in fact, be offered. The stern-looking woman pushing the cart made sympathy seem a less likely prospect.

"Are you the professor who's going to lead this group?" the woman who now knew the difference between the two libraries asked Susan.

"No, I'm a student."

"If you're a returning student, this is the group you're looking for."

Surprised by the voice, Susan stepped backward and onto the foot of her Victorian literature professor. Cordelia Brilliant grimaced. "Ms. Henderson . . . I wondered if you might be here."

"Henshaw."

"Oh, yes, Henshaw, I apologize. So many new students. It's almost impossible to learn everyone's names right away. And are you here for the returning students' support group?"

"Yes. Exactly." If she was honest, Susan would have to admit that Cordelia Brilliant scared her. Ever since the professor had walked into the classroom on the first day, dropped a large pile of notebooks and texts on the lectern at the front of the room, and asked a young blond in the first row how, exactly, one would define a minor Victorian woman writer, Susan had been terrified of being called on. That day, student after student had been asked the same question. Answers had varied from a simple "I have no idea" to the rambling statements of people who seemed to believe that they would hit upon the correct answer if they just talked long enough. While the young man next to her was babbling away, apparently under the impression that Tennyson was a female, Susan had begun to quake. She had no idea what to say. In fact, she had just braced herself to be called on next when Dr. Brilliant had wheeled around to the blackboard and, chalk dust flying in all directions, had written these words:

THERE WERE NO MINOR FEMALE WRITERS IN VICTORIAN ENGLAND. MEN HAVE DESCRIBED THEM AS SUCH IN AN EFFORT TO BELITTLE THEIR WORK AND THEIR LIVES. PERIOD.

Susan, relieved to have avoided making a fool of herself,

had flipped open her notebook and diligently copied down this statement.

"Those of you to whom this is not obvious might be happier in another class."

Did the fact that she needed to write down the statement mean it was less than obvious to her? Susan looked up guiltily—right into the eyes of her professor. "I'm talking about you," those eyes seemed to be saying.

"Well, Ms. Henshaw, would you like to take a seat?"

Susan returned her attention to the present. "I . . . Susan. Call me Susan."

Dr. Brilliant raised her eyebrows. "Susan Henshaw? Aren't you connected with the murder everyone is talking about? Didn't you find the body?"

"No. No," Susan protested. "My backpack was used to kill her." She heard the gasps of the women behind her. "I . . . I wasn't there at the time. I mean, it didn't have anything to do with me. I hardly knew her."

"I thought the campus paper said you were held for questioning," a suspicious voice accused.

"That was because of my backpack. That's all. I had nothing to do with it," Susan repeated.

"But I've heard of you. You're the woman who solves murders in one of those ritzy towns on the coast, aren't you? Are you going to solve this one?" one woman asked.

"Oh, yes, do. Prove to these kids that we oldsters can still do a thing or two that they can't." A woman with a silky gray cap of hair spoke up.

"Well, that's what we're all here to talk about, aren't we?" Dr. Brilliant, like a good professor, returned the group's attention to the present situation. "We're here to help one another adjust to the problems of returning to school after being out of the academic world for a while."

"For some of us, more than a while," said the gray-haired woman Susan had just sat down beside. She looked around the room with piercing blue eyes. "Some of us have been out of school for longer than most of the students around here have been alive."

"That must be why they treat us as though we don't exist.

I was almost run over by a long-haired kid on a skateboard on the way here."

"The ones on bikes are the worst. I don't understand why the campus police don't enforce the rules against riding on the sidewalks."

"Enforcing rules isn't a big thing on this campus." Another woman spoke. "I could swear I smelled pot last night. It was practically billowing into the window of the library, where I was studying."

"In the Carn or the Darn?"

"Why? Are you interested in joining the party?" The woman who had been complaining about skateboards turned to the woman who had asked the question.

"I have a friend. She has cancer and the chemo is making her miserable. Everyone says marijuana helps control some of the side effects. I just thought . . ."

"That's the way things are around here. You're worried about your friend who is dying and these kids have nothing better to do than get high."

"I think it's about time I interrupted this lively discussion. You've all brought up some interesting issues and there is obviously a lot to discuss. And as group leader I'm not sure how I can help. I'm neither the person who instigated these meetings nor the person who usually acts as facilitator. She is a psychology professor. My field, as a few of you know, is Victorian literature."

As Cordelia Brilliant continued to introduce herself and explain the purpose of the group, Susan looked around at the others in the room. The first thing that struck her was that they were all women. Didn't men return to school as well? Or did they not join support groups?

She got up to get some tea and continued to consider her companions. They all seemed to be around her age; certainly those who weren't going gray were going to their hairdresser regularly. As they all got up to get refreshments (most of them making a comment to the effect that they really didn't need the extra calories), they rearranged themselves at the table. Susan found herself seated next to the woman who had been encouraging her to solve the murder, thus proving the abilities of older students. The conversation at their end of the table became more general.

"You're in my creative writing class, aren't you?" the woman asked. "I'm Jinx McCulley. I mean, Jinx Jensen. I keep forgetting that I'm using my maiden name again. As though maidenhood is something you can regain." She smiled and wrinkles crinkled around her eyes. "You probably don't recognize me. I sit in the back of the class."

Susan grinned. "Then I guess you get there before I do. I usually end up in the front. Those are the only seats empty by the time I arrive. I . . . I usually stop in the ladies' room on the way. To be frank, Dr. Hoyer scares me to death. A fresh coat of lipstick usually helps—a little."

"I know exactly what you mean. I had a conference yesterday with my social psychology professor and I swear I spent more time dressing for it than I did for my first date after the divorce. And the conference was just about as successful."

"Not good?"

"Dreadful. Although different. I bored my professor to death, I could tell. Almost as much as my date bored me."

"I hope you've found other, less boring men since then," Susan said politely.

"Not yet," her companion said cheerfully. "But I'm learning to enjoy my own company. Not a bad thing, I think."

"No, of course not." Susan sipped her tea. It was terrible. Lukewarm and bitter. She put down the mug.

"Dreadful, isn't it? I generally bring my own bags and stick to hot water, but today I forgot. Say"—Jinx Jensen took a deep breath—"would you like to come over to my house and have some tea? It would be nice to get to know another student in the same situation I am. And maybe we could commiserate about creative writing class. I've barely begun my writing project and I know that more than a few of the other—younger—students have turned theirs in already."

Susan wondered if Jinx was lonely after her divorce and had returned to college to make friends.

"I live only a few blocks from campus," Jinx added.

"Sounds wonderful," Susan said impulsively. Cordelia Brilliant was explaining that the group would meet once a week at this time and they were encouraged to come and bring up anything that was bothering them. After that more tea was offered, which Susan and Jinx refused. The group broke up and Susan wondered how Jinx planned to get home.

"I usually walk to school—I'm trying to lose some weight. Actually, I'm trying to lose the same ten pounds I've been trying to lose for the past ten years. Once in a while I have a terrible feeling that I would miss them terribly if they actually went away."

Susan laughed. She really liked this woman. "If you're anything like me, you won't get the chance to find out. Unless there's a problem with parking, why don't I drive us over to your house?"

"Oh, a bad influence. Just what I've been looking for." Jinx laughed and scooped up a huge straw purse, which she flung over one shoulder. "I'll bet you're just the woman to talk me into opening a package of Mint Milanos to go with our tea."

"You buy Pepperidge Farm cookies when you're dieting?"

"They were on sale," Jinx explained.

Susan didn't know about the other returning students, but she sure felt better when she left the room than she had when she entered it.

Jinx and Susan ended up choosing wine and cheese over cookies and tea. Jinx served the food in the eclectic living room of her small townhouse.

"I moved here the day after my divorce became final. At the time I didn't know if the move was permanent or temporary, but now it feels like home to me, so I guess I'm staying," she explained, handing Susan a heavy homespun linen napkin.

"You seem to be quite settled." The walls were crowded with paintings and art prints. The long couch and two chairs were piled with pillows. There was a small rigid heddle loom set up in one corner, and she spied a potter's wheel on the balcony. There were also enough plants to keep the surrounding few miles oxygenated. "How long ago was your divorce?"

"Two years." Jinx looked around her surroundings and smiled to herself. "Yes, this is home. I've even gotten used to the bedroom. . . ." She stopped speaking and grinned. "You have to see what I did in the bedroom. Bring your wineglass. You may need to take a swig or two."

Susan followed Jinx down a short hallway, through one of three doors, and into a bedroom quite unlike what she'd seen of the rest of the apartment. The bed was brass, as ornate as its Victorian makers could manage. And it was covered with pillows made of various fluffy materials. Lace and satin ribbons decorated large shams. Embroidered throw pillows literally covered half the bed. There was an old-fashioned dressing table with the requisite crystal perfume bottles, and piles of fabric were draped about the windows. The only discordant note was a huge drawing of a house and a tree done in crayon on construction paper, which was pinned over the bed.

"My granddaughter's work. It's her image of the house I used to live in."

Susan looked at the drawing. The house had four windows surrounding a perfectly symmetrical door. Smoke rose from a chimney dangerously tilted toward the ground. A sun was in the sky and a row of flowers marched along the horizon. It looked like the drawings of almost every kindergarten student she had ever known.

"She's in nursery school," Jinx added.

"Then she's advanced."

"We like to think so. So what do you think of my bedroom?"

"It's very feminine."

"Ha! It's tacky. The female equivalent of those single-male pads with a bed that falls out of the wall and lights that dimmed automatically that were popular in early sixties movies. I hate it. And it shows exactly how screwy my self-image was after my divorce. Follow me." She led Susan to the next doorway. "This is where I sleep. It's the reason I bought this townhouse, in fact. This is where I feel comfortable."

Susan looked at the book-lined walls, a bay window full of plants, and a daybed, which was covered with so many magazines and newspapers that she couldn't make out the pattern on the spread covering it.

"Now you know the real me. Dedicated bookworm."

"Wonderful." Susan wandered over to the desk, which held a computer and a laser printer. A pile of papers was sliding to the floor and she automatically straightened them. " 'Chapter three,' " she read from the top sheet. "You're a writer!"

"No, but I'm finding that turning the story of my divorce into fiction is very therapeutic."

"You're doing it! You're turning your life into fiction, exactly like Professor Hoyer told us to do!"

"It's easy. I use what happened in my life and who did what to whom. My characters even look like they do in real life—but then I change their names."

"Interesting." Susan nodded. "I may just try that."

Jinx took a deep breath. "Look, I want to level with you. There is a reason I invited you over here. You see, I overheard those women talking about how you solve murders and . . . And I think I know something about the girl who was killed. Something not many people know."

SEVEN

"WHY DON'T YOU COME BACK TO THE LIVING ROOM SO I can refill your glass and explain," Jinx suggested.

"Fine." Susan didn't even glance at her watch. She'd told Jed she had research to do in the library and would be late for dinner. She hoped it would encourage him to take a more active role in getting the meals prepared. And this was, after all, research of a sort.

Jinx waited until they had settled back on the couch before beginning her explanation.

"I never planned to get divorced," she started, and then laughed at herself. "I suppose not many people do. But what I'm trying to say is that I didn't figure I'd be single at this stage of my life." She sipped her wine and looked up at Susan. "I'm just confusing you, so why don't I begin at the beginning? You see, my husband left me. Fell in love with a coworker. Same old story. I know. The trouble is that just because a situation is old doesn't mean you know what to do when it happens to you."

"I can understand that."

"So when Ed—that's my ex-husband—said he had found the love of his life, I kicked and screamed—literally—then hired the best divorce lawyer I could afford and started attending a support group of women going through the same thing."

"Good idea."

"It wasn't quite that simple. In fact, I was falling apart so badly that a friend almost had to kidnap me to get me to that first meeting. But I was a convert before refreshment time."

"I'm glad it made things easier." Susan really was, but she was also wondering exactly what this had to do with the murder.

But Jinx answered that question immediately. "That's where I met the girl who was murdered. Although I know I should call her a woman. She must have been close to thirty years old. I'm afraid that seems almost like a child to me."

"You met her at this meeting for divorced women?"

"Yes. She wasn't actually getting a divorce . . . at least not when she started attending."

Susan, sensing some hesitancy, sat quietly and waited for the rest of the story.

"Look," Jinx began, running her hands through her gray hair, "we're not a twelve-step program. I mean, we're not dealing with addiction in our group. But we do promise at the beginning of each meeting to protect the privacy of the other people in the room. But . . ."

"But Merry is dead."

"Yes. And I suppose she would want me to talk about this. To tell someone who might be able to help, someone who can make sure justice is done."

"I don't know . . ."

"I know, I sound like a nut. Just let me tell you what I know and then you can decide what to do. Okay?"

"Fine." She was reluctant but curious.

"Well, when I first started going to these meetings, I thought it would be a good place to moan and whine and blame my husband for ruining my life—and I suppose I did do a bit of that at first."

"I can understand that."

"But the group doesn't let that go on for too long. The point is that it's your life and you have to make it a good one."

"Easier said than done," Susan commented.

"Definitely. But I had it so much easier than so many of the women there. My only child is grown up and settled. I'm not rich, but I have the means to keep myself comfortably. Many of the women in the group have young children. And, of course, the divorce disrupts the children in many ways and it's almost always the mothers who have to deal with that on a day-to-day basis."

Susan nodded. Jinx was right. It was an old story.

"And as time went on, I listened to everyone else and realized exactly how lucky I was. Besides, once Ed had moved out and our home was for sale, I suddenly began to realize how much freedom I had. And that I could finally do exactly what I wanted to do with my life. When I stopped being hurt and miserable, I recognized that I was actually going to be happy. In many ways happier than I had been since my daughter was a child. If I want to spend all night reading or working on my weaving, I can do it. If I decide that all I want for dinner is a bag of microwaved popcorn and a glass of wine, it's just fine."

Susan smiled wistfully. She'd miss Jed, of course. . . .

"And I could go back to school. Every time I mentioned that to Ed, he made fun of me. Said I was trying to regain my lost youth."

"How awful!" At least her family had been supportive.

"Of course, I know now that I should have gone ahead and done what I wanted to back when I was still married. I could have. I just didn't. I guess being on my own has forced me to take control of my own life. To grow up."

"So it hasn't been all bad."

Jinx smiled. "Haven't you been listening? It's been great! A few of the women in the group were connected to the college and really encouraged me to go back to school! And I'm having a wonderful time there!" But when she continued, she had a more serious expression on her face.

"Merry wasn't happy with it at all."

"Her husband left her, too? For another woman?"

"Well, he didn't admit to another woman, which made it all the more insulting, I guess."

"What do you mean? Was it a man?"

"No. Personal growth and development. PG&D is what we called it in group."

"I have no idea what you're talking about," Susan admitted.

"Then you're one of the lucky women. You see, men don't leave their wives for anything as outré as a midlife crisis these days. They leave because they wake up one morning and realize that a wife and family have limited their life. They discover the need for personal growth and development."

"Which can't take place within the marriage?"

"That's what they claim."

"And that's the reason Merry's husband left her."

"Apparently. At least that's what we were told the first few times she spoke up in a meeting. But . . . well, I really hate to say this about someone. And, strangely enough, it seems worse to say it about someone who is dead, but Merry was a liar. A compulsive liar, some people in the group thought. I'm not comfortable putting labels on people, frankly."

"But she did tell lies."

"Definitely. And they were lies, not just exaggerations. Which is what I thought at first. You see, the meetings were led by a professional therapist who gave everyone an opportunity to speak without allowing any one person to spend the entire time emoting. Which is what we all wanted to do at first. It's the natural result of being in a bad marriage—in a bad marriage no one listens to you, so a lot of us had a lot of talking to catch up on."

"But you all got a chance to speak."

"Yes, we did." Jinx grinned. "I am getting to the point. Honest.

"You see, some of us told some pretty gruesome stories. There are women in that group who came home from work and discovered their husband in bed with their kid's baby-sitter. And women who were married to men who were seri-ously abusive. Both physically and mentally. And women married to drunks and addicts—although our leader usually steered them to Al-Anon and Nar-Anon meetings so those particular women tended to disappear after a while. But gen-erally the women told these horrible stories and then slowly, as the weeks went by, they stopped talking about their hus-bands constantly and began to focus more on their own lives and how they were going to manage after their divorce.

"Of course, not everyone follows the pattern. There are some women in that room who are going to be whining on the day they die—and they'll have absolutely no idea that they've wasted their life. They simply do not get it, as the kids say these days."

"And Merry was one of those women?"

"No, Merry was . . . well, at first I thought she was just reti-cent. Then odd—this is a stressful time of life for a woman and it doesn't bring out the best in most of us, at least not immedi-ately. Then I realized she was lying, purely and simply lying."

"About what?"

"I'm not really sure. I mean, I don't know that much about her life."

"Then how did you know she was lying?"

"Because she started telling other people's stories. Oh, she changed the details a bit, which is probably why it took me so long to catch on, but they were the same stories." She looked at Susan. "You don't understand. Let me give you an ex-ample. I remember exactly the tale she was telling when I realized I'd heard it before.

"The meetings sometimes seem to take on a topic almost extemporaneously. In the meeting I'm thinking about, one of our newest members started explaining how her husband was using his ample financial assets to manipulate her into agreeing to a divorce. And then everyone started talking about money.

"Money was one of the problems we all shared. Even women who had worked during their entire marriage worried about how they would manage to live, raise their children, and retire now that they were single again.

"So we're all contributing to the conversation and Merry starts talking about how her husband had moved the money from their joint accounts into a single account right before he left home. She said he even emptied their safe deposit box and rented a new one with only his name on the deed. It was the last detail that struck a chord.

"You see, we had a few extremely wealthy women in the group, women with valuable jewelry. And one of their husbands pulled that stunt with her safe deposit box."

"Merry had valuable jewelry?" asked Susan. The young woman she had known had worn some heavy silver bracelets, but nothing valuable.

"Probably not. That's what clued me in. She came to the meetings complaining about her husband, and one of the things she had said in the beginning was that they were so poor she had to borrow to pay her tuition because her husband was always following one guru or the other around the country and couldn't keep a job."

"So why did they even have a safe deposit box?"

"My thought exactly. Of course, I didn't speak up. But I began to listen more and more closely to the stories she was telling. And week after week they began to sound more and more like stories people had told previously."

"You're kidding."

"Nope. At first I thought it was me. I was pretty stressed out, but not so that I would imagine things, believe me. And I realized that her complaints about her husband changed. He started out as a pretty typical PG&D man. Self-centered, selfish, immature. And as time went on he got worse and worse. In fact, he seemed to develop the rotten personality traits of all the husbands of the women in the room. It was pretty incredible."

"It must have been."

"And, of course, I wasn't the only person who began to wonder exactly what was going on. But one of the rules of the group is that we don't criticize one another. We're supposed to be encouraging rather than negative."

"You probably needed all the encouragement you could get."

"You said it. But Merry was strange. And, after a while, we all knew it."

"Did anyone say anything?"

"Actually, yes. But I wasn't at that meeting and only heard about it later."

"What happened?"

"Nothing major. It was a big meeting—we sometimes had as many as fifty women attending—and when there are that many people, there tend to be splinter conversations in the room."

"I don't know what you mean."

"Well, people chatting together when someone else is talking."

"Oh."

"Merry was talking, telling the group I don't know what about her husband, when she overheard another woman laughing about having heard Merry's story before and apparently someone else said that she had not only heard Merry's stories before, she had lived some of them, which was more than Merry herself had done."

"I assume Merry got upset," Susan commented.

"That's not the word for it. She blew up. Screamed at the women who were talking about her that they had no idea what they were talking about. That they had no idea what she had suffered. That her husband had tried to kill her and would do it again."

"And you think he did."

"I have absolutely no idea. I just thought someone should know about it."

"You could go to the police."

"I know, but I don't feel comfortable doing that. You see, I find myself feeling sorry for the guy," Jinx explained.

"Really?"

"Yes. And, believe me, he's just about the only man whose wife came to those meetings that I would say that about."

"Because of all of Merry's lies."

"Yes. And because I got such a bad feeling about her. Why did she need to make him so evil? Why did her problems have to be worse than anyone else's? It just wasn't right. And so maybe he had good reason to want a divorce—and maybe he was one of those men who leaves a marriage and treats his ex-wife as honorably as possible. And I'm afraid if I go to the police with the story I just told you, they will automatically assume the worst about the man. And he could be perfectly innocent. On the other hand . . ." Jinx stopped and stared down at her still-full wineglass.

"On the other hand, Merry might have been telling the truth this one time. And he might actually have been the one to kill her."

"Exactly."

EIGHT

Susan drove home happy. She had made a new friend. She might have discovered the identity of Merry's murderer. It had been a productive day. But she was about to remember what her children had known for a while. No matter how well the day goes, when you haven't done your homework, the evening sucks. (Their description, not hers.)

It began well. When she walked from the garage into her kitchen, Clue was happily finishing a bowl of her favorite kibble. Better yet, Jed was standing near the microwave, the table was set for two, and at each place a full glass of wine awaited.

"Something smells good."

"I stopped on the way home at that gourmet shop downtown and picked up dinner," Jed announced. "Braised lamb shanks, Greek spinach pie, pecan rice pilaf, and chocolate cream pie for dessert! I'd never been there before. It's wonderful. They have a great selection of food and everything comes with re-heating instructions. You should try it sometime."

Susan didn't bother to tell him that she had been shopping there for years. The meal smelled wonderful and, except for the pie, everything was exactly what she would have chosen. She preferred lemon to chocolate. "Sounds fabulous. How was your day?"

"Well, I . . ."

"Jed, you won't believe what happened!"

Jed smiled, opened the microwave, and rotated the food. "What?"

"Well, I went to this meeting for returning students. Sort of a support group. And . . . You know, only women showed up. Don't you think that's strange?"

"Well, I suppose—"

"Maybe men are just more interested in competing with one another than in supporting one another. Would you ever go to a support group?"

"Is there one for men whose wives won't let them finish a sentence?"

"What?"

He laughed and pulled the dish from the microwave. "Nothing. Sit down, drink your wine, and I'll serve this culinary creation. Okay?"

"Great. Well, Jinx—"

"Who?"

"Jinx. She's another woman in my returning students' support group. I told you."

He wasn't going to argue. "Okay. A woman named Jinx."

"Yes, she told me this story about Merry, the young woman who was murdered."

"Right." He put two filled plates on the table, and Susan told him about her afternoon while they ate.

"Sounds like you may be on to something. But may I make a suggestion?" Jed asked as they were finishing their meal.

"Sure. What?"

"Why don't you do the easy thing this time? Why don't you just call Brett for the information you want?"

"He's not—"

"I know he's not part of their police department, but he has sources. At least he might be able to find out the identity of Merry's ex-husband and where he is now."

"Jed, what a good idea!"

"Try harder not to sound like I rarely have them."

"I—"

"I'm just kidding. You know," he added, scooping up the last bit of phyllo dough on his plate, "this is almost as good as your spinach pie."

That was probably because she had been a regular customer of that particular gourmet shop since the week it opened. However, she decided that honesty was not always the best policy. Jed had taken her hint and provided dinner. What more could she ask? she wondered as she reached for the phone. She dialed Brett's number as Jed cleared the table and cut generous slices of pie for them. Susan knew he would finish hers as well as his own.

Brett answered on the second ring.

"Hi, Brett. Susan." She listened a moment. "Yes, we had a wonderful time, too. Next time Erika and I will cook and you and Jed can sit back and enjoy life. Yes. Yes. Well, actually, there is a reason for my call. I need some information and I think maybe you can get it for me." She stuck her fork in the mound of whipped cream topping as she listened to his response.

"Well, it's not exactly like I'm investigating. I'm just trying to help make a friend feel better—no, she had nothing to do with the murder. Nothing at all." As she spoke, Susan realized she didn't actually have the facts to back up this statement. "But my question does have to do with the murder. It's about Merry. Merry's husband, to be more exact. I was wondering what you could find out about him." She licked the cream off her fork as she listened to his answer.

"I don't know anything about him, really. Other than that he threatened to kill Merry. No, no. I'm wrong about that. She said he threatened to kill her. See, that's why I'm calling you and not the police in charge of the investigation."

Jed stopped eating long enough to make a suggestion. "Maybe you should explain about Jinx and the divorced women's support group. Like you told me."

Susan nodded, listening to Brett repeat his demand that she stay out of the investigation of Merry's murder. "I am not investigating," she insisted. "Jinx came to me. Why don't I explain?" And as the whipped cream melted into the chocolate filling, she did just that. "So what do you think?" she concluded. "Can you track down the guy and check him out? Privately? Without anyone having to know about that scene in the support group?"

There was silence on the other end of the line.

"Why would the other police department even know you were checking?" Susan asked.

More silence.

Susan played her only card. "It's okay. If you can't do it, I'll just have to find the man myself."

Jed grinned and finished off the last of his slice. He knew Brett was once more agreeing, reluctantly, to Susan's request.

"He'll do it!" she announced, hanging up with a smile on her face.

"Good for him. Now, how about another piece of pie?" He reached out for the plate.

"I don't . . . Well, okay, but I'll take it with me. I really have a lot of studying to do tonight."

"Would you like me to make some coffee?"

Susan had had her husband's coffee before. "Not unless you want some. I'll make tea later if I get desperate for caffeine."

"Fine. You get to work and I'll clean up in here."

Susan headed to her husband's study. In college, she had done most of her studying sitting on her bed in the dorm. But not now. Not only did she suspect that Jed might not want to share their bed with the ephemera of homework, but she found she possessed a remarkable propensity to drift off to sleep while trying to concentrate on the complicated formulas that seemed to control the stars.

She had opened and closed the door to Chrissy's room, thinking she might find a spot to spread out on the large antique desk she had given her daughter for her sixteenth birthday. The desk was virtually hidden under piles of wedding gifts, which couldn't fit in the small apartment Chrissy and her husband shared with their two huge dogs in west Philadelphia. Susan hadn't even considered Chad's room. Every time he came home from Cornell, he promised to clean it, but . . .

The guest room had been the logical answer. But it was immaculate, awaiting a promised visit from Jed's mother. Susan was sure that Claire would appear the very moment she allowed a speck of dust to land on the dresser. The door was kept closed: Clue found clean bedspreads irresistible.

So Jed had offered his desk and Susan had reluctantly accepted. She would have preferred someplace more private, finding that she was self-conscious about studying. It was one thing to sit reading in a chair, another to lean over a desk, writing away in her notebooks. But Jed stayed out of the room while she was at work and had even cleared out one of his desk drawers for her. In just a couple of weeks, a few hours at the desk during the evening was becoming a habit.

Tonight she couldn't concentrate and found herself writing notes about Merry's death. She was hard at work when Jed stuck his head in the room.

"I'm going to take Clue out for a walk around the block. Want to come?"

"No, I'm . . ." She looked down at the opened notebook. "I'm working."

"Hey, looks like you're really getting into the story you're writing. Are you going to let me read it?"

"Not until it's done."

"You're too busy to walk?"

"Sorry. I'd like to work on this for a bit longer."

"Okay. Come on, Clue."

Susan felt a twinge of guilt. It was probably chilly outside. She should have offered to keep Jed company. She shouldn't have let him think she was doing homework when, in fact, she had wasted the last hour writing a scenario in which Merry's husband was a murderer and Merry was . . . She put down her pen with a start. A murder mystery! She would write a murder mystery and turn it in as her project in creative writing. She knew a lot about murder after all, more than Jinx, who was planning to do the same thing. And everyone told her to write about what she knew. Susan grinned and got up. One problem solved! She decided to treat herself to a cup of hot blackberry tea and an early night. She could work on her astronomy assignment in the morning.

But her morning started with a call from Brett. Who explained that he had done a bit of research and come up with a surprising result. There was no grieving widower. There was no grieving ex-husband. Merry, in fact, had never been married.

NINE

Introduction to Creative Writing
Hoyer Tues/Thurs 12:00–12:50
Academic II, Rm 1609

"How does the writer draw a character from scratch, think of an appropriate name, flesh him out so that he becomes real both in the writer's mind and to the reader?"

Not a hand was raised in response. In just two weeks, Susan realized, everyone in the class had come to understand Professor Hoyer's fondness for rhetorical questions.

"I have devised a method—a model, in fact—which I call the character satellite. It does, I believe, answer this question." Professor Hoyer turned and drew a small circle on the green chalkboard behind him. "Let's say this is your character. Let's call him Joe Smith. We may, of course, rename him when we get to know him a bit better. So let's continue. What does Joe Smith have? Parents?" A line and a dot extended out from the first. "A wife?" Another line, this one ending in a suggestive little womanly shape. "Perhaps a mistress?" A line with an even more suggestive and definitely not little womanly shape. There were a few appreciative chuckles from the men in the class. "Children?" Two more lines. "But is this the sum total of a man? I think not, and so will your readers if you should be lucky enough to have readers.

"So we must continue. But why am I doing all this work? Mr. Jenkins!" A long-haired young man, who had been huddled in his heavyweight hooded sweatshirt, seemed to wake up with a start. "Besides his relatives, what makes a character, Mr. Jenkins?"

"Ah . . . parents and grandparents maybe?"

"I would include those as relatives, but we can put them on our model, of course. Anyone else?"

"His religion?" A woman in the front, who on the second day of class had read an essay explaining why she had left a convent, spoke up.

"His religion." A line pointed upward with a cross at its farthest point.

Suddenly realizing that actual answers were required of these particular questions, the students came to life and made suggestions.

"His profession?"

"Education?"

"Where he went to school?"

"Hobbies?"

"What teams he watches?"

"Television shows?"

"Music? Rap? Rock? R&B?"

And then suggestions into the philosophical and metaphysical.

"Beliefs?"

"Hopes?"

"What he's afraid of?"

"Dreams?"

"Plans for the future?"

The satellite now looked a lot like a spherical sea urchin and Professor Hoyer had a huge grin on his face. "Now. What is the problem with this?"

Dead silence. Perhaps the class thought they were back to rhetorical questions.

"The answer is obvious. Unless you are intending to produce a many-volumed work, how are you going to introduce so much information about just one character? And what about the other characters? Are they going to be squeezed out by our Mr. Smith?

"No? Well, then, remember this rule of the Hoyer character satellite. It's not just what you put in that makes a character real. It's also what you leave out. And the other thing to remember: Character is motivation. Your creation is going to do things as well as be things. Say you are writing a murder mystery." Susan, alerted, began to take notes. "Now what about our Mr. Smith's character would make him a good victim—or a murderer?"

Susan had no idea.

"What would make a person kill another person? Their relationship?" He drew lines around his model connecting the mother-in-law and the daughter. "Possibly his psychological makeup?" Another line. "Perhaps he's afraid of the person he kills?" There was a connection to the list of Joe Smith's fears.

The wall clock ticked and then the class ended. Professor Hoyer began to erase the now incomprehensible diagram.

"I hope you are all working on your short story. The long work is not due until the week before the end of the semester, but I expect you all to have read at least one assignment in our critique group before midterms.

"Class dismissed."

Italian Language I
Amato MWF 12:00–12:50
Anderson Hall, Rm 412

"And you, Ms. Susan Henshaw. Do you have anything to read to the class?"

The assignment had been to write a short paragraph describing a close friend. Susan had chosen to write a short version of her first assignment for creative writing.

It had been decades since Susan had been required to read aloud to a classroom full of people. She started to sweat before the first words were out of her mouth.

"Clue *è un'amica. Lei è di* Princeton, New Jersey. *Lei è molto bassa e molto grassa. Lei è bionda. Lei è simpaticis-*

*sima e molto esuberante. Lei non parla italiano. Lei è un po'
stupida.* Clue *è un cane."*

"Ah, *bravissima,* Susan Henshaw. You write about your
dog. Very clever. Very, very clever. You have a dog named
Clue. There must be a story there. Perhaps you will tell it to
me sometime."

How, Susan wondered, did Italians make an ordinary leer
seem so . . . so personal?

"Now, you all have your books and you have all marked
the place I indicate on page thirty-eight. *Trentotto.* Thirty-
eight. If you know all that, you will do just fine on the midterm examination."

Introduction to Astronomy
Forbes-Robertson MW 1:00–1:50 Night Laboratory
    Thurs 8 pm
Connecticut Science Building, Rm 101

"You will, I'm afraid, be working with a slight handicap
for the next few months, Ms. Henshaw. I understand your lab
partner will not be returning this semester."

"Or any other," someone added from behind Susan.

"No. I don't think so." Susan waited quietly, hoping Professor Forbes-Robertson would suggest she join another two-
some. Apparently, she was going to have to wait for a long
while. The professor had called the class to order and was
writing another of her incomprehensible formulas on the
blackboard. Susan picked up her pen and dutifully copied
down the numbers and letters. They didn't mean anything to
her, but she figured it was the least she could do.

This was the only class she was having real trouble with.
Oh, she didn't have a natural flair for languages, but she could
memorize vocabulary words and grammar rules in Italian.
And although she wasn't exactly the star of her Victorian lit
class, she loved every minute of it. Creative writing was a
worry. Although it was less and less as time went on. The critique groups were revealing, and she thought—hoped—she
could write as well as some of the youngsters in the group.
She began to think again of her short story. A murder should

start with a victim, she decided, and began to draw one of the Hoyer satellite models. . . .

Five minutes later she looked up and discovered an almost identical design on the blackboard. But Professor Forbes-Robertson wasn't talking about imaginary characters.

"So you understand that what happened in the night sky over a year ago is still affecting the movement of the stars even as we speak. Any questions?" Madeline Forbes-Robertson looked straight at Susan.

"No, no, of course not," Susan lied.

Minor Victorian Women Writers
Brilliant MWF 11:00–11:50
O'Dool Building, Rm 3

"We should probably begin our discussion of the author of *Middlemarch* with a question. Why did George Eliot feel it was important to disguise her sex when, in the same period, both Mrs. Gaskell and Mrs. Humphry Ward were apparently quite comfortable writing under their own names? I see by the expressions on some of your faces that you question these women for using not only their married names but the titles that went along with them. We will, I assure you, speak of that later in the course.

"But first I want to concentrate on this huge marvelous novel . . ."

Susan smiled and settled down to listen. Who cared who was married to whom? Who cared what names these women took when they declared themselves to be the authors of these wonderful books? The class was getting down to business and talking about the novels. She was content.

PART II

MIDTERMS

TEN

"**W**HAT IF I FLUNK?" SUSAN PUSHED HER DANISH PASTRY away. She was too worried to eat.

"You're not going to flunk." Jinx, apparently having given up trying to lose those ten pounds, took a large bite of her jelly doughnut.

"I've failed three quizzes and only got a C on the fourth."

"You won't flunk if you analyze what you just told me. What did you do differently on the test you didn't fail? Study harder? Concentrate on the textbook more than the class notes? What?"

"It was the first quiz. There was an easy section with some vocabulary words and a diagram where we had to label the parts of a telescope. The quizzes after that have been theories and math. Tough stuff."

"You're kidding! Why is it that astronomy sounds so romantic? Sort of a staring-at-the-stars-with-a-loved-one-by-your-side-type of class?"

"That's what I thought. And, boy, was I wrong. It's science, science all the way. And it's driving me nuts. I wish I'd dropped the course when I had the chance."

"Astronomy? Oh, I took that last year. Boring. Boring. Boring. Nothing about sun signs or your horoscope or anything at all interesting. I hated it, but I aced it." The two women had been joined by another student from their creative writing class. A junior.

"Hi, Vicki. Have a seat," Jinx said politely (and unnecessarily, as Vicki had already taken one chair to sit in and was plunking her backpack down on another). Susan said nothing.

What could she say to someone so obviously her mental superior?

"Don't you have a degree already?" Vicki asked, turning her attention to Susan.

"Well, yes, but . . ."

"So are you planning on going for your master's?"

"No."

"Then what difference does it make whether or not you flunk a course or two? If I weren't working on a degree, I'd never pick up a book." She leaned forward and stared at the Danish pastry still sitting in the middle of the table. "Is anyone going to eat that?"

Susan pushed the plate toward the young woman. "Feel free."

"So why do you care?" Vicki persisted, her mouth full of buttery dough.

Susan and Jinx exchanged looks. "I guess it's just compulsive behavior," Susan said.

"I'm working on a degree, but I'd feel the same way if I weren't in a degree program," Jinx said.

Vicki looked skeptical. "I guess maybe it has something to do with being old . . . older . . . more mature. You know what I mean."

"Yes. Old."

"Old. Definitely old." Jinx agreed with Susan. "Don't worry, hon. When you get to be our age—"

"Now that's one of those phrases I never thought I'd use," Susan interrupted.

"Well, hang on, because you're going to hear it again. When you get to be our age, you want to do things the right way."

"When you get to be our age, you hate the thought of someone saying you can't do something because you're our age," Susan added. "If you know what I mean."

"Sure. Of course," Vicki replied, sounding like she meant the opposite. "So why are you having so much trouble? All you have to do is make sure you've memorized the information that is highlighted in the course synopsis, the one old Forbes-Robertson handed out the first day of class, and you won't have any trouble."

"You're kidding!"

"You didn't know?" It was obvious that Vicki's opinion of Susan's mental abilities was getting lower by the minute. "My lab partner and I realized that the second week of class."

"Oh, well, I don't have a lab partner," Susan explained, as if that was an excuse.

"She was murdered," Jinx added.

"Merry Kenny was your lab partner? Wow! Did she ever say anything that might give you a hint as to who killed her?"

"No . . ."

"I think it was a boyfriend. I knew she was always having trouble with some guy she was seeing. She sure could pick the wrong men!"

"You knew her?" Susan asked.

Vicki answered Susan's question. "We shared an apartment off campus last year. Well, for half the year. I moved out and into an apartment with this guy. . . ." She sighed and Susan got the impression that the young woman was hoping for an opportunity to pour out the story of this particular part of her life to them.

"You were friends?" Jinx asked.

"Not really. Merry was going to room with someone else and I was all set to move in with my boyfriend. At least that's what I thought at the end of my freshman year. But we broke up over the summer and I hadn't signed up for a dorm room. So I was stuck. I went to the housing office. They put us together. Then my boyfriend and I got back together and I moved out and in with him. Stupid of me. I should have known that a guy who will dump you over the summer isn't to be trusted. He was seeing someone else the entire time we were together. Well, I wasn't going to put up with that, so I'm living alone this year and—"

"But you and Merry remained friends after you moved out of her apartment?" Susan interrupted to ask.

"We stayed in touch."

"Was she ever married?" Susan asked.

"Married? Merry? Are you kidding me? She didn't plan on ever getting married. Said she didn't believe in it. And if you ask me, she meant that. She was involved with more married men than anyone else I know. I think she liked breaking up marriages. That's the truth, if you ask me."

"I met Merry in a support group for women getting divorced," Jinx stated flatly.

"Oh, that. That was different." Vicki looked distinctly embarrassed.

"Different?" Jinx repeated.

"Yeah. That was her social psychology project last year."

"Going to a support group was a class project?" Susan asked. If only she had signed up for that class!

"Yeah. Sort of." Vicki became uncharacteristically reticent.

"What do you mean, sort of?" Jinx asked, leaning on the table.

"Well, she started out studying groups. The traditional kind. Like Alcoholics Anonymous."

"So she went to meetings and claimed to be an alcoholic? Or was she really an alcoholic?" Jinx persisted.

"She didn't. And she wasn't. Oh, wine with dinner and a little weed on weekends to relax. You know." Vicki hesitated. "Or maybe you don't. At your age and . . . and all."

"We've heard of such things," Susan said, trying not to smile.

"Yes. Although we called it pot and listened to the Dead while we smoked," Jinx told her.

"The Grateful Dead! Sure. We listen to them, too."

"I'm glad we all have something in common, but to get back to what we were talking about," Jinx persisted. "Merry was going to support groups, where she didn't belong."

"It wasn't like that. She only went to open meetings of AA. She said that you don't have to be an alcoholic to go to that type of meeting. And everyone there knows that . . . I guess."

"But that's not what happened at the group I went to," Jinx said.

"You mean you were a member of that group of women who were getting divorced?" Vicki asked.

"Exactly. And those weren't what you call open meetings. She didn't tell us she was there because she was taking a course. We all thought she was there because she was going through a terrible time in her life and needed help. At least that's what she claimed." It was obvious to Susan that Jinx was furious.

Vicki picked up the message, too. "Hey, don't blame me. I didn't have anything to do with it. I don't even know much about it. She just told me a little about some of the meetings."

"What? What did she tell you?"

"I told you. Not much. She said that the women . . . uh, got together once a week and—"

"You started to say something else. What was it?" asked Jinx, who had picked up on the pause.

"Look, she's dead. I don't want to say anything that makes her sound mean or anything."

"As you say, she's dead," Jinx stated more gently (probably, Susan thought, because she realized that Merry's death might have been a serious loss to this young woman). "But it wasn't a natural death. She was murdered. And this woman here"—she pointed to Susan—"is trying to find out who killed her. You don't want the murderer of your friend to go free, do you? Other people might get killed."

"No, I don't. Of course not. But I don't want to hurt your feelings, either."

"You don't have to worry about me. I benefited a lot from that support group. And my personal opinion of what Merry was doing doesn't really matter much now that she's dead."

"Well, I guess. I don't know where to start."

"Just tell us what you know," Susan suggested.

Jinx was more direct. "Tell us everything."

"Well, Merry went to some open AA meetings thinking she would do a report on them, but she changed her mind almost immediately. This was early in the semester."

"And?" Jinx prompted.

"And somehow she heard about these other meetings. The women getting divorced support group. I don't know what you called yourselves," she added apologetically to Jinx.

"Unlucky to start with."

"Huh?"

"Stupid joke. Never mind. Go on."

"Well, to tell you the truth—"

"Which is what we're waiting to hear," Jinx mumbled.

"Well, Merry didn't want to study the people in AA. She said they had real problems, but that the divorced women's group was full of whiners who couldn't keep their men." She looked anxiously at Jinx. "That's what she said."

"That's not, however, what she said at the meetings, where the rest of us were doing some pretty serious work trying to put together lives torn apart by men who didn't give a damn anymore."

"Merry said that, not Vicki," Susan reminded her friend, reaching out and putting a gentle hand on her arm.

"I . . . of course. I'm very sorry." Jinx blushed. "Guess I'm a bit more sensitive about the entire thing than I thought I was. Go on. I'll listen quietly."

"There's not that much more to tell." Vicki shrugged. "She went to meetings regularly throughout the semester and then wrote a report. Must have been a good one, too. She got an A."

"Did you read it?"

"Read someone else's term paper? Are you kidding? I try to forget my own the day after I turn them in. Unless, of course, I can recycle them."

"What do you mean?" Susan asked.

"Oh, you know. Write a paper for one class, then the next semester choose a similar topic for a different class, change the paper just a bit, and turn it in again. Recycled work. Everyone does it!"

"But you don't learn as much as you would if you had done two original papers," Susan protested.

"No, I guess not." Vicki looked as through she couldn't imagine anyone caring.

"About the class Merry wrote the paper on support groups for." Susan returned to the point. "I don't suppose you know who her professor was for that class?"

"I sure do. Professor Laker. She had an affair with him that lasted through about half of the semester."

ELEVEN

"I'D LIKE TO SEE PROFESSOR LAKER, PLEASE. IT'S IMPORTANT."

The young woman manning the desk in the reception area of the psychology department looked skeptical. "Is it about your midterm? Professor Laker told me to tell his students that grades would be posted over there." She nodded toward a large bulletin board that was hanging on the wall across the room. It was covered with notices of available jobs and the office hours of various professors and their teaching assistants. Susan hoped the professor taught small classes; there was little room available. "Frankly," the young woman continued, "I wouldn't worry if I were you. He's an easy grader."

"No, we need to see him. It's not about midterms. I'm . . . we're . . . neither of us is in any of his classes," Jinx explained.

"Then why are you here?"

"We need to see him about something personal," Susan said.

"You're not married to him, are you? I mean," the young woman continued, apparently realizing she had just accused the man of bigamy, "neither of you is married to him, are you?"

"No. We just need to ask him some questions. About a class he taught last year."

"Well, I suppose you can knock on his door. He might be in. Room six. Down the hallway." She pointed.

"She should have just pointed us in the right direction when we came in," Jinx hissed, following Susan down the narrow hall.

"But then she would still be wondering if one of us is the esteemed Mrs. Laker," Susan replied. They had arrived at an

71

open door with a large six painted on it. "Hello, are you Professor Laker?" she asked the man sitting at the desk.

"It's my office. Who else would I be?"

Susan and Jinx exchanged looks. Susan didn't know what Jinx was thinking, but she couldn't help wondering how this could be the man who had inspired passion in Merry. He was huge. Fortunately, he had long arms, or he would never have managed to reach around his belly to the pile of books and papers covering his desk. Susan guessed that he was around her age. His graying hair was pulled back into a skimpy ponytail, which snaked down the back of his ragged chambray shirt. Blue jeans and worn running shoes completed his outfit.

"I'm Susan Henshaw and this is Jinx Jensen. We would like to ask you some questions."

"About what?"

"About Merry Kenny. The student who was murdered," Jinx answered bluntly.

"Was Merry a friend of yours?" Professor Laker asked.

"Not a friend exactly," Jinx answered. "We both knew her, though. And she was Susan's lab partner in astronomy."

"Not exactly a close bond."

"She was murdered with my backpack," Susan added.

"I think almost anyone would consider that a unique bond," he said seriously. "And it might make you interested in her murder, but I'm still not sure why you think it entitles you to ask questions of people whose relationship with Merry was of a more intimate nature."

"I am trying to find out who killed her and why," Susan stated flatly, hoping that he wouldn't ask her why.

"Why?"

Damn! "Because—"

"Because the police have been threatening to arrest Susan," Jinx lied. "She is just trying to defend herself with the truth."

"An interesting idea in our system of justice, but I have no reason not to help you. Ask away." And he leaned so far back in his chair that Susan was afraid he would fall to the floor.

"You . . . uh . . ."

"If you're going to ask about my relationship with Merry, I should tell you that our affair was no secret. Many of my colleagues know that it happened and they also know that it was over long before her death."

"Why?"

"Why do these things end? I suppose Merry and I just were not meant to be."

"I mean," Susan said, trying not to sound angry at the arrogance of this man, "why did your colleagues even know about your relationship with Merry?" Had he been bragging about going to bed with a young, attractive coed? she wondered.

"I am an adult and I am discreet. But Merry told everyone she knew. I can only assume that she was proud of our relationship."

Jinx was scowling. "Could we start at the beginning of the story?" she asked. "Like how did your relationship start? We understand she was in one of your classes."

"Two of them, actually. She took my Introduction to Social Psychology in the fall last year and then Social Psychology II in the spring semester. We . . . ah, we became involved in the spring."

"How did that happen?" Susan asked.

"Aren't you married?" Jinx spoke at the same time, looking down at the gold band he wore on his left hand.

"How does anything like that happen? Merry and I had some student-teacher conferences, met for coffee a few times; we had a lot in common and . . . well, frankly, we were attracted to each other. And I was separated from my wife at the time. Not that it's any business of yours," he added to Jinx.

"Was Merry a good student?" Susan asked.

"Exceptional. Much more creative than average."

"Creative? How?"

"Let me give you an example. Most of my students turn in the same old term paper year after year. But Merry decided not to just research her paper in the Carn or the Darn but to live her paper. She did research in the field, so to speak. Remarkable for a student in a lower-level undergraduate class."

"Are you talking about the research she did on support groups?"

"Oh, you know about that?"

Both women nodded.

"That's exactly what I'm talking about. She positively flung herself into that project. Her idea was that support groups are frequently used by the members of the group for purposes to which they were not intended."

"Like dating people in your AA meeting," Susan suggested.

"Not exactly. Dating is an outgrowth of propinquity. You date those you know. And if you're busy going to four or five AA meetings a week, the people you know are going to be the people in those meetings. That doesn't mean anyone would join AA thinking it was a dating service. No, Merry's thesis was a bit more sophisticated than that. She felt that some people use the meetings to find a truth in their lives and others use them to verify their own lies. If you understand what I mean."

"No, I don't."

"We don't know anything about social psychology, I'm afraid," Susan explained, in case Jinx's comment had sounded too abrupt.

"Well, then you probably won't understand what Merry was trying to prove—what she did, in fact, to my complete satisfaction, prove. That sometimes a support group ends up supporting the exact opposite of what it intended."

"How did she do that? Did she find a support group for something she felt she needed? Like Overeaters Anonymous—not that Merry was fat," Jinx added quickly.

"Which support group Merry chose to study doesn't really matter. What matters is that she felt she had begun to prove her premise. And that is very rare in a student, I can assure you."

"You know, Professor, I understand that Merry joined a group and then pretended to be an ordinary member rather than someone studying group dynamics. Is that ethical?" Susan asked. She thought that she really sounded as though she knew what she was talking about.

"Well . . ."

"It seems to me that a person who joins a group under false pretenses, such as studying the group rather than receiving support from the group, might, in fact, change the dynamics of the group she is studying."

"I don't think you know what you are talking about, frankly. Merry was quite capable of acting as though she had a real reason to be in the group she chose. I don't believe her presence would have changed the experience for any of the other members."

Susan realized that Professor Laker was going to stonewall them and that, in fact, they weren't really learning anything more about Merry. She could also feel Jinx's irritation increasing. Time to change the subject. "Was Merry in love with you?" she asked, hoping to flatter him into talking about the relationship.

"She claimed to be. I am, I believe, a realistic man. I know I'm no longer a young stud and Merry was charming, intelligent, attractive. She didn't have to settle for a man she didn't want. If she wasn't in love with me, why would she have become involved?"

"Maybe—"

"I like to think we met as two people interested in the same things, who had a lot in common beside our mutual love."

"But you were married at the time," Jinx reminded him.

"Separated."

"Why?"

"I certainly don't see what business that is of yours."

"I just wondered if Merry was one in a long line of young female students whom you seduced, or whether your affair with her was unique," Jinx replied.

Susan assumed he would refuse to answer—if he didn't actually throw them out of his office. But, surprisingly, he became a bit more subdued. "The committee sent you, didn't they? You're not here because of Merry. You're not interested in Merry at all, are you?"

Susan didn't know what to say. "What are you talking about? Why else would we be here?"

"We only care about Merry," Jinx said. "We have nothing to do with any sexual harassment committee."

Susan was getting confused. She looked over at Jinx. "What sexual harassment committee?"

"Don't you read the *Clarion*?"

"The student newspaper?"

"Yes. Stories about the formation of a committee to process complaints of sexual harassment on campus have been on the front page every week all semester."

"I hadn't noticed." Hell, since she had returned to school, she barely managed to glance through the *New York Times* most days.

"There are people on campus who seriously believe that an affair between a professor and a student is almost always a case of sexual harassment. Because of the inequality of the people involved—the professor in his position of power over the student. Trading grades for sex."

"I have never done that, and I certainly never will do anything like that!" Professor Laker roared.

"We're not accusing you of anything," Jinx insisted. "I'm just explaining the committee to Mrs. Henshaw."

"And we have nothing to do with any official—or unofficial—campus investigation," Susan added. "I can assure you that it's only Merry we're interested in. Nothing else. No one else. Not even your marriage, except as it relates to Merry. I'm trying to avoid being arrested for murder, Professor."

"Well, I had no reason to murder Merry. We fell in love. We had an affair. We fell out of love and I went back to my wife. I rarely saw Merry after that. When we passed on campus, I was cordial. That's all. That's it. End of story." He stood. "And I think it is time for the two of you to leave my office. I have work to do, you know."

"I have just one more question, Professor Laker," Jinx said as the two women followed the professor's lead and stood. "How did a woman who was never married pick a support group for women going through a divorce to study? What was it about that particular group that interested her?"

He stopped, his hand on the doorway. "You know, I wondered about that myself. I thought . . . But what I thought was not important because it turned out not to be true. I suppose she just saw a notice about the meetings and went to one." He looked at the two women carefully, as if finding them of interest for the first time since they walked into his office. "Why do you ask? Are you under the impression that the support group had anything at all to do with Merry's murder?"

"Not really," Jinx said.

"We're just curious," Susan admitted. "There's just one other question. Nothing about your relationship."

He sighed, his stomach distending even farther. "One more then."

"Do you have any idea why anyone would want to murder Merry?"

He seemed to consider the question seriously, as though it was somehow unexpected or unique. "No. None."

TWELVE

"GOD, I FEEL LIKE A FOOL," JINX ANNOUNCED WHEN THEY were back in the lobby of the psychology building.

"Why?"

"I thought I'd come to terms with it all. You know, with men having affairs, leaving their wives for younger women. The whole bit. And then I saw that fat old man just reveling in the fact that a young woman had found him attractive, and I started to burn. And when he announced that his wife had taken him back after all that had happened . . . I'm sorry. I wanted to rip his lungs out."

"Seems to me you should be mad at his wife," Susan suggested.

"Why?"

"She took him back."

"Hey, I don't blame anyone for making a different decision than I did. That's one of the things I learned in group. I mean, my marriage was pretty much over. My husband and I hadn't had much of a life together for years. That's part of what the group taught me. I listened to women talking about how they missed lying in bed at night and discussing the day with their husband. How much they missed his support—and I don't mean financial. And listening to them I suddenly realized that I wasn't getting either. When it came right down to it, we had been living separately in the same house for years. He shouldn't have had an affair; I blame him for that. But I never even considered forgiving him and staying married."

"And a lot of women did?"

"Yes. I was surprised by how many. And according to the therapist who ran our group, a lot of those women end up with very strong marriages. For me the opposite happened. I kicked my husband out of the house and cried and screamed and mourned, and then one day I woke up and realized I was not only better off without him—like a lot of my friends had been saying—but I was happier without him. I wouldn't go so far as to say he did me a favor when he got involved with that bimbo—my ego took a while to recover—but things have turned out just fine."

"And what about your ex? Is he happy with the woman he got involved with?"

"Okay, let's be honest," Jinx said, opening the door for Susan. "She got fed up with him after a year and took off with a new, and younger, man. I practically celebrated when I heard the news."

"Poetic justice?"

"Sounds like it to me!" Jinx laughed, and ran smack into a man trying to enter the building they were leaving.

"I'm sorry."

"I can't say that I am. You may have saved me a trip to the suburbs. I was looking for your companion."

Jinx glanced at Susan, who was staring at the good-looking young man who had just spoken.

"I remember you. Your name is Reilly. Mark Reilly."

"Michael O'Reilly," he corrected, moving out of the way as three giggling coeds pushed by them to get through the doorway. "Maybe we could go someplace more private?"

"Why do you want to talk to me?" Susan asked.

"Who are you?" Jinx sounded substantially less hostile.

"It's midterms week, you know," Susan added, not moving. "I'm very busy."

"I am perfectly aware of what week it is. I'm a student here, too. And I have midterms as well. But I also have a job to do. A full-time job."

"What do you do—" Jinx began to ask.

"Officer O'Reilly is one of the police officers investigating Merry's murder," Susan explained. "I didn't realize he was a student as well."

"I'm working on my master's. And I'm planning to start law school next year."

"Sounds like you're the classic overachiever," Jinx said.

"My father spent his entire life walking a beat. I have no intention of doing the same." His tone didn't encourage further exploration of the subject.

"Why do you need to see me now?" Susan asked, standing her ground. "Can't it wait?"

"Well, I was going to return your backpack. . . ."

"You're kidding. Why didn't you say so?" Susan asked, a big smile appearing on her face. "I need one of the things in there—a class syllabus for my midterm in astronomy. That's good news!"

"And I need to ask you some questions."

So it wasn't all good news. "Here?" Susan asked.

"I was hoping for someplace a bit quieter, frankly. And more private." He looked at Jinx.

"How did you know Susan was here?" Jinx asked, ignoring his hint with more presence than Susan would have had.

"I . . . well, actually, I am here to interview someone else about Ms. Kenny's life."

"If you just happened to run into Susan, surely your need to speak with her couldn't be all that urgent."

Susan tried not to smile. Jinx was really something!

But apparently Michael O'Reilly didn't agree with her assessment. "I am a busy man, Mrs. Whoever-you-are. And I heard enough of your conversation with Mrs. Henshaw to realize that you are not fond of men. In my business, I often see women who have been abandoned by men who turn against the entire sex—"

"Excuse me?"

"I said—"

"I know exactly what you said and I also know that you know nothing at all about my life and have absolutely no basis to make any sort of judgment about me or my feelings about the opposite sex. You . . . you arrogant idiot!"

"Jinx, he's a policeman."

Jinx stopped and looked at Susan. "Is there a law against insulting a policeman?"

"I don't know, but it's probably not a good idea."

"It's a very bad idea," Officer O'Reilly told them. "Your backpack is in my car. What I have to do shouldn't take more than an hour. Where can we meet?"

"Can't you just give it to me now? I really need that syllabus."

"No, I can't. There are certain formalities we must go through. You must check your property and sign some papers."

"Well, then, how about the Student Union?" Susan suggested without thinking about it much.

"Why not someplace a little quieter? And more private. You're taking astronomy? How about the foyer in the old science building?"

"I guess." Susan would have preferred a place with chairs in case he was late, but on the other hand maybe the laboratory would be open and she could do a little studying there. "Okay. One hour."

"Yes. And I think this should be a private discussion."

"I can leave you alone," Jinx offered.

"Please do." And with that Michael O'Reilly spun around on the heels of his well-polished cordovan loafers and entered the psychology building.

"Boy, he's a pain in the butt, isn't he?" Jinx said. "On the other hand, he's awfully good-looking."

"He makes me nervous," Susan admitted.

"Why? You didn't do anything wrong. It's not your fault that Merry picked up your backpack instead of her own and that it just happened to be handy when someone was looking for a murder weapon."

"I know that, but a lot of things bother me about it all."

"Like what?" Jinx asked, following Susan down the steps.

"In the first place, the murderer hasn't been arrested."

"You know, I read someplace that if a murderer isn't arrested in the first twenty-four hours after the murder, the chances are less than fifty-fifty that he or she will ever be found. I don't remember where I read it, and it must have been a while ago, because I do remember thinking that I could kill my ex and probably get away with it."

"That may be true in a big city, where there's lots of crime, but I don't think it's necessarily true in Connecticut. I think the police here are going to investigate until there's an arrest. And I sure don't want to be the person they arrest."

"You started out wanting to investigate the murder."

"Yes, but Brett—he's the chief of police in Hancock—talked me out of it. And I've been busy. Getting back into the habit of studying is more difficult than I imagined it would be."

"I know what you mean. Although I'm having a wonderful time writing my novel now."

"You're going to turn in your novel!"

"Yup, it's about my husband. I'm writing a murder mystery with him as the victim! Although I think I'm going to have to do a lot of editing. Right now he's tortured to death—and the description of that alone takes nine pages."

"That may be too much," Susan suggested.

"Yeah, but it was such fun to write! I especially like the part where his nose hairs are pulled out one by one!"

"Oh, yuck!"

"You think it's a bit much?"

"Just a bit."

"Then I won't tell you what I did—what the character in the story did—to his armpits."

"Spare me." Susan paused. "But if it's a murder mystery, how are you going to disguise the suspects? Won't everyone know it's the ex-wife who killed him?"

"In the story I'm writing there are lots of ex-wives and ex-lovers, and they all hate him. The detective has a lot of suspects to choose from."

"How long is your story going to be?"

"Right now it's 148 pages single-spaced. And I haven't even figured out who my detective is. I plan to use an amateur detective. I want someone interesting, but I think everyone has been done. Housewife, cleaning woman, caterer."

"How about a dentist? I've never read a mystery where the sleuth is a dentist."

"Forensic dentistry. Been done."

They were walking by the Student Union and a poster of Colorado fluttered in the breeze. "Ski instructor?" Susan suggested, staring at the icy mountain slopes. The next poster announced an upcoming visit from an alternative rock group. "Or how about a rock 'n' roll singer?"

"Good thoughts. I just wish I knew a bit more about skiing or rock music."

"Why don't you write about what you know? I know it's a cliché, but it's been working for people for years. Have your detective be a weaver or a potter or . . ."

"Or how about a middle-aged dilettante who has gone back to school to try to learn to be a writer?"

"Sounds good to me! Are you planning to try to get it published?" Susan asked, impressed.

"Why not? If I ever finish it. Maybe I'll be the next Mary Higgins Clark."

"And just think, I'll be able to say I knew you when you were a nobody."

"Thanks. Do you want me to wait for Officer O'Reilly with you?"

"No. You've got work to do. We don't want to leave your fictional murder unsolved, do we?"

"No, I think it's better, in this case at least, if art does not imitate life."

THIRTEEN

SUSAN WAS HARD AT WORK ON YET ANOTHER LIST OF IDEAS for her short story when Officer O'Reilly finally made an appearance. "You said you'd be here in an hour," she commented, looking at her watch.

"I discovered there was more information to be gotten in the psychology department than I imagined. You and your backpack are only a minor part of this investigation, you know."

"I can't say I'm sorry to hear that," Susan admitted.

"Which doesn't mean you're not a suspect."

"Why in heaven's name would I still be a suspect? I didn't have a motive. I wasn't anywhere near the murder scene, so I also lacked opportunity. Just because my pack happened to be used as the murder weapon? If I loaned my car to a neighbor and she then used it as the getaway car in a bank robbery, would you arrest me for robbing the bank?"

"No. But I might suggest you be a mite more careful about who you loan your car to."

What business it was of his, she didn't know. Too angry to speak, Susan held out her hand for her backpack.

"We need to go through it first."

"How do you expect me to go through it if you won't give it to me?"

"Why don't I empty it on the desk over there and you can check the contents?"

"Fine."

They both headed over to the old wooden desk apparently abandoned in the hallway near the door to a science lab. Without further ado, he dumped the backpack upside down and papers, pens, makeup bag, and even an empty water bottle fell out. It was the latter item that first attracted Susan's attention.

"The bottle isn't mine. I don't drink that brand of water."

He picked it up and twirled it around in his fingers. "It's not imported."

"That's right. I prefer San Pellegrino, but I do drink other brands."

"But they're all imported, right?"

"No. You are not right. They are not all imported. I just don't know this brand. I bring my water from home each day; I don't buy it out of those expensive machines. So I know this isn't mine."

"Interesting. It would be even more interesting if the young woman had been poisoned, but of course we both know that isn't true."

"Maybe she was poisoned before she was strangled. You know, a Mickey Finn or something. Maybe she was unconscious when she was killed. And the . . . whatever is in a Mickey Finn . . . was in that bottle."

"There was an autopsy. She was not poisoned. There was nothing but water in this bottle." But Susan noticed that he didn't just toss it into the nearest wastebasket. He did, however, pull a notebook from his back pocket and write something down.

"Let's just check this with the list, shall we?"

"What list?"

"The contents of the pack were recorded at the scene of the murder. We need to make sure that everything that was there then is here now."

"What about the water bottle? Does it say what brand of water was in the pack? Was the same brand there the day Merry died?" Susan asked, getting excited. This was the first clue she'd found and the police were ignoring it!

"You seem to be pretty obsessed with this water thing." Michael O'Reilly sounded bored.

"Does your list show Pellegrino water or this brand?"

"See for yourself."

Susan took the sheet of paper he handed her and scanned it. The brand listed was the same as the bottle. "Interesting."

"Why?"

"Because this isn't the brand of water I drink," Susan repeated. "Someone must have put this bottle in the pack."

"That doesn't make it interesting in my book. Look, the lady is thirsty. She opens her pack and pulls out the bottle of water you say you put in it at home—"

"I did put it in at home!"

"I'm not questioning your story. I'm trying to be accurate."

"Well, that's what it sounded like. So go on."

"So she drinks that bottle of water and then, still thirsty, she goes over to one of the many machines that sell water on campus, tosses out the empty bottle, and buys this one."

"This brand is sold on campus? Are you sure of that?" Susan asked.

"Positive. I see those little blue bottles every time I go for a Coke. I always wonder why the hell anyone would buy water in a plastic bottle when there are fountains in each building spouting the stuff for free. But that's just my opinion."

"Yes, it is." And Susan wasn't particularly interested in it. She continued to look through the list.

"Is everything here?" he asked.

Susan didn't answer for a moment. "I think so. It's been over five weeks and a lot has happened since the murder, but I think I can honestly say that everything I remember being in this backpack is still here. With the exception of the water bottle, of course." She started to put everything back in the pack. "If that's all you need me for . . ."

"It's not. I want to go over your statement again. The one you made at the time of the murder."

Susan held out her hand for it.

"Why don't I just go over it with you?"

She shrugged. "If you want to, but I do have to study."

"As I think I told you, so do I. And I don't get off from work for four hours."

Susan didn't think she would win a game of "I'm busier than you are" with him, so she decided to let him start as he wished. "So read." She jumped up and sat on the edge of the desk.

"According to this, you think you and Merry accidentally traded backpacks in the astronomy laboratory in . . ." He looked up and seemed to recognize their location for the first time. "In this building, in fact."

"In that room, in fact," Susan added, pointing to the doorway behind her.

"This one?" He reached out and turned the doorknob as he asked the question.

The door opened as she answered. "Yes."

"Why don't we . . ." He started into the room without waiting for her answer.

"Fine with me." She hopped down, swept the last of her possessions into her old backpack, and, carrying two packs, hurried after him into the lab.

"So where were the two of you sitting when this switch happened?"

"We were lab partners. We were sitting at our seats. Over there." Susan pointed to a double table in the middle of the room.

"And which seat were you in?" he asked, walking over to the table Susan had pointed out.

Susan pointed again. "And Merry was in the other one, of course."

"Were your seats assigned?"

"Yes. And we didn't choose to be lab partners, either. That was assigned on the first day of class. I mean, I didn't know Merry before I came to school. We didn't pick each other."

"So you always sat on the aisle and Merry always sat on the inside." He continued his questions as though nothing she said was of interest to him.

"Oh, no. We were assigned to a certain table, but we could sit in whichever seat we preferred."

"And you were sitting here the last time you saw Merry alive."

"Yes."

"And you say in your statement that you both put your backpacks on the floor."

"I did? I don't remember now. But if I said it then . . ."

"You think you were accurate?"

"I'm sure I was accurate."

"Okay. So why don't you explain exactly how you came to pick up Merry's pack and she yours."

"As well as I can remember, they were both sitting on the floor. Merry and I were talking about meeting later at a coffee shop off campus that she knew about."

"It says here that you were going to study together. Wasn't it a little early in the semester for a study date? Most students were still buying books at that point."

"You've never taken a class from Professor Forbes-Robertson, have you? She plunges right in. And Merry and I were to be the second group up at the telescope the following night—the first night our class was scheduled to meet at the observatory."

She paused for a moment and remembered that terrible evening. Flustered without her lab notes or a partner, she had flubbed her way through the assignment, embarrassing herself horribly. She had gotten the impression that Professor Forbes-Robertson had enjoyed writing a large red F in her grade book beside "Henshaw, S."

"Anything wrong?"

"Just a bad memory. It doesn't have anything to do with Merry," she added quickly.

He looked as though he didn't believe her, so she continued on quickly.

"See how dark it is on the floor. And our packs were both old and blue. Mine belonged to Chad, my son, when he was in junior high school and was probably even more worn than Merry's. I think that whoever reached down first just grabbed the first black nylon strap her hand touched and assumed that it was her own."

"You say here that you don't know who grabbed first."

"No. And if I had no idea then, I sure haven't got an idea now."

"And you say you didn't look in your backpack until you were at that coffee shop."

"Right."

"What about your car keys? Did you drive to the restaurant?"

"Yes. They were in the pocket of my jacket."

"Do you ever carry a purse as well as a backpack?" He looked at her elegant Spanish leather pack now sitting on the table next to them.

Susan reached into the pack and pulled out a small Dooney & Bourke bag. "Yes, but sometimes I'm carrying the one that fits into my pack and sometimes I'm not."

"Why do you change purses?"

"Because it goes better with what I'm wearing. Or I need to carry things in it when I'm out shopping or something," she answered impatiently. "But when I'm carrying a small purse and I have room, I put it in my pack. Which is what I'm doing today. But that day I was carrying most of my textbooks, and the professors had given out syllabuses, and . . . Well, anyway, my pack was stuffed and I didn't have my purse and . . ." She stopped speaking.

"Something wrong?" he asked suspiciously.

"I . . . No, not really. I just thought of something. Nothing important probably."

"What?"

"Well, I had Merry's pack, remember."

"Because you'd switched them, yes."

"There were keys in the pack I had—in Merry's pack. She didn't carry a purse; most of the younger women don't. They just use a pack. And there were keys in the pack I had. I didn't think much about it at the time."

"And why do you think it's so significant now?"

"Because how could she have gotten into her apartment without her keys? And you see what that means, don't you?"

"I'd love to hear what you think it means."

Susan wondered if that was sarcasm she heard in his voice. "Because if she didn't have her keys, the person who killed her must have let her in. The person who killed her must have had another set of keys. Don't you see? It's a clue."

"There is, Mrs. Henshaw, another possibility."

"What?"

"You had her keys. You could have gone to her apartment and opened the door. You could be the murderer."

FOURTEEN

"I COULDN'T BELIEVE IT. THE MAN WAS PRACTICALLY ACCUS-
ing me of murder." Susan appeared in the doorway between
the bedroom she shared with Jed and the bathroom, waving a
toothbrush to emphasize her point.

"Hon, it's almost midnight. Don't you have a midterm tomorrow? Shouldn't you get some sleep?" Her husband's
voice was muffled by the down comforter he had thrown over
his head.

"Jed, it won't do me any good to get an education if I end
up in prison!"

"Oh, I understand some prison systems have quite extensive education programs . . ."

Well, if he wasn't going to take her seriously! She scowled
and returned to the bathroom. The vocabulary lists taped
around her mirror had become almost ornamental in the last
few weeks as various colors of notecard came into use. Susan
thought that if she ever started to study a new language again
she would get organized from the beginning, creating a
system where pink cards were printed with verbs, green for
nouns, white for adjectives and adverbs. Not, she reminded
herself, that she was ever going to learn another language. If
traveling in another country without even knowing a smat-
tering of the local dialect condemned her as an ugly American, so be it! She couldn't take this!

Her midterms were spread out over the next week and a
half. But Thursday was reserved for critique time in creative
writing. She hoped her last short essay wouldn't be one of the
ones critiqued. It seemed to her that her first midterm exams
in almost thirty years should be enough grief for one week.

She rinsed out her mouth, tied her flannel robe more tightly around her, and picked up the notebook she had been studying during her bath. It was slightly damp along the bottom. She yawned. The bath had made her sleepy rather than waking her up; apparently, the aromatherapy bath salts labeled "pick-me-upper" had not done the trick. Maybe a cup of tea would improve her concentration. She looked around, but her slippers seemed to have vanished. Sighing, she left the bathroom, tiptoed through the bedroom—she knew Jed would sleep through the night, but she sure didn't want Clue to wake up and decide a midnight walk was just the thing—and headed downstairs to the kitchen.

The shelf where tins of Earl Grey, orange pekoe, and Constant Comment normally sat was filled with tins with labels that were printed with names like Tea of Tranquillity, Memory Master Mango, and Ageless Asago Gingko. The labels were all beautiful and artistic and everything looked so healthy and intentional that she always felt guilty adding artificial sweetener to her tea, wondering if bees were at that very moment feeding on organic and rare flowers to produce the perfect honey to gently sweeten these effete brews.

But she was exhausted and beginning to panic. What if that young woman today had been wrong? What if knowing the material on the syllabus wasn't enough? She had spent the last twelve hours taking notes, revising her notes, studying her notes. She was pretty sure she knew everything she had been told she needed to know ... But, she asked herself again, what if she needed to know more than what was on the syllabus? What if she needed to know—in fact, to understand—all the material that had been confusing her ever since the first day of class? She had to get a good grade on her midterm! She was so far behind that she might actually fail the course even if she did get a good grade on the midterm. She gave up on herbal tea and reached for the coffee beans and her grinder. She didn't know what the questions would be, but she was sure that caffeine was at least a part of the answer.

But by the time the coffee was ready, she had begun to wonder if a break wasn't in order. Every time she read through the material she seemed to know it. Maybe if she just thought about something else for a few minutes and came back to it, she would be able to judge her own knowledge more objectively. And definitely, she decided, she would be able to concentrate a bit better once she had done a little constructive thinking about what was really on her mind!

She got up and went over to her old backpack. She had dumped it on the counter when she came home, knowing Jed's idea of cleaning rarely included lifting before wiping.

She opened it slowly, wondering again if Officer O'Reilly had noticed anything unusual in her reaction to his insistence that she examine her pack. She had been honest, however, in saying that nothing was missing from her pack except for her bottle of water. Luckily, he hadn't asked if anything had been added!

She pulled out the sheets of paper she'd discovered stuck inside her Victorian literature text. They were printed on an anonymous dot-matrix printer, so there was no reason that anyone looking at them would not assume they belonged to Susan. No one except Susan, who was positively sure they weren't hers!

She only wished she knew exactly whose they were. Not that she was sure what they were. At first glance, she had decided they were a creative writing project. Then she'd decided they were pages of a letter to an unidentified person. If only there were more pages . . . What she had in her hand contained neither a salutation nor an address.

She read through the first few lines for the third time that evening.

He approached me after class. I was sitting at my desk, organizing the notes I had taken during the lecture, when I became aware of his presence. There was a suppressed sensuality about him and I remember shivering slightly with anticipation. . . .

Susan stopped reading, thinking Merry might have pursued a career as a romance writer if she had lived.

But Merry was a sociology major. Could this have been a part of her work? A project she was doing? Like the research she had done last year on Jinx's support group? Maybe even a recycling of the material in last year's term paper, as Vicki had suggested was a common student practice? Well, Susan decided, she could ask Jinx about it tomorrow. After her astronomy midterm. She looked at the pile of notebooks on her table and remembered something her son said frequently.

"You don't want me to overstudy, do you, Mom?"

She had thought it was bull at the time. But now . . .

"Oh, hell," she said aloud to the empty room. "Maybe the kid was right after all." She left everything where it was and headed to bed. She'd set the alarm for five A.M. Everyone knew studying in the morning was more efficient than working late into the night.

The alarm came as a relief, waking Susan from a nightmare in which she was taking a midterm for a class she had not attended all semester. For some reason, she had thought it appropriate to attend school that day completely naked.

"Susan, what time is it?" Jed, waking up in the dark room, asked in a sleepy voice.

"Too early for you to be up. Just go back to sleep." He didn't argue, rolling over and resuming his rhythmic snoring.

Susan got dressed quickly and was about to tiptoe from the room when she realized that the accompaniment to Jed's snoring was Clue's tail, thumping on the floor in happy anticipation of an earlier-than-usual morning walk.

Susan sighed. "Okay, but we're going to make it short this morning. And," she added, following the dog downstairs, "I'm going to take my notes and a flashlight. No reason I can't get an early start like I planned."

Walking a dog in the chill October darkness and reading class notes was more difficult than she had imagined it would be. And sort of spooky, too, she decided, as Clue bounded into the crispy leaves blown into piles by the bitter north wind.

The wind also blew her papers and Susan had almost given up the attempt to read when a white sedan pulled up to the curb by her side.

"Susan? What are you and Clue doing out so early?" The

driver's window was rolled down and Brett's handsome face appeared.

"Brett. I got up early to study and Clue . . . Well, you know Clue."

He chuckled as Clue, recognizing a familiar face, jumped onto the side of the patrol car.

"Down," Susan ordered ineffectually.

"No problem. This car is scheduled to be replaced in January. A few more scratches before then won't matter." He patted the dog's golden head.

"Why are you out so early?" Susan asked. "Anything wrong?"

"Not really. There was a fire over on Orchard Street and I got beeped. Nothing serious," he added as Susan mentally ran down the list of people she knew who lived in that section of town. "Chimney fire. Apparently the owner closed the flue before going to bed without realizing that a few live embers were left. They scorched an antique Oriental rug. Smelled like hell, but except for a slight kippering of the living room's antiques, the alarm went off before any serious damage was done. What are you reading?"

"I'm studying for my first midterm. Astronomy."

"That's the class you were taking with the young woman who was killed."

"Yes."

"Any idea how the investigation is going?"

"Fine, I guess."

"Does that mean you haven't heard anything official?"

"I got my backpack back yesterday. Sounds silly, doesn't it?" She giggled. "Don't mind me. I'm so worried about this test that I'm a bit punch-drunk from lack of sleep. You wouldn't believe the dream I had last night."

"Susan, I need to talk with you. I was going to put it off. I called your house the other day and Jed answered and told me how busy you were, but if you have a few minutes this morning . . ."

"Is it about Merry?"

"Sort of. I've been in contact with the local police over

there and ... Well, frankly, their attitude is beginning to worry me."

"What attitude?"

"Look, I don't want to get you worried unnecessarily."

"Why don't you come back to the house with me? You can explain over coffee," she suggested.

Brett reached over the driver's seat and opened the rear door of the car. "Hop in. I can do a lot of explaining on the way over. It will save time."

"Great," Susan said. She had stopped worrying about her midterm. Now she was wondering whether or not she should tell Brett about the extra papers she'd discovered in her pack.

FIFTEEN

"SO HOW DID IT GO?"

Susan grinned at the concerned expression on Jinx's face. "You know, I think it went really well. I actually studied the material that was on the test and I honestly think I knew it all." She frowned. "You don't think this could be a classic example of self-delusion, do you?"

"When do you get your grade?"

"Next week."

"So you'll find out then. Why don't you just not worry about it for now? Do you have time to go have a glass of wine or something? We can celebrate getting your first midterm out of the way."

"Why not? I may as well hope for the best. And I could use a drink. I'm completely worn out. Besides, there's something I want to talk to you about. Something a little odd," Susan added.

"Sounds good to me. Do you know a bar or restaurant around here?"

"No, and I'd rather we went someplace quiet." And private, she added to herself.

"Then why not my place? The wine is good and I actually vacuumed this morning. Of course, you'll have to put up with Maggie."

"Your granddaughter?"

"No, my granddaughter's golden retriever. I'm dog-sitting this week."

"I've never met a golden I didn't love," Susan assured her.

"The problem with goldens is that they never meet anyone they don't love. The most codependent breed in the entire universe." She looked at Susan. "Where's your car?"

Susan laughed. "What happened to your diet?"

"The same thing that always happens this time of year. I bought my Halloween candy early and ate an entire bag of miniature Almond Joys."

"Maybe you should only buy candy you don't like," Susan suggested.

"I think that's an oxymoron. There is no candy I don't like—except, of course, for the candy that I love."

Susan chuckled. "My car is in the day-student lot. It's a hike, but some days it's the only exercise I get."

"So tell me about your midterm," Jinx continued as the two women headed to the parking area. "Do you really think you did well?"

"I do. I really do. I can't believe it! I went through all my notes, all those complicated theories and equations, and pulled out just what was referred to on the class syllabus. And, you know, that's what was on the test. It was amazing. I feel like I've been wandering around in a fog that's suddenly been lifted."

"This is the syllabus that was in your backpack? The one the police had been keeping all this time?"

"Yes. I could have asked Dr. Forbes-Robertson for another copy, but I really never thought I needed one. The week's reading assignments were always written on the board."

Besides, she had been trying to avoid any personal contact with her professor.

"Incredible. So how many midterms do you have left?"

"Two. Italian and Victorian lit. What about you?"

"You wouldn't believe. Remember the sociology class I told you was going to be so easy? Well . . ." The two women discussed their classes all the way to Jinx's townhouse, where a large golden retriever bounded out of the opened front door and headed down the block, causing a momentary distraction.

"Maggie! Maggie! Come back!"

"Run the other way," Susan urged.

"What?" Jinx looked at Susan as if she had gone mad.

"Run away from her! Goldens can't stand to think they're missing something. Come on! Maggie!" Susan yelled, and started running in the opposite direction from the dog.

It only took a few seconds for Maggie to realize she was being ignored and turn around. Jinx grabbed the dog's collar as she dashed in Susan's direction. Together the two women tugged the happy animal back home.

"Well, at least she's done everything she needs to do," Susan said as Maggie squatted on top of the last living impatiens of the season outside of the townhouse's door.

"And I think we deserve some cheese and crackers with our wine after that little burst of exercise. Why don't you make yourself at home in the living room while I fix us a snack?"

"Sounds good to me."

As Maggie followed her sitter to the kitchen, Susan plopped down on the comfortable couch, leaned back, and closed her eyes. The next thing she knew a dog was licking her face.

"Clue. Stop that, Clue."

"Down, Maggie. Get off the sofa!" ordered Jinx.

"I've been kissed by a dog. Clue's going to be jealous," Susan said, laughing, as she finally managed to push the large ball of fur to the floor.

"I'd like to tell you that she would be better trained if she was mine, but it would be a lie. We used to have a Newfie when my daughter was little. One hundred and forty pounds of unbridled enthusiasm. A complete mess. But we loved her."

"Are you allowed pets in this condo?"

"Yes. But I'm not even going to consider it. I want to be free to take off and travel around the world if I want to. I won't, of course, but I want to be free to do it, you understand. Red or white?" She held up two bottles of wine.

"White, thanks." While Susan napped, the coffee table had sprouted wineglasses, a basket of crackers, a plate with two different pyramids of goat cheese, and a small bowl of olives. "Hmm. Looks delicious."

"It is. Help yourself."

She did, and the two women munched and sipped happily for a few minutes, talking about their classes, comparing anxiety levels during this difficult week.

"How's your short story going?" Jinx asked.

"Not badly. The problem is, I can't judge my own work. Either I think it's a work of genius and I'm certainly going to top the bestseller list for at least a year or I think it's trash and I should zap it right out of my computer's memory before anyone reads it."

"That's the point of the class critique group, remember. They're supposed to have more perspective than the author."

"I haven't had anything read out loud in class yet."

"Lucky you!" Jinx said. "My touching description of childbirth was torn up so badly that I skipped the next few classes. I was completely humiliated."

"I really don't want to hear that!" Susan cried, putting a pillow over her head.

"Well, don't worry. When it happens you can dash right over here and I'll pour you a drink." Then Jinx reminded her, "You said you wanted to tell me something."

"Actually, I want you to look at something. It's here in my backpack." She yanked the ratty bag toward her and pulled out the sheets of computer paper she had found among her things. She passed them to Jinx.

Susan had finished her glass of wine and was resisting pouring herself another when Jinx put down the papers and looked up. "You didn't write this, did you?"

"Heavens, no! Frankly, I'd be embarrassed to show it to you if I had."

"It's certainly a little sentimental. I suppose you could excuse that if the woman who wrote it was really in love with this guy. I remember when I met my husband—"

"I think Merry wrote it." Susan interrupted before Jinx could get sidetracked by her memories.

"That's interesting." Jinx frowned and started to reread the papers. "You know what?" she said slowly. "Some of this is vaguely familiar. It sounds a bit like a story I heard in my support group."

"Are you sure?"

"I think so. It's not that unusual a story. I mean, we all talked about the beginnings of our relationships—the hope, the promise, the sex. Of course, that all changed. Who do you think this was being written to? And why?"

Susan shrugged. "I haven't the foggiest."

"It's weird, isn't it?"

"What?"

"Well, if this is the same story Merry told in the support group—and I'm pretty sure it is—then it means that Merry is . . . is what? Using the same material over and over again?"

"I don't understand."

"Well, I told you she came to my group last year, right?"

"Yes."

"And if this is about the man she claimed was her husband, she's still telling the same story."

"What about this year? Wasn't she still going to your group when she died?"

"I sure don't think so. I don't go anywhere near as much as I used to. My life is in order and the crisis is pretty much over. But I still attend at least once a month. To remind myself of all I went through and keep from slipping back into old habits—and to help women who are newly alone and just starting to think about putting their lives back together."

"And Merry hadn't been there recently?"

"Well, she could have been there when I wasn't, of course. But I think I would have heard about it. I have friends who go to meetings much more frequently than I do. One of them, in particular, would have mentioned Merry's presence. I'm sure of it."

"Why?"

"She can't stand her. In fact, if you need to know if Merry was still attending when she died, I could give Barbara a call. She goes to all the meetings."

"Why?"

"Well, she got her life together after her first husband dumped her for a younger woman. She even met another man, fell in love again, and got married. Only . . ."

"Don't tell me," Susan said, seeing what was coming.

"Yup. He left her, too." Jinx surprised Susan by smiling. "There were some members of the group who thought she re-married too quickly. Barbara says if she ever even thinks about marrying another man, she's going to make sure every single woman in the group approves."

"Sounds like it might not be a bad idea. Would it be possible for you to get in touch with Barbara? Or do you have to go to a meeting to see her?"

"No, I can give her a call."

"Would you? Right now?"

"Sure. Who could resist such an opportunity? Gossip for a good cause." She reached out for the portable phone on the coffee table. "Want another glass of wine?"

"Just half."

Jinx poured with one hand and dialed with the other. Susan was sipping wine when Barbara answered.

"Hi, Barbara, it's me. Jinx. How are you?"

Apparently, Barbara took the question seriously. Susan was wondering if she shouldn't have that other half glass of wine when Jinx managed to get a word in edgewise. "That's great. Why don't we get together for lunch on Saturday and we can catch up. The reason I'm calling, Barb," she added quickly, "is to ask you a question. About Merry Kenny. You remember her."

Barbara evidently not only remembered, she wanted to reminisce.

"Yes, well—" Jinx tried to ask her question.

"Yes, well—" She tried again.

"Did she come to any more meetings before she died?"
She made it.

"Really? . . . Really? . . . Are you sure? . . . Really? . . .
Fantastic! I'll see you on Saturday!" And Jinx hung up, a
huge smile on her face. "Well, isn't that amazing?"

"Tell me! I'm dying to know. Amazing or not."

"Merry stopped coming to group because she was asked to
leave."

"Asked to leave? Why? By who? Whom?"

"Our group leader. At least that's what Barbara said. Apparently, she missed the meeting where the announcement
was made."

"Tell me what announcement before I start to scream!"
Susan urged.

"Our group leader said that Merry had been asked to stop
attending group. One of the members had come to her complaining that Merry was trying to blackmail her."

SIXTEEN

Susan PUT DOWN HER GLASS AND STARED AT JINX. "BLACK-
mail? Isn't that a motive for murder?"

"That's exactly what I was thinking." Jinx picked up her
wineglass and drained it. "Barbara didn't know any details."

"But your group leader might. I don't suppose . . ." Susan
glanced at her watch.

"What?"

"It's late. You probably have to study."

"I'm pretty much caught up on all my work, so if you want
to ask me to do something that might help your investigation,
I'd be happy to," Jinx assured her. "In fact, I'd be thrilled. I've
been thinking about Merry recently. I didn't like her, but she

didn't deserve to die. You know, I've never thought much about murder before. I mean, it isn't exactly fair, is it? One person shouldn't decide whether another person should die."

"So how hard will it be to get in touch with the therapist who ran your group?"

"Piece of cake. She must have office hours."

"She has a private practice?"

"I don't know about that, but she's an adjunct professor at the university. I've never been to her office, but she probably has one somewhere in the psychology building."

"You're kidding! She's a psychology professor? Then don't you think Professor Laker would know her? And if he knew the person who ran your group, why didn't he mention it when we talked to him?"

"Good question."

"We need to talk with him again, but first I think we should try to get in touch with . . . What did you say this woman's name was?"

"Dr. Wesley. We call her Lillian. You know, I could call the psychology department and see if she's there."

"Good idea. Since she knows you and all . . ."

"No problem." Jinx started dialing as she spoke.

Susan looked around the attractive room as she listened to Jinx explain their need to someone on the other end of the line. "Well?" she asked as Jinx hung up.

"Lillian's regular office hours start in fifteen minutes. The secretary said she is very dependable—that if she's scheduled to be in her office, she will be."

"So I guess the only question is, do you want to come with me?"

"I was just waiting for you to ask!"

"You know," Susan said, gently lifting Maggie's head and removing her backpack, which the dog had been using as a pillow, "at this rate, we would probably lose weight if we walked back and forth to the campus."

"Only if we stopped eating."

Susan laughed. "Well, I don't think that's likely to happen." She paused and then changed the subject. "Would you mind telling me about Lillian on the way?"

"I'll tell you what I know. She runs the group, but she doesn't talk all that much about herself. She's divorced. I do know that. But not the details. Oh, once in a while she refers to her own life. But doesn't really talk about herself."

"Such as?"

"Well, one of the women would start talking about how her ex-husband had . . . uh, I don't know . . . smacked her or something. And Lillian would say something like, 'Well, my husband never hit me, but if he had . . .' and then she would go on to talk about what she thought the proper response might be."

"So you don't know why she was divorced?"

"Not really. And I don't remember her ever talking directly about her ex. She does talk about herself as an independent woman, though. She went back to school after her divorce to get an advanced degree. I know that, but I'm not sure if it was her doctorate in psychology or something else. She is phenomenally well educated. Quotes famous writers. Can recite long bits of poetry. It's amazing."

"Do you know why she started the group?"

"Oh, she didn't. She took over when the original leader and the founder of the group left."

"Do you have any idea why she left?"

"No. Come to think of it, I don't even know that she did leave. She could have died for all I know. What I do know is that Lillian started in the group as a member, not the leader."

"You mean she came to learn to cope with a husband who had left her, just like everyone else?"

"Yup. And I don't know about everyone else in group, but I really appreciated that. I mean, Lillian's brilliant. She has a great career. She's got to be in her midfifties at least, but she's fabulous-looking—almost like a model. Not that there are a whole lot of middle-aged models."

"She sounds perfect."

"Doesn't she? We'd all probably hate her if it weren't for the fact that she had gone through the same thing we had. That her husband had dumped her."

"For another woman? Or was he a case of PG&D?" Susan asked, impressed with the fact that she remembered the term.

"I knew you were going to ask me that and, frankly, I'm

not sure. I got the impression that it was a case of PG&D. But that may be because I have a difficult time imagining a man leaving Lillian for another woman. I've thought about it, of course. But I just don't know exactly what broke up her marriage."

"So she really doesn't talk much about her own marriage."

"Never directly. Like I said, she only mentions things to . . . well, I guess you could say to show that she could understand what someone was going through or that she could relate. Mostly, she sits back and once in a while she puts in a word or two of comfort or tries to get two group members to relate to each other's condition and learn from it."

"She doesn't suggest topics for discussion or anything like that?"

"You've never gone to a support group other than the one for returning students, have you?"

"No," Susan admitted.

"Well, I don't know about other groups, but in our group there is always someone who is in the middle of an immediate crisis."

"And that person just starts talking or what?"

"Let me explain. The group meets on Monday night at seven-thirty."

"Where?"

"In a room in Academic I. It's an art history classroom during the day, so it's hung with lots of bright posters and art-work. Sometimes the contrast between the artistic exuberance and the sadness of the women in the room is stunning. I wrote a short story about it, but I could never bring myself to turn it in in creative writing."

"Maybe you'd let me read it?"

"I'd love it." Jinx grinned and then continued her explana-tion. "So we all get to the group around seven-twenty or seven-twenty-five. And we stand around and talk in small groups. You know how any meeting is before it's called to order."

"Yes."

"But the difference between that group and the one for re-turning students is that there is usually someone—and some-times more than one person—clutching a handkerchief and sniffling as she holds back tears. Lillian calls the group to order by suggesting gently that it's time we started and we all find seats. Whoever has been weeping silently will burst into tears and start to talk. Usually, whatever she wants to talk about will pretty much become the topic of the meeting. On the rare occasions that no one is in the middle of a crisis, Lillian reminds us of something that happened during the previous meeting or how someone had said that this week she was going to make some sort of change in her life. Dye her hair or get a new job—anything—and Lillian asks if the plan has turned out or if the woman has changed her mind about what she wanted to do. And the group takes it from there."

"People aren't shy about talking over what's happening in their lives?"

"I know what you're thinking. If someone had told me that I would be telling a group of women I hardly knew—and when I first started going I didn't know anyone—all my personal problems and the truth about my marriage, I would have denied it backward, forward, and upside down. But what you don't realize is how desperate you are when something like that happens. The women in that group understood, and once I started going, I wasn't alone anymore. There were people who could help. It was an incredible relief."

Jinx was silent for a few minutes and Susan waited for her to continue in her own time. She had seen this woman as strong and together, but for the first time she saw the pain that Jinx had gone through to get to where she was now.

"Not everyone felt like I did." Jinx resumed the story. "And Merry was—or appeared to be—one of the women who didn't seem to get better." She stopped speaking again. "I'm not explaining very well."

"I don't understand exactly what you mean," Susan admitted.

"Well, there are women who don't benefit from coming to group for one reason or another. There are women who have problems that need to be taken care of elsewhere."

"You mentioned that Lillian sent some members to Al-Anon. For families of alcoholics, right?"

"Yes. If the problem in the marriage is that the husband is a substance abuser, Lillian thinks that Al-Anon and groups like it are more appropriate for the wife. Although not always. When the wife is determined to make a separate life for herself, our group can really contribute. And there are women who are alcoholics as well. I remember one who always reeked of alcohol when we met, and when she finally admitted she was drinking too much, she blamed it on the fact that her husband had left her. It took a while for Lillian to get her to confront her own problem and join AA, but I can tell you that everyone in the group was happier the day that happened. What a whiner."

"And were those the only women who left?"

"Heavens, no! I've never kept track, but I'll bet that at least a quarter of the women who show up the first time never come back or come back for only one or two more meetings." Jinx shrugged. "Probably some of them decide they don't have the type of problem the group could help. I'm sure some of them just cannot bear to tell complete strangers the intimate details of their lives. A few just don't belong. I remember watching a young blond woman who was upset because her husband liked to watch sports all day on the weekends. She came to the group talking about how it was abusive to ignore your spouse and how she just couldn't stand seeing him stretched out in front of the TV for one more minute. One of our members whose husband was absolutely impossible—he'd had affair after affair ever since the second month of their marriage—told her to just count her blessings that she knew where her husband was and what he was doing there. The blond never came back. I've often wondered if she took Lillian's advice."

"Which was?"

"To either learn to enjoy watching sports with him or find something to do on weekends that she enjoyed and that would take her out of the house."

"Good advice."

"Lillian is very practical as well as compassionate. You'll see."

"Two more questions," Susan said as they arrived at the now familiar psychology building.

"Sure."

"Do you have to be married to come to the group? I mean, what about women in serious relationships who aren't married and the men leave them? Are women like that welcome?"

"Definitely. But it's different if you're not married. You don't have as many legal hassles, at least not in this state."

"And you said there are women like Merry who don't seem to get better . . . to feel better? I don't know how to phrase it."

"Change their life for the better. That is the entire purpose of the group, although women come just wanting to feel better. No, there are some women who just come and whine. Month after month and year after year."

"Does Lillian ask them to leave?"

"No. I don't know whether she's just optimistic that they'll see the light eventually and get their lives together or such a compassionate person that she figures if they get some benefit from coming—even if it isn't visible to everyone else in the group—they should be allowed to continue to come."

"Well. Here we are," Susan announced as they walked up to the main bulletin board in the foyer of the building. "Is her office number on that list?"

Jinx perched her bifocals on her head and scanned the list. "Can't see without these damn things, can't see with them," she muttered. "Oh, here it is. Professor Lillian Wesley. Room 212. That must be on the second floor."

"Sounds right to me," Susan said, heading for the well-worn stairs on one side of the building.

They climbed the stairs slowly, winding their way through students who were propped against railings and perched on the stairs themselves.

"Sorry," Jinx said as her purse smacked into a young man's blond dreadlocks.

"Huh?" He looked up, apparently unaware of any assault.

"Nothing."

"Here it is!" Susan exclaimed. "Room 212." She knocked.

"Come in," a voice trilled.

"Professor Wesley . . ."

"Lillian . . ."

Susan and Jinx became silent as the woman sitting at the

desk looked up. Her welcoming smile turned into a scowl as she recognized one of her visitors. "Well, well, Jinx Jensen. Are you here to try to do just a bit more damage to my career?"

SEVENTEEN

"I COULDN'T BELIEVE IT. AND JINX WAS ASTONISHED."

"What did she say?" Jerry Gordon asked. Susan and Jed had been invited to dinner at Kathleen and Jerry's house to celebrate the halfway point in the semester, and over dessert Susan was filling them in on the details of her encounter with Lillian Wesley that afternoon. (Alex and Alice, the Gordons' eight-year-old and four-year-old respectively, having left the table by this time.)

"Well, Jinx did exactly the right thing. She tried to make sense of what was going on. She asked if they could talk privately, but Professor Wesley refused to talk. Just like that. She said that she was very upset and refused to talk things over when she was so upset and that she would appreciate it if we would leave her office immediately."

"And what did Jinx do then?" Kathleen asked, pouring coffee and passing around generous slices of sour cream apple pie.

"What could she do? I said something stupid about being sorry we bothered her. And we turned around and left. I couldn't believe it," she repeated.

"And you have no idea what this Jinx did to elicit such an incredible response?"

"Jinx didn't do anything! I was there. I know."

"Well, it seems to me that either this professor is nuts or someone did or said something you don't know about," Jed suggested calmly, looking around for cream for his coffee.

"Susan said you weren't using cream anymore," Kathleen explained. "I can get some skim milk."

"No, don't bother. My wife is learning a new language and all about the stars. She's becoming an expert on Victorian literature. And maybe even becoming a writer. And I'm learning to drink my coffee black. It's all part of getting old."

Everyone laughed.

"A published writer?" Jerry picked up on what Jed had said.

"No way," Susan denied. "I'll be lucky—very lucky—if I do well in my creative writing class. It's a lot more difficult to write fiction than I thought it would be."

"Can't you write nonfiction? Essays?"

"Yes, but the class is creative writing and our professor believes that means fiction. Some students are working on poems, but I thought a short story would be easier."

"I took a creative writing class in college—well, two, actually," Jerry reminisced. "I loved them. They gave me an opportunity to emote, to tell the world what was in my innermost soul."

"Well, I'm too old to expose my innermost soul to a class of almost complete strangers," Susan explained. "Although most of the other students would agree with you. They're emoting all over the place. Love poems, stories of religious conversions, the pain over the loss of a beloved gerbil . . ."

"What?"

"I kid you not. One young man wrote a tribute to Hamlet, his gerbil, who fell down a heat vent and died." Susan paused for a moment. "Or at least he seemed to think the poor thing had died. I've been wondering what will happen when the heat is turned on in the dorms."

Jed and Jerry laughed.

"So what do you write about?" Kathleen asked.

"Well, right now I'm working on this cute idea . . . well, I think it's cute. One of our assignments is to write a description of someone or something we love."

"And you're writing about your husband, I assume?" Jed asked.

"Not to disappoint you, but I'm writing about Clue. It

worked in my Italian class, and in creative writing so many students are gushing on and on about their one true love—"

"Who will probably be out of their lives in less than a month," Jerry interjected.

"Exactly. But I'm trying something different. I don't say it's a dog I'm writing about until the end of the piece. I start out by talking about how she understands me and pleases me and then I talk about how the sun glints off her golden hair. And then the last line of the piece just slips in the information that I'm describing a dog."

"So up until that point anyone reading it will think you're a lesbian?" Jed asked, a smile on his face.

"Not necessarily. I could be writing about my daughter." She frowned. "It was very successful in my Italian class. Paolo loved it. And Professor Hoyer is the only person who will read this version—unless it's my turn to read aloud to the class. So far, that hasn't happened."

"You don't seem to be looking forward to that," Kathleen said.

"I'm dreading it."

"What about the murder?" Kathleen asked. "Are you and this Jinx trying to solve it? Isn't that why you wanted to talk to the professor who ran the support group?"

"Yes, but . . ." Susan looked up from her pie. "It's not like you and me trying to find a murderer. Jinx doesn't have any police experience and . . . and it's just not the same. I never would have gotten involved in this if that horrible Officer O'Reilly hadn't practically arrested me when he found my backpack. I mean, it's not as if I'm not busy."

Kathleen opened her mouth to say something, but a child screaming took precedence over everything else. "Sounds like bedtime for the kids," she announced, getting up from the table.

"I'll get them ready," Jerry offered.

"No, I'll get them ready and then you can read them their story and tuck them in." Kathleen was out of the room before anyone could make another suggestion.

"And why don't I clean up here," Susan said, starting to collect the dirty dishes into a pile.

She refused the men's half-hearted offers of help and headed to the kitchen, her hands full.

Kathleen didn't love to cook, so her meals, while excellent, tended to be comprised of dishes that took a minimum amount of time and effort to prepare. The sink was not piled with pots and pans, as it would have been after one of Susan's dinner parties. Susan rolled up her sleeves and got to work and within fifteen minutes the dishwasher was running and the counters were sparkling. Susan peeked back into the dining room. Jed and Jerry, who saw each other almost daily at the advertising agency where they both worked, were engrossed in a conversation concerning a coworker. Kathleen was apparently still upstairs with the children. Susan decided not to interrupt anyone. Jed and Jerry were happy and the children might just decide that another appearance of Auntie Susan tonight was an excuse to delay their bedtime. She sat down on a stool near the counter and poured herself a last glass of wine.

She was, she realized suddenly, feeling a bit lonely. She had wanted to come to dinner tonight and talk about how worried she was about her classes, how hard she was finding the return to school. She had wanted sympathy, damn it. And she hadn't gotten what she wanted. Kathleen was more wrapped up in her children than ever. Jerry had spent the first part of the meal talking about whether or not he should volunteer to be a Little League coach in the spring. And Jed was probably sick and tired of listening to her complain about school and her studies. He had related tales of coaching Chad's elementary-school soccer team and commiserated with Kathleen about Alice's entry into nursery school. After beginning the meal with a toast to her for completing half of the semester, no one had paid very much attention to Susan at all.

She swirled the wine in her glass and thought. There was, she admitted, the terrible possibility that she was becoming a bit of a bore. She had wanted to go back to school. And these three people had supported her decision. That didn't obligate them to listen to her whine about how much harder it was than she had expected it to be.

Except, she reminded herself, that's what friends and family did. They listened.

The door opened and Kathleen walked in. "Jed said you were in here. Are you all right? My miserable dinner didn't make you ill, did it?"

"No. Your dinner was wonderful and you were sweet to ask us over. We could have gone out—"

"No, we couldn't. Every single sitter we have is in the middle of midterms, too." Kathleen reached for the wine bottle.

"I don't think there's any left," Susan said.

"That's okay. I've had enough. I have to be up early tomorrow. I've got the garden club's annual bulb planting in the park."

"You do that every year. Couldn't you skip this year?"

"Nope. This year I'm running it."

"You're kidding! Kathleen, that's great. But you must have been incredibly busy this week—organizing volunteers and picking up bulbs and stuff. You should have put off dinner tonight."

"Oh, no. We've been planning on this meal since you registered for classes. I couldn't . . . Sounds like another bedtime crisis," she said as a wail from the second floor made its way into the room. "I'd better go help Jerry."

Alone again, Susan polished off her wine and then took a last dab at the kitchen counter before joining her husband.

Jed was sprawled in a chair in the living room, his eyes closed.

"Are you asleep?" she asked gently.

"Yes." Eyes still closed, he smiled.

"Then I guess I'll have to drive home."

"I guess you will. But shouldn't we say good-bye to Kathleen and Jerry?"

"I think Kath is going to be busy for a while." Jerry appeared in the doorway. "Alice is having a minor breakdown. Apparently, Alex told her that the gardeners were going to bury bones with the tulip and daffodil bulbs tomorrow. Kathleen is trying to figure out a way to be honest with the child and still explain what bonemeal is made from."

"Sounds like she has her work cut out for her," Jed said.

"Will you tell her how wonderful it's been to have a home-cooked meal with you guys? And thank her for all the work."

"Sure. And good luck with the rest of your midterms, Susan."

"Thanks. I'll need it."

Susan didn't speak again until she had successfully backed Jed's car out of the driveway. "I have been cooking for you, you know."

"I didn't say you hadn't. Thanking Kathleen for the home-cooked meal didn't mean you don't cook. It meant that she rarely does and I appreciate it. That's all."

Susan didn't answer.

"Susan? You're not mad at me about that comment, are you? There's no reason to be. Believe me, I know how hard you're working on your classwork and I don't expect you to cook the same way you did before. . . . Susan? Are you listening to me?"

"Sorry. I wasn't paying attention. Jed, is the speedometer on your car broken?"

"No, it's fine. Why?"

"I was just wondering why we're being stopped by the police."

EIGHTEEN

IF YOU HAVE TO GET STOPPED BY A POLICE CAR, IT'S NICE IF you know the officer inside. Ten minutes after Susan rolled down her window to talk to Brett Fortesque, he was sitting in her kitchen waiting for the coffee to be made. And lecturing her.

"I keep telling you that you're treading in dangerous waters here. According to my contact, this woman is serious."

Clue's entrance into the room and her greeting of one of her favorite people interrupted them, and by the time the dog had been coaxed onto her expensive (and monogrammed) down-filled bed in the corner, Jed had joined them and the three adults were provided with large mugs of decaf.

"That professor that Jinx and I tried to see this afternoon is threatening to file a complaint against Jinx," Susan said to her husband.

"To have her arrested?"

"No, no. Nothing like that. The worst that might happen is a court order preventing this Jinx from having any contact with the complainant—and we're a long way from that," Brett explained, putting three spoonfuls of sugar into his coffee and stirring.

"But Jinx could be arrested if she violated that court order, right?" Jed asked, ignoring his coffee.

"Jed, there isn't even a court order right now! I told you. She threw us out of her office almost before we were in it! And this is just a rumor, really. I mean, nothing has happened yet."

"One of the younger guys in the department was out with some friends tonight at a bar over near the campus. He graduated from the academy a few years ago and he ran into one of his old classmates. For some reason they stopped talking about girls and football and started talking about your wife and her friend."

"Don't look at me like that, Jed! It isn't my fault if people talk about me!"

Her husband didn't reply and Brett continued. "Anyway, it turns out this other officer was a bit pissed because he had been busy taking a statement from this professor and had gotten to the bar late. It was a statement that concerned your wife."

"Because she was with Jinx?"

"Well, that's what interested me. Now, mind you, I don't know this officer. And I certainly can't tell you if he had too much to drink. But the story he told my man is that this Professor—"

"Everyone calls her Lillian," Susan interrupted.

"Fine," Brett said with a smile. "So, as I understand it, Lillian just happened to have a conference with Michael O'Reilly right after Susan and Jinx were in her office and she was very upset by their visit."

"So?"

"So the story I was told was that she wanted to know what it would take to get a court order that would keep Jinx away from her."

"But not me, right?" Susan asked.

"Apparently, this Jinx Jensen was the only person mentioned."

"That's strange," Jed said, playing with his untouched mug.

"It's more than a little strange," Susan stated. "It's nuts. And that means it's not her idea—it's that damn O'Reilly's idea. I don't know what he has against us."

"Maybe he just doesn't like women who get involved in murder investigations," Jed suggested.

"But how would he know about me?"

"There have been articles in various newspapers about you investigating crimes in Connecticut over the years, right?" Brett asked.

"Yes. The last two even printed photographs of her," Jed said.

"Dreadful photos," Susan muttered automatically. The last photo had caused her to stock up on Slim Fast, much of which was still in her kitchen cupboard.

"But why are you here? Do you really think this is serious?" Jed asked.

"Not now. Susan and I were talking while you were walking Clue and she tells me that she's only seen Lillian this one time. There isn't a single judge in the entire state who is going to act under those conditions." Brett answered Jed's question before turning to Susan. "But you should stay away from her. Who knows what sort of connections she might have—personal or political—and every time you're in the same place she is, there's an opportunity for her to claim harassment or even to say she's being stalked. I don't think you want to take any chances," he added.

"You know what bothers me?" Susan said.

"That it's after midnight?" Jed muttered, yawning again.

"That it took an hour for her to call the police department. You said she called the police at five-thirty, right?"

"That's what I was told," Brett admitted.

"And Jinx and I were at her office no later than four-thirty. Maybe even a bit earlier," Susan said.

"And you think that might be significant?"

"It could be. What happened between the time we left and the time she called that made her decide to try to get this court order against Jinx?"

"Maybe nothing. You said she had regular office hours, right? And this is midterms week. Maybe she had a lot of students who needed to see her and she didn't have time to get to the phone." Jed, usually the most patient of husbands, was beginning to sound annoyed—and completely exhausted.

Susan stood up quickly. "Why don't you let me think about this overnight and we can talk in the morning, if you're free."

"Sounds good to me," Brett said, taking the hint.

"You go on upstairs," Susan told Jed. "I'll lock up down here."

"I will, if you don't mind. It's been a long week," Jed said. "Thanks for stopping in tonight," he added to Brett. "We appreciate the fact that you go out of your way for us like this."

"Don't mention it," Brett assured him. "I'll call tomorrow if I hear anything," he added as Jed started up the stairs.

"I'll be up in a bit," Susan called to her husband's back. Even from here he looked worn out, and she felt a twinge of guilt. As soon as her midterms were over, she was going to start taking better care of the man she loved! But right now there was just one more thing she needed to talk over with Brett.

"Let me grab a coat and I'll walk you to your car," she offered.

"I think Clue wants to go along," Brett told her, as the dog pushed her nose against the door in an effort to escape.

"Don't open it until I have her leash attached," Susan warned, and she put on the dog's leash. It turned out that Clue's enthusiasm for the outdoors was prompted by her apparent need to uproot the chrysanthemums planted in urns on either side of the front door, and Susan pulled the animal toward the street as she and Brett chatted.

"The squirrels play in those planters and Clue is just outraged by the fact that they seem to disappear when she walks out the door." She tried to excuse the animal's bad behavior.

"Poor Clue," Brett said, bending down to scratch her head. "Don't you know that some things seem to be forever just outside our grasp?"

Susan was surprised to hear something quite so philosophical coming out of Brett's mouth, but he changed the subject before she could respond. "I'm curious about one thing, Susan."

"What?"

"How long have you known this Jinx? And is that her real name?" He asked the second question before she could answer his first.

"I have no idea. But I can't imagine calling a baby Jinx, can you? I mean, it's sort of an interesting name for an adult to have. But it would be mean to attach that label to a two- or three-day-old."

"You've never asked her?"

"Well, to answer your first question, we haven't known each other all that long. She's in my creative writing class. But we really met in the returning students' support group, which meets on campus."

"That's what you have in common? One class and that you joined the same support group?"

"And she knew Merry before Merry was killed."

"How?"

Susan explained about the divorced women's support group, where Jinx and Merry had met and Lillian's involvement in it.

"What is this Jinx? A support-group junkie?"

"I don't know why you would say that! After all, the first support group worked for her when she was trying to change her life after her husband left her, so when she was doing something frightening and stressful—and, believe me, returning to school when you're over forty is both—and there was a support group available, she joined."

"And that's all you know about her."

"I know she's an interesting person. She has lots of fascinating hobbies and . . . and she has a granddaughter and her daughter has a golden retriever named Maggie."

"Okay, I'll admit that owning a golden retriever is an excellent recommendation. But this woman is connected with a murder, a murder you're involved with, if only by the fact that you were the last person to admit to being with the victim."

"What?"

He peered at her in the darkness. "Susan, you didn't know?"

"I left her in my lab. There were people around. In the hallway. On the stairs. On campus."

"Yes. But you were the last person the local police—or the campus cops—can find who actually spoke with Merry. I thought you knew that."

"I had no idea. None. Did she go straight to her apartment? We were supposed to meet at a coffee shop off campus."

"But she might have gone home for any number of reasons. Although I think the theory is that she was meeting someone there."

"Before meeting me?"

"Susan, I have to be honest. One of the theories is that she was meeting you at her apartment. And that you lied about the coffee shop."

"And I used my own backpack to strangle her and then left it behind so that I could be easily connected with the murder."

"Well . . ."

"Brett! Are you telling me they think I'm an idiot as well as a murderer?" She wasn't sure which she found more insulting.

"I told you about O'Reilly's opinion of . . . um, suburban housewives."

"That they're idiots and murderers?"

"Well, not all murderers, of course. Susan, this is exactly why I'm so worried. It almost looks to me as though there's an organized effort to connect you with this murder. And when I heard about that professor and her attempt to get a court order . . . Well, it's a stupid idea, but even if it mentions only Jinx, it's also just one more strike against you."

Susan peered through the darkness at her companion. "You don't think I'm going to be arrested for Merry's murder, do you? I hardly knew her. Why would I kill her?"

"Susan, it's been five weeks since the murder. No one has been arrested. And the case is complicated by the fact that there are two police departments competing with each other. I hear feelings are running so high that there was a liaison appointed to work with the two groups."

"Who is this liaison?"

"Officer O'Reilly." He looked at the shocked expression on her face. "You didn't realize that?"

"No. And you think that complicates things?"

"I know it does. So you will be very, very careful, won't you? And stay away from that professor."

"I . . . Yes, I will. Good night, Brett. Come on, Clue." She pulled her dog away from the police car as the engine started. It wasn't until she was once again urging her dog away from the chrysanthemums that she realized she hadn't talked to Brett about the main thing that was worrying her.

NINETEEN

SUSAN HAD PLANNED TO STUDY AT HOME OVER THE WEEKEND. Jed was going to be busy doing errands—closing up the pool; cleaning out the gutters; putting away all the expensive gardening equipment, which had provided them with sixteen tomatoes, three green peppers, and five or six salad bowls of mesclun over the summer; and running the mower around the lawn one last time. She knew he would spend as much time at

Hancock Hardware as working. And if the weather held, he planned to golf on Sunday.

But Susan couldn't concentrate. When she sat down in Jed's study, her eyes wandered from Italian irregular verbs toward the pile of Christmas catalogs accumulating on top of the VCR. Hoping fresh air would revive her, she bundled up in an old wool sweater, grabbed *Middlemarch*, and plopped down on a lounge on the patio. But the falling leaves, Clue, and the crisp air all conspired to make her daydream of long walks in the woods rather than Dorothea's naïve choices.

Finally she gave up and, filling her pack to the brim, headed off to the local library.

Hancock Public Library was one of Susan's favorite places in town. A historic church and three modern wings made it a warm and friendly place, especially since she had had a hand in solving the one murder to take place within its walls. She loved the stacks overflowing with current and classic fiction, its extensive collection of cookbooks and shelter magazines, the comfortable chairs provided for browsers. And since she started school, she had come to appreciate the lone row of carrels tucked in behind the biographies. They were quiet, private, and situated right over a line of heating vents set in the floor. Susan headed for them after greeting the librarian who was manning the checkout desk.

There were seven desks and four were already occupied. Susan, inwardly sighing (she was, after all, in a library), chose the empty one between two long-haired readers. Determined to work and not chat, she piled her study materials up and opened a notebook without even glancing at her fellow workers. First Italian. Then reread the piece she had to turn in to her creative writing professor this week. Then a quick review of *Middlemarch* and three of Elizabeth Gaskell's novels. Then Italian, Italian, Italian.

First those irregular verbs. Then nouns. Lots and lots of nouns. For some reason she had little trouble remembering the words for boot, shoe, and sweater, possibly because she could imagine herself walking down the Via Tornabuoni in Florence, dropping into the elegant boutiques, and trying on clothing. *"Gli stivali rossi, per favore."* She could almost say it. But was *rosso* red or pink? Did she mean *verdi*? Wasn't that green? Not that it wouldn't be nice to have green boots, but her favorite winter coat was black and she sort of had her heart set on red boots. On the other hand, she certainly did not want pink boots. . . .

This was getting her nowhere! She pushed her notecards and textbook to the back of the desk and pulled out the folder marked CW. She reread the descriptive essay she had thought so clever. Only this time it seemed flat. Boring. Silly even. She imagined reading it in front of the class and hearing the snickers as the young students thought they were listening to her describe a female lover. . . .

She ripped the sheets of paper in half and tossed them into the wastebasket the library had thoughtfully provided near her feet. What she needed was a new idea. A really good new idea. She had to describe something . . . or someone. The someone appealed to her, but who? Maybe someone who didn't actually exist . . .

Brilliant! It was such a good idea that she almost said that word aloud. Merry's husband. Merry's imaginary husband. The man she claimed had threatened to kill her. Susan picked up her pen and wrote.

She could almost see him. Not too young, not too old. Thirty-one or two. And good-looking. Blond hair that just touched his collar, green eyes, and a mouth that seemed to fall naturally in a sneer. Tan skin, muscular build, and—she added, inspired now—a tattoo, one of those that circles the biceps. Not interested in displaying his marital status for the world to see, he didn't wear a wedding band, his only jewelry a gold watch . . . one of the ones that pilots were supposed to wear . . . What was that brand? Susan frowned. Well, she could fill that in later after a trip to the magazine shelves. No issue of *Vanity Fair* was complete without a full-page color ad for it.

Jeans, a soft chambray shirt, cowboy boots, and a black leather jacket completed his outfit. And sunglasses. He definitely wore sunglasses. Aviator glasses, in fact.

Susan frowned. Any minute now she would have this man flying secret missions for the CIA. Not the image she was aiming for. Sunglasses, but not aviator glasses; those thin ones from Ray•Ban. The ones with the lenses that reflected your own image rather than allowing a peek at the wearer's eyes. He looked good in them and wore them even when the sun wasn't shining. Conceited bastard! What did he have to hide?

Maybe he really had threatened to kill Merry. Maybe he had gone up to the apartment he had shared with her and was waiting for her when she came home from class to change her clothes for a date later that night. But she had made an appointment with Susan and she was late. Fatally late, because she wasn't careful and didn't realize her husband was waiting there . . .

Susan slammed her pencil on the desk and pushed her chair back. "Damn. Damn. Triple damn."

"Excuse me?" The woman to her left sounded concerned.

"Excuse me?" The young man (with a ponytail) on her right used the same expression to express irritation.

"The key. I'd forgotten all about that key in the backpack."

The woman next to her looked around as if expecting the pack Susan was talking about to appear. The young man on the other side frowned. "Lady, I'm gonna flunk my geology midterm if you don't shut up. And if I flunk that test, I'll lose my financial aid. And if I lose that money, I'll have to drop out of school and get a job. What I'm saying, lady, is if you don't shut up, you could change the course of my entire life."

"Oh, I . . ."

"Young man, why do you think you're the only person here with important work to do?" Another woman's voice cut through the air.

"I don't think that. I . . . Oh, hell, I'm going to find someplace else to study." The young man gathered his papers and books and stormed off into the stacks.

"Well, he was certainly rude, wasn't he?" Susan's other neighbor said.

"I guess I've been sort of loud," Susan admitted.

"Maybe you'd like to get some coffee?" A familiar face peered over the carrel and grinned.

"Jinx! How long—"

"Shhhh!" The tolerance of Susan's neighbors had been put to the test and lost.

"Good idea," Susan whispered, gathering her things. She followed Jinx out of the library.

"What are you doing here?" Susan asked when they were standing together on the front steps.

"Looking for a book. What else? What about you? I thought you would be home studying the entire weekend."

"I was planning on it, but I couldn't concentrate there. But, Jinx, that's not important now."

"Your midterms aren't important?"

"Well, yes, but I had a thought that might be more important. Besides, I can't study when there's something else on my mind." Deep in her heart, Susan knew she sounded a whole lot like her kids making up excuses not to do their homework. She just hoped Chad and Chrissy never discovered how little distance they had fallen from the tree.

"Something about Merry's murder?" Jinx asked, catching on quickly.

"Yes. Her key was in the backpack!"

"Her key was in your backpack?"

"No, her key was in the backpack that I mixed up with mine. In her backpack."

"So what's odd about that?"

"Nothing, but how did she get into her apartment? It must have been unlocked by someone who had a key! I mentioned this to that awful Officer O'Reilly and he turned it into evidence against me! But I think maybe I should find out who else had a key. Because that person may have let Merry into her apartment the day she was killed. That person may, in fact, have killed her!"

"Unless her landlady let someone in?"

Susan frowned. "How do you know she had a landlady?"

"I don't. But that's what I did when I was living in an apartment and I forgot or misplaced my key."

"I wonder where she lived," Susan said, hitching her heavy backpack up on one shoulder.

"In an apartment about a mile from campus. I drove her

home once after group when her car was in the shop," Jinx added, seeing the surprised expression on Susan's face.

"Do you have the time to go there now? I mean, maybe we could talk with her landlady and clear up this one point. Then I can get back to studying."

"Fine with me. It's about twenty minutes from here. Why don't I drive?"

"Great. Would you mind if I went over my Italian again on the way?"

"Not at all. Do it out loud. Maybe I'll sign up for an Elderhostel to Rome or Florence in the spring."

Saturday traffic was bad. There were six high school football teams and dozens of soccer leagues playing that afternoon, and Susan had reviewed all of her vocabulary and most of her verbs before they arrived at Merry's apartment. Or, to be more exact, on the block where Merry's apartment was located.

"I dropped her off here. I think," Jinx added, peering out the windshield. "It was nighttime and I remember thinking that there weren't any large apartment buildings in this area, but Merry said all the homes had been divided into apartments and dozens of students lived on this block."

The block was populated with old and mostly run-down Victorians, each displaying multiple modern metal mailboxes beside old, ornate front doors.

"The place where I dropped Merry was in the middle of the block and had old-fashioned carriage lamps on either side of the door. There it is! At least I think that's the one."

"I suppose all we can do is knock on doors and see if anyone knows if Merry lived around here," Susan suggested, looking over her shoulder at the house Jinx had indicated as the other woman parked the car.

"Let's give it a try," Jinx agreed.

The concrete sidewalk to the house was broken and chipped, but the wood stairs to the wraparound porch were sturdy, and the large house had been recently painted. Susan wouldn't have chosen navy and puce, but at least it looked cared for. There were six remarkably ugly black mailboxes hanging underneath an elegant brass lamp. Susan tried to read the names.

"I don't see how we will know which one is the landlady or owner or . . . Oh, look! We're in luck!"

The highest mailbox had a little Post-it note stuck to its rusting top. APT 4 RENT RING 5.

Susan interpreted the sign to mean that the person in apartment five was the person in charge. She rang the bell and waited for a response.

"Yo. You looking for me!" A young man with many tattoos instead of hair stuck his head out a window on the second floor.

"Is that a question?" Jinx whispered in Susan's ear.

"Yes. We have some questions—"

"You have an apartment available?" Jinx asked.

"Yeah. Wanna see it?"

"Yes. We would like that very much," Jinx answered, while Susan, surprised by this tactic, remained silent.

"It's not here. It's out back. In the carriage house. I'll be right down." The shiny head disappeared only to reappear again, almost instantly. "You two ain't superstitious, are you?"

They exchanged glances. "No, I don't think so," Susan said, becoming more and more confused.

"Good. I have midterms, you know. I don't have the time to be showing that apartment to people who are afraid of dead bodies."

TWENTY

"**W**HAT OTHER KINDS OF BODIES ARE THERE?" JINX whispered, her eyes widening.

"Live ones, I suppose. And, frankly, I think I'm more afraid of some of them," Susan whispered back as the man who had called down from on high opened the door and joined them on the porch. He might be studying for midterms now, but he certainly had been pumping iron rather than hitting the books for the last few months. The man's muscles bulged from every piece of clothing he wore.

"I understand exactly what you mean," Jinx answered.

"You gotta follow me," the man told them as, ignoring the stairs, he jumped off the porch.

And follow they did, around the corner of the house, shuffling through leaves that no one had bothered to rake, across a tiny backyard to . . .

"Where are you taking us?" Susan finally asked.

"The apartment. It's a garage apartment. Like the ad in the paper that said, 'Garage apartment.' Can't you read?"

"It's in the garage?" Jinx asked.

"It's over the garage. There's cars in the garage."

"Did Merry live over a garage?" Susan asked Jinx. Their guide had no interest in slowing down so that they could keep up.

"I have no idea. She never mentioned it, but she never really mentioned anything about where she was living. But if someone died there, it's probably Merry's apartment."

Jinx and Susan followed their guide and soon they were standing in a surprisingly spacious studio apartment. Twin dormers on opposite sides of the room let in lots of light. A small Pullman kitchen and a door presumably leading to a bathroom were at the end of the long room. There was a daybed, covered with an old army blanket, four wicker chairs with tattered checkered cushions, a coir rug, and a coffee table displaying a Chianti bottle with what must have been years and years of candlewax dripping down its sides. Brick and board bookshelves ran under the slanted ceiling and a battered desk and an even more battered chair completed the room's furnishings.

"It's rented furnished?" Susan asked as Jinx wandered around the room, picking up the books from the shelves, peeking inside the covers, and then putting them back again.

"Didn't you read the ad? 'Garage apartment, furnished, nine hundred dollars a month, utilities extra.' That's what it said. That's what it meant. And it's not negotiable. It's late in the year, but some broad will break up with her boyfriend and need a place to stay. You know."

"Yes. This place wasn't really cleaned out after its last tenant, was it?" Susan continued to make conversation, Jinx having vanished into the bathroom. She could be heard opening and closing the medicine cabinet.

"I have a full schedule and they don't pay me extra for stuff like that. Besides, the . . . uh, the relatives of the broad who used to live here have looked through all this. They don't want anything. They told me to call Goodwill to cart all this junk off. I figure the new tenant can do that as well as I."

"Oh, well, it actually looks pretty clean." Susan tried to placate him. She walked to the kitchen and opened the oven. It didn't look pretty clean. It looked like it hadn't been cleaned in about a decade, maybe longer. She shut the door and reached for the refrigerator. The handle came off in her hand.

"Lousy landlord!"

Susan was startled. "You don't own this place?"

"Do I look like a property owner? Do I in any way re-semble a pillar of society?"

She didn't want to insult him, but there was only one an-swer to that. "I guess not," she admitted.

"What is your friend doing? Taking a shower?" The water that, with much clanking of pipes, had been running was sud-denly turned off.

"I . . . She wants to make sure this is a place where she can live. She wants to, you know, feel the vibes," Susan ex-plained, feeling that she was speaking his language.

Apparently not. "Lady, come off it. Your friend is looking for someplace cheap and this either is it or it isn't. I'll be in my apartment. Just buzz."

"I . . . Yes, we will!" Susan called to his back as he loped down the stairs.

"Is he gone?" The bathroom door opened and Jinx ap-peared, a filthy towel dangling from her hand.

"Yes. What did you find?"

"This is it! This really is Merry's apartment!"

"How do you know?"

"Look in the books! Her name is in the one on top of the pile on her desk!"

Susan walked over to the shelves and picked up *The Anthropology of the Arctic Indian*. Sure enough, "Merry Kenny" was scrawled on the flyleaf. "Strange that her books are still here. I mean, there aren't any sheets on the bed."

"Maybe they were used to cover her body. There are towels in the bathroom."

"What about the closet?" Susan walked over to the one door no one had opened and looked inside. "Son of a gun!"

"What?"

"Clothing. It's full of clothing."

"Really?" Jinx came to Susan's side and stared in the closet. "You know what I think we should do?"

"What?"

"Go through everything. See if we can discover any clues."

Susan shrugged. "We're here. We may as well, but I can't imagine what we're looking for."

"Maybe we'll know it when we see it."

"I hope so. Do you want to work together or split up?"

"Who knows when that young man will be back. I think we should split up. It will go more quickly." Jinx was pulling shoe boxes off the closet shelf as she spoke. "Is that okay with you?" she added when Susan didn't reply.

"Sure. And you're right. We'd better get going. I'll take the desk and the bookshelves."

"Be sure to flip through each book. You know how people stick things between pages."

"Good idea." She got to work. The desk drawer was empty except for a broken pencil and a few stray paperclips. She turned her attention to the bookshelves.

It turned out that Merry was a real aficionada of the art of sticking things between pages. Susan was only halfway through the top shelf and she already had a two-inch pile of notes, receipts from the campus bookstore, empty Twizzler wrappers, a Popsicle stick, and an ad for a free Clinique makeover. "How's it going?" she asked, glancing over her shoulder in Jinx's direction.

"Hey! That's the backpack!" she exclaimed.

"Yours or hers?" Jinx asked, holding it out to Susan.

"Hers. Mine is at home. And it took the police a ridiculous amount of time to get it back to me. I wonder how long she's had hers. I mean, I wonder how long hers has been here."

Jinx had emptied the pack on the floor and was sorting through its contents. "Does it look like anything is missing?"

"How would I know . . . Oh, you mean since I had it before . . . when Merry was murdered."

"Uh-huh."

"Heavens, I don't think I remember everything that was in it." But Susan stared at the pile with interest. "Look, the keys are there. I knew they would be. . . . I don't believe it!"

"What?"

"We forgot what we were doing here! We didn't ask that guy if he let someone into Merry's apartment the day she was killed."

"Well, we had to make sure this was her apartment first. And I don't know about you, but now that I've seen him, I'm not sure I have a whole lot of faith in anything he says. What about you?"

"Hey, what are you two doing, going through all this stuff? You're not some more freaky friends of Merry's, are you? Or maybe you're murder junkies." The caretaker was back. And he looked angry.

"Huh?"

"Yeah, that's what you are. You two are like those freaks who used to come here the weeks after Merry was murdered, wanting to see this place, wanting to drink in the atmosphere, one of them said. Sick. That's what I call it. You may look like middle-aged housewives, but you're both sickos."

"That's not true," Jinx protested.

"It isn't true at all!" Susan chimed in. "We're students, not housewives!"

"You're telling me you're not here because Merry was killed in this place?"

"We—"

"We're investigating Merry's murder. This is Susan Henshaw. She is famous in this state for investigating and solving murders."

"Yeah. Like that other old lady. Miss Marple. I've seen her on the boob tube."

"I am not ol—"

"Exactly like Miss Marple," Jinx interrupted. "And you could be a big help."

"Yeah? And why would I want to do that? Would I get paid?"

"I don't think—" Susan began.

"You never know," Jinx interrupted again. "It could, of course, depend on what your information is worth. And whether the murderer is convicted, naturally."

"Yeah. Naturally." He pronounced the last word as if it had only two syllables.

"So how well did you know Merry?" Jinx asked.

"We weren't what you call intimate. I mean, I didn't sleep with her or anything."

"We're not accus—" Susan started to say.

"I could have, maybe. I didn't want to. I mean, I was involved at the time she was living here and I believe in what you might call faithfulness. I mean, one woman at a time should be enough for any man, right?"

"Right," Jinx agreed fervently.

"How long did she live here?" Susan asked, hoping to find some information in the waves of self-aggrandizement.

"Well, let's see. I been living here for three years now and Merry . . . Well, she came here when I had just changed my dissertation topic and that was two years ago in the summer. So say two years give or take a month or two."

"You're getting a graduate degree?" Jinx asked, clearly astonished.

"How did Merry find the apartment?" Susan asked quickly. They really didn't need to know any more about this man. "Did you—or the owner—put an ad in the school paper?"

"Nah. That was late July or early August. Everyone's looking for places to live that time of year. Ya just list your place over at the campus housing office and the hordes come out of the woodwork. You know?"

"And she lived alone?"

"Well, she signed the lease, but that don't mean all that

much. She had friends who came to stay once in a while and more than once in a while, if you know what I mean."

"Men or women?" Jinx asked.

"Men friends. Merry was no bi, if you know what I mean."

"If you mean she wasn't bisexual, we know exactly what you mean," Susan assured him.

"Any man in particular?" Jinx asked.

"You ladies notice anything on the way back here?"

"Aside from the appalling condition of the backyard?" Susan asked, annoyed by his habit of answering a question with a question.

"Go out on the porch. You'll see what I mean."

"What do you mean?" Jinx asked.

"What porch?" was Susan's question.

"That little landing thing at the top of the stairs. What do you call it if not a porch?"

A landing, Susan thought, but she kept the thought to herself and went out the door to stand beside Jinx on the little six-by-eight platform at the top of the stairs.

"So what do ya see?" He swept one thoroughly tattooed arm in a circle.

What they saw was an ill-kept yard with a cracked macadam driveway on one side and a crumbling sidewalk on the other. The back of the house had not been painted as recently as the front and Susan's first sight of the roof made her worry about whoever was living in the apartments on the third floor.

"Do you see anything special?" Jinx asked Susan.

"I . . . No."

"Yeah. Some detectives you two are. Your Miss Maple would know what I'm talking about."

"Miss Marple," Susan corrected him automatically.

"What would Miss Marple see that we don't?" Jinx asked.

"Tall fence. Not many windows at the back of the house. No one overlooking the garden."

"What garden?"

"I'm not talking about flowers or grass or nothing. I'm talking about privacy. This is a very private apartment. Once someone drove in that driveway and parked the car, only someone looking out of one of the three windows at the back of the house could see who was coming and going."

"And that was important to Merry?"

"Yup. Got it in one. Privacy. That's one quality Merry was looking for in an apartment. She told me that on the phone when she called to inquire about the apartment. Too bad, as it turned out, though."

"Why?"

"If she'd lived someplace a little less private, a little more public so to speak, someone might've seen who killed her."

TWENTY-ONE

SUSAN AND JINX STARED DOWN AT THE GROUND, DIGESTING this information.

"Am I right or am I right?"

"Yes. You do seem to be," Jinx admitted.

"Who can see out those three windows?" Susan asked. There were two on the second floor of the building and one on the first.

"The one on the bottom is over the sink in apartment 101. The women living there are what you might call party people—always out at clubs or going to raves. Bet no one cooks in that kitchen for weeks at a time. And if no one cooks, no one is likely to be cleaning up, right. The window to the left is in the apartment of a computer nerd—guy never looks up from his computer screen."

"And the third window?" Susan asked.

"That's my place. So I guess me or anyone who is visiting me can see out that window." He grinned.

"And did you?"

"Did I what?"

He was playing a game and Susan didn't see what choice they had but to play along with him. "Did you see anything unusual the day that Merry was murdered?"

He leaned against the doorjamb and his grin got even bigger. Susan felt a barely controllable urge to slug him. "Know what's interesting?" he asked.

"What?"

"The police asked the same question. The very same question. So what I want to know is, Why are you amateur sleuths so much better than the police?"

"What I want to know is, What did you say to the police?" Jinx asked.

"What I want to know is, Did you tell the police the truth?" Susan stated flatly.

"Do I look like the kind of man who would lie to the police?"

Susan and Jinx exchanged looks. "He's wasting our time," Jinx said.

"I didn't think he had a lot of time. It being midterms week and all," Susan answered. "And I know I don't have a lot of time . . ."

"No one saw anything. That help you any? No one saw anything, and that's just what I told the police."

Now they were getting somewhere. "Does that include the women who live on the first floor?" Susan asked. "Did they also tell the police that they saw nothing?"

For the first time they got a straight answer. "They wouldn't tell me. I asked and I asked. But they wouldn't tell me. Them's teases in more ways than one, if you know what I mean."

Susan glanced down at the window belonging to the apartment of the women in question. It was open a crack and a breeze blew the curtains back into the room. Surely no one would go out and leave a window open? When they were done here, they might as well take the time to stop in. Then she would get back to her studies.

"You let us into this apartment with a key," she said, returning to the subject.

"Yeah, but only because I thought one of you two wanted to rent the place. I don't just let anybody inside."

"Are you the only person who has a key?"

"I am the only person who has a key officially, you might say."

"What do you mean?" Jinx asked.

"Well, I have a key and I have a copy of the key, which I give to whoever rents the place. See?"

"Yes."

"But I don't have any way of knowing who the person who rents the place gives the key to or how many keys she has made and then passed out to every Tom, Dick, and Harry."

"Do you have the locks changed between tenants?"

"Does this look like one of those fancy condos in Greenwich?"

"So you don't have the locks changed."

"Lady, I don't do anything. I don't have to do anything. This is what is known as a very desirable neighborhood. It's close to campus. There's on-the-street parking. And you can find someone to party with any night of the week. These here apartments sell themselves. I just hang around my apartment, take the first and last month's rent payment, and go about my own business. And I think you two might want to do the same thing."

"Actually, we were wondering if you would mind if we went back into the apartment to look around for a bit. There might be a clue. . . ."

"I do mind. You have no business in there unless you're potential renters, and since you've admitted that you're not, I suggest that you both be on your way."

"Fine. Thank you for your time."

Susan, unable to be as polite as Jinx, merely nodded and started down the stairs. Maybe the ladies on the first floor would be more cooperative. Not even bothering to see if Jinx was following, she headed around to the front of the house and rang the doorbell of apartment 101. She read the names affixed to the mailbox while waiting for an answer. The occupants of 101 had played it safe. C. Meyers and H. Hansen. No one looking for single women would find any indication of their sex. Although, she wondered, how many men would decorate their nameplates with little stars and moons? And, she looked closer, tiny teddy-bear stickers. Maybe one of the women had a child?

Before she could wonder about it anymore, the door was opened by a girl so lovely she looked as though she had been hired from Central Casting by someone looking for the perfect coed. Long golden hair shimmered around a face with almost impossibly even features and clear skin. Blue eyes, of course, and a perfect little pert body. "Hi, I'm Heather," she said.

Susan had guessed Tiffany, but Heather would do. "Hello, I'm Susan Henshaw. . . ." She stopped. She had done this before, gone up to a perfect stranger and asked for information. Someday she would think of a convincing opening line. But for now the old reliable would have to do. "I'd like to ask you some questions."

Heather's parents had brought her up well; she was instantly on her guard. "Why? Are you doing some sort of survey? Or from some government agency? The Census Bureau or something?" She looked over her shoulder. "I'm not alone here. My roommate . . ."

"Look, I'm investigating the murder of the young woman who was killed in the apartment over the garage. Merry Kenny."

"Are you a policewoman?"

"No, I'm doing this privately. Like a private investigator."

"Are there really such things?" Heather asked, seeming interested.

"Of course there are. Did you think they only existed in books?"

"I . . . well, I don't read mystery novels . . ."

"Or any type of novel, in fact. Our Heather is not exactly a book person." The voice came from the hallway and Heather visibly relaxed as she was joined by another young woman.

"This is my roommate. This is Susan . . ." Heather raised her eyebrows.

"Henshaw." Susan supplied the missing name.

"I'm Courtney. Nice to meet you. Would you like to come

in?" Heather's roommate was almost a photo negative of her. The hair was long and shiny but dark brown, as were the luminous eyes. Her skin was perfect but tanned, and the highlights were apricot rather than pink. Their bodies were almost identical and Susan wondered if they shared a single wardrobe. "Are you really a private investigator?"

"No, but I am looking into Merry's murder," Susan admitted. "I didn't actually say I was a P.I."

"Oh, well, jumping to conclusions is sometimes the only exercise Heather gets. Come on in. I gather you've already spoken to our idiot superintendent?"

"Yes." Now it was Susan's turn to look over her shoulder. What had happened to Jinx, for heaven's sake? Then she had another thought. "You don't think he could be dangerous, do you?"

They seemed to know exactly who she was talking about. "Our living masterpiece? Not a chance!" Heather said.

"We call him that because of his tattoos. He once told us his body was his art gallery," Courtney explained. "Are you looking for him?"

"No, Jinx . . . That's my friend. I left her talking with him. I . . . Oh, here she is."

Jinx mounted the steps to the porch, a scowl on her face. "That young man is a complete idiot. We should find out who the owner of this place is and make a complaint." She saw the two girls and smiled. "Hi, I'm Jinx Jensen."

"This is Heather and this is Courtney." Susan introduced them.

"We were just going to go inside," Courtney said. "Would you like something to drink?" she asked as the older women followed the younger through a hallway filled with bicycles, skateboards, and skis awaiting the first snow of the year. Heather opened a door and they were shown into a large living room. The sun was shining through a big bay window onto a worn but polished hardwood floor. The room was furnished with two couches and three chairs, all upholstered in sunny blue and yellow chintzes, surrounding a large coffee table of faux Oriental origins that was enameled burnt sienna. The combination was surprising, but it worked. Off-white paper shades hung in the windows and posters of important exhibits of Impressionist painters were displayed on the walls.

"Charming," Susan said. "This is really charming."

"Heather did the decorating—and upholstered all the furniture as well," Courtney explained after suggesting they all sit down.

"I hope you're getting a degree in interior decoration," Jinx said. "You'll be able to make a fortune when you graduate."

"No, the college doesn't offer that. I'm an art history major. But I hate it," Heather added, as though it made absolutely no difference.

"Heather's parents said she has to do two years here before they'll pay her tuition and living expenses at Pratt in New York City. She's really, really talented."

"You do seem to be," Susan said. "Why did your parents insist you come here?"

"That's my parents," Heather said, sighing in the manner of all youth at the incredible ignorance of their elders. "They were afraid I would be killed in New York—which really is the center of the design industry in this country—and my mother went to this school." She shrugged her cashmere-clad shoulders. "Anyway, I only have one more semester after this one."

"And next year we'll be in our own little pad down in Greenwich Village or SoHo," Courtney enthused.

"Courtney is going to study acting. You're looking at the future Meryl Streep," Heather announced proudly.

"Katharine Hepburn," Courtney contradicted.

Jinx laughed. "How long have you two known each other?"

"Forever," Heather answered.

"Eleven years." Courtney added, "We met at camp the summer I turned eight."

"And we've been friends ever since."

"Best friends."

Heather suddenly seemed to remember that Jinx and Susan were there for a purpose. "Would you like something to drink?" she asked. "I could make some . . . ah, some tea. I think there's tea around here somewhere."

"I'm fine," Jinx said.

"Me, too. And I do have to get back to my Italian," Susan replied. "But I'd really appreciate it if you would tell us about Merry. She . . . my backpack was used as the murder weapon," she added as though that might explain her interest.

"You're kidding. How awful for you," Courtney said, pulling a pillow from behind her and hugging it.

"We didn't know her all that well," Heather said. "She was nice to us when we moved in here."

"When was that?" Susan asked.

"Last January."

"We both lived in the dorm for our first semester."

"My parents again. They insisted," Heather explained.

"But we hated it and one of the women who rented here was an instructor in my Intro to Philosophy class and she happened to mention one day during class that she was going to study for a year at Oxford and she'd be leaving the day before Christmas. Well, I had come over here to pick up an assignment I'd missed and so I immediately asked her if her place was going to be empty. She said yes. I dashed right over to get it before anyone else did."

"And I loved it the moment I saw it," Heather added. "So we moved in right after the holidays."

"You were a sublet?"

"Boy, you haven't rented around here, have you? There's no such thing as a sublet. You leave, you forfeit your deposit, your place is rented to someone else."

"So Merry was here when you came."

"Yes. And she helped us a lot. We didn't know anything about getting phone service or having the utilities put in our names. Merry stopped in and helped us out."

"Good thing, too, since all our masterpiece was interested in was hitting on us."

"And he's not exactly our type."

"So Merry became a good friend?" Jinx asked.

"Nope. Not at all. She was friendly but involved in her own life. We waved when she came in and out, and we kept talking about getting together for dinner. But you know how those things go. We talked about it, but we never did it."

"Did you know who her friends were? Who came to her apartment?" Susan asked, thinking of that back window.

"Not by name. She was going with this old professor for a while. We couldn't figure out what she saw in him." Heather looked at Courtney as she spoke.

"Then she traded him in for this really good-looking guy with a motorcycle for a while," Courtney said. "My bedroom is on the driveway side of the house and he used to arrive and leave with a dull roar. But he vanished in early June of last year and we haven't seen him since."

"So she could have been dating either of them when she was coming to our group," Jinx said.

"What?"

"Nothing. How about this year? Anyone special in her life?"

"No one I knew about," Heather said.

"But we were both away for the summer, and school had only been in session for a couple of weeks when she was killed."

Susan frowned. "What about keys? Did Merry ever give you a key to her apartment for any reason? You know, to open the door for a delivery or anything?"

Both girls denied this ever happening.

"So if anyone had a key to Merry's apartment, it would have been someone Merry gave it to?" Susan asked. "Or the guy you call the masterpiece."

"Yes, as far as we know," Heather said. "We're not helping much, are we?"

"Well, it does help to eliminate possibilities," Jinx said.

Susan didn't say anything. As far as she could tell, the possibilities were endless. Every time they talked with someone, more people were added to the list labeled "men who might have been in possession of a key to the dead woman's apartment."

TWENTY-TWO

WHEN SHE RETURNED HOME, SUSAN WAS SURPRISED TO DIScover Kathleen sitting at her kitchen table. Surprised and, she had to admit, a little dismayed. She didn't want company; she had to study. Didn't anyone know she had to study?

Kathleen stopped petting Clue's head and smiled up at Susan. "I knew you'd be busy today, so I brought dinner."

"You brought . . ." Susan was astounded and embarrassed. How could she have thought Kathleen didn't care! "Kath, thank you so much. I've hardly studied at all and I'm falling so far behind. You're wonderful!"

"Well, you know I'm not a gourmet cook, but I think you may like this. It's chicken chili—made with strips of white meat and lots of fresh cilantro. You don't need to hear the entire recipe. It's in a microwave dish in your refrigerator. All you have to do is heat it up. Is there anything I can do to help you study? Maybe ask you questions and see if you know the answers? Then you'd know what you need to concentrate on."

"I'd love it if you would go through my Italian vocabulary with me," Susan said sincerely. "I made flash cards, but I can't seem to keep myself from cheating—you know, turning them over to peek at the answers."

"Sure. Do you want some coffee while we work?"

"Actually, I missed lunch completely. I hate to take the time to raid the refrigerator . . ."

"Why don't you give me your flash cards and I can ask you questions while you put together a meal?"

"Good idea."

An hour later Susan had three empty plates in front of her. Kathleen had two piles of index cards. "I know more than I thought I did," Susan said, sipping from a steaming mug of coffee.

Kathleen smiled. "You know what interests me? You know what you can relate to."

"What do you mean?"

"Well, you know almost all the food words."

"But I've been eating in Italian restaurants and cooking from Italian cookbooks for years."

"But have you been shopping in Italian stores?"

"That little deli over in Greenwich has a lot of imported items from Italy and—"

"I was thinking of clothing stores. You had no trouble at all when it came to remembering the Italian words for skirt, suit, blouse, shoes, boots, silk."

"I know. I have visions of shopping my way through Italy in the spring," Susan admitted.

"Then you'd better brush up on your numbers. Because your tendency to confuse one million with one thousand could get you in a lot of trouble in those exclusive Italian boutiques."

Susan laughed. "I guess. It's always nice to be able to tell a bargain from a splurge."

"True." Kathleen stood. "I'd better get going. Do you want me to walk Clue before I go?"

Clue leaped to her feet, tail wagging.

"She knows how to spell two words. Walk and cookie. And she's not going to get a cookie. After all, you ate at least a quarter of my sandwich," Susan told Clue, smiling fondly down at her dog and then up at Kathleen. "If you have time, why don't we walk her together?"

"Great."

It took only a few minutes for the women to put on their coats, but Clue managed to give the impression that she had been waiting forever by the time the door was opened for her.

"You have some dog," Kathleen commented as they followed the tugging animal to the street. "I thought she was supposed to be a lot calmer by the time she was two years old."

"That's what the kennel told us. But they lied. She still

thinks she's a puppy. She has just as much energy as the day we got her. How about Licorice?"

"The original couch potato. I think she's missing Alice. Although maybe I'm projecting. I know I'm missing her. I keep thinking I put her in nursery school too young."

"Kath, all the kids in her play group were signed up. She wanted to go and it's only three mornings a week. She likes it, doesn't she?" Susan asked, suddenly guilty. In the past, she would have known all about this.

"She loves it! And I think her teacher is a genius. Alice is actually beginning to read. And she's barely four years old."

"Sounds like Alice is the genius."

"Well, Jerry and I like to think so."

"How does Alex like school this year?"

"Well, that's another story. He claims to hate his teacher."

"That doesn't sound like Alex. Does he say why?"

"Just that she doesn't understand men."

"What?"

"I kid you not. Apparently, she didn't allow him to chat about the weekend's soccer game during their social studies lesson, told him his team T-shirt wasn't appropriate garb for school, and suggested he pick a writer other than Matt Christopher for his book report."

"I can understand the first two restrictions, but why not Matt Christopher?"

"The assignment was to write about a book written by an author the student had never read before. I don't think she believed Alex when he claimed not to have read anything by the most popular writer of sports stories at the elementary level—and she was right about that. He went through every Christopher book in the library last summer."

"I assume you've been in to talk to her."

"Yes, I dashed in the second week of school determined to have it out with this woman who was ruining my only son's chance at Harvard," Kathleen admitted ruefully.

"And?"

"And it turns out she's wonderful. She says Alex is very bright. So bright that he's just coasting along getting good grades. She wants to challenge him a bit more."

"That's what you said all last year!" Susan exclaimed. "She sounds like the perfect teacher for him."

"She is. I was completely embarrassed."

"What's her name?"

"Mrs. Sweeney."

"Kathleen! She's one of the best teachers in the world! Chrissy had her for third grade, but by the time Chad came along she had left to raise her own children. I didn't know she had started teaching again. You should have called me and talked about this before going to the school."

"You've been so busy. I didn't want to bother you," Kathleen answered quietly.

"Oh, Kath, you know you're never a bother." Susan's guilt level was going up by the minute.

"I guess I should have called. But everything's all right now. In fact, I'm going to be a class mother."

"Oh, Lord. What's the third-grade class trip?"

"The Mystic Aquarium in the spring. Why?"

"Well, that's better than some of them. At least it's outdoors. I remember one trip I chaperoned to the Museum of the City of New York. Not only did three kids get lost but one girl broke her arm falling down the stairs. Very exciting. The aquarium should be much easier—unless, of course, it rains."

"Maybe I could plan to be ill that day."

"I think major surgery is the only excuse for the absence of a class mother on the day of the big class trip. And it better be an emergency, not something that's been scheduled for a while."

"Now you tell me. Well, there's no reason to worry about that now. I just might die of boredom at one of Alex's soccer games long before then."

"That bad?"

"Well, I had a great time last year. And Alex really is one of the better players. Still, it's just little kids kicking a ball around the field each and every Saturday until Thanksgiving."

"If he's good, he could end up on one of the league teams—they play other towns in the state. And they play all winter . . . inside."

"You're kidding. Did Chad do that?"

"Nine years in a row."

"Did you go to every game?"

"Well, not after the first three years," Susan admitted. "And I can give you an important bit of advice."

"What?"

"Tell whoever is organizing the league games that you don't cook, you don't drive, and you don't make phone calls asking for money."

"Can I get away with that?"

"Probably not. But it's worth a try." Susan looked at her happy dog, who was leaping from leaf pile to leaf pile. "Do you have time to walk another block or two?"

"Sure. Might as well give Jerry a taste of what it's like to be a mother."

"I was always trying that with Jed when the kids were little," Susan admitted. "But it didn't work. He would have a great time playing with them on weekends, but then he went back to work on Monday and I had to take over and do the dull things like laundry."

"And class trips."

"Oh, believe me, there's nothing dull about class trips," Susan said. "Did I ever tell you about the time Chrissy's teacher took the class to eat sushi?"

"I don't remember."

"You would remember. Anyone would remember a tale of thirty-four kids with diarrhea and upset stomachs."

"Food poisoning?"

"Turned out to be the flu, but we were in a panic for a while, believe me."

They crossed the street and continued around another block, enjoying the leaves falling from the trees, the crisp air, and each other's company. They were on the way back to the house by the time Kathleen had finished talking about her kids and school, and Susan broached the subject of the murder.

"Jinx and I spent most of the morning over at the apartment where Merry was murdered," she started, and then proceeded to tell her friend what little she knew about Merry, her home, the support group she had attended with Jinx; about the papers of Merry's that she had found in her backpack when the police returned it to her, the strange reception she and Jinx had gotten from the professor who had run their support group, and the adversarial relationship she seemed to have with Officer O'Reilly, through no fault of her own.

"Wow, you have been busy," Kathleen commented as they turned a corner and Susan's home came into view.

"Hmm. But I sure wish this murder hadn't happened. Not only did I lose a lab partner, but I haven't been able to immerse myself in my studies the way I hoped I could. Slow down, Clue," she ordered the dog, who was straining at the leash.

"That is too bad, but you know what strikes me?"

"What?"

"Well, I'm outside of this for the first time . . ."

"So? Your opinion may be even more valuable because of that," Susan said when Kathleen appeared reluctant to continue.

"Yes, but I don't know anyone involved except for you."

"Yes. And . . . ?"

"Well, has it occurred to you that Jinx is somewhat interwoven with everyone who is involved with the murder? I mean, are you sure she is exactly who she says she is?"

"I . . ." Susan started, with every intention of defending her new friend. Then she thought about what Kathleen had said for just a moment. "No. In fact, I hadn't even considered that. But you're . . . I guess . . . I suppose you're right," she admitted, looking at her old friend strangely.

TWENTY-THREE

"SUSAN, THIS IS FANTASTIC!"

The Henshaws were sitting on the couch in the study, a tape in the VCR, their dinners in their laps. "It is good, isn't it?" she said, putting a large chunk of chicken in her mouth.

"How you can cook like this and study for tests at the same time is a mystery to me."

"I didn't," Susan admitted. "That is, I didn't cook this. Kathleen brought it over today. It really is delicious. I'll have to ask her for the recipe."

"Guess that cooking class she's taking is paying off. Jerry says he's never eaten better."

"Kathleen is taking a cooking class?" It was the first she'd heard of it.

"Yup."

"Where?"

"Someplace in Westport. You didn't know?"

"No . . . Jed, has Jerry said anything about me? You know, anything that Kathleen has said?"

"You mean, has Kathleen been complaining about you to Jerry?"

"Exactly."

"If so, he hasn't mentioned it to me."

"Do you think she might have reason to complain?"

"Do you?"

"I haven't meant to ignore her!"

"Susan, no one said you had."

She realized she'd been sounding just a bit defensive. And her husband seemed to be having a difficult time looking her in the eye. "Jed? Do you think I'm ignoring her?"

He sighed. "I know how hard you've been working and I know that making a success of school is important to you. But, well, since you asked . . . it wouldn't surprise me if Kathleen thought she had been replaced by this woman Jinx."

"Jed! That's not true."

"I didn't say it was. I said that Kathleen may think that. You think about it. You didn't even know Kathleen was taking this cooking class."

"Well, I don't know all of the classes Jinx is taking. . . ." She stopped and put down her spoon. "I'm being stupid. Kathleen's a good friend. I shouldn't be giving her any reason to even worry about my friendship. And she must be worried. Otherwise, why would she have said what she did this afternoon?"

"What did she say?"

"Well, I don't remember the words exactly, but she practically accused Jinx of being untrustworthy. I didn't want to argue with her, so I didn't say anything to defend Jinx, but I thought it was a little strange. If Kathleen is jealous, it all makes sense."

"What are you going to do about it?"

"You think I should sit down with Kathleen and tell her more about Jinx?"

"No, I think you should spend more time with Kathleen, talking and doing the things you and she used to do—and leave Jinx out of it completely."

Susan didn't like to hear criticism any more than anyone else, but she knew that Jed was fair and that he wouldn't say anything to hurt her unless it was important. "I . . . I guess you're right. I'll be done with these tests on Wednesday. Maybe I should call Kathleen right after dinner and suggest a shopping day. I could use some new boots."

"Two women in a shoe store. Sounds like a plan."

But it wasn't. Susan called while Jed was loading the dishwasher, but Kathleen, more immersed in her children's school activities than she had admitted to Susan, was busy all week.

"Looks like I'll just have to pick up those boots at the pre-Christmas sales," Susan said, grabbing her backpack from the kitchen table.

"Going to study? I thought we were going to finish watching the movie."

"I think it's more your type of movie than mine. All those car crashes and such. And I really—"

"Should study. I know." Jed surprised her by interrupting.

"Oh, Jed . . ."

"Susan, I know what you're going to say. And you're right. You've been ignoring me, too. But we've been married a long time and I know how many times I've been obsessed with something at the agency and not paid enough attention to you or the kids. You deserve to take this opportunity to become involved in what you're doing. Go ahead and do what you need to do. I'll finish the movie and take Clue for a walk."

Susan's smile was interrupted by a yawn. "Thanks. Maybe I'll go to bed early and set the alarm. I did some really good work this morning, and the library at the college is open twenty-four hours a day during midterms. I could head over there and get a seat early before they're filled, study for a while, and then come home early. Maybe we could take Clue for a walk in the park tomorrow afternoon before it gets dark. If it's sunny, it will be a gorgeous day."

"Sounds great. But if you don't get back in time for a walk, please don't worry about it. Clue and I will manage."

Susan went upstairs with a smile on her face. She was a lucky woman to be married to someone like Jed.

She was an idiot. She should have stayed up late last night and studied. She wasn't a morning person. She'd never been a morning person. Why she thought she would be able to concentrate at six A.M. rather than late at night was beyond her. Not particularly surprising, since everything was beyond her this morning. Besides . . .

Susan muttered angrily all the way to the parking lot by the Carn. Then she found she had an additional complaint: The lot was closed overnight. She had no choice but to drive about a half-dozen blocks to the commuting students' parking lot and then walk the entire way back to the Carn. By the time she arrived, stomping up the worn granite stairs, she was awake but still furious with herself. Then she passed through the hideous security barrier and into the large rotunda of the old building and its charm worked on her once again.

Susan loved the Carn. Except for its size, it reminded her of the library she had gone to on Saturday mornings as a child. Built at a time when grandeur indicated seriousness of purpose, every inch of the building was carved or gilded. And this morning joining the scent of old books was the aroma of freshly brewed coffee. Susan looked around hungrily.

"Hi, would you like some coffee?"

She wondered for a moment if she was hallucinating. Could that plaster angel guarding the stacks be speaking, offering her the manna that, at this moment, she desired more than anything?

"Excuse me, ma'am. We're over here. Would you like some coffee?"

Out of the corner of her eye, Susan spotted a young man and a young woman sitting behind an old wooden library table in an alcove. On the table was what seemed to be a huge coffee urn . . . probably was a huge coffee urn if the accompanying paper cups, jug of milk, and chipped bowl of sugar was any indication. As if winged, Susan's feet took her to the table. "You're selling coffee?"

"No, we're giving it away. But you can make a donation to the library fund if you like." The lovely young woman pointed to a frayed basket into which assorted coins and a dollar bill or two had apparently been tossed by students as thankful to find this table as she.

"Could I have some? Black."

She was promptly handed a thick cup. "If you're planning on using library materials, we would appreciate it if you waited to get them until you're done with this," the young man suggested.

"You mean, you don't care if I spill coffee on my papers, you just want to protect the library's property."

"You got it."

"Don't worry. I'm just here to study." Susan rummaged in her pack, found a bill, and dropped it in the basket. "How long are you going to be here?" she asked.

"Just until eight. That's when the Student Union opens."

"I'll be back before then," Susan promised.

The young woman eyed the five-dollar bill Susan had donated. "We'll save you a cup."

"Or two," Susan replied, pulling her pack back up on her shoulder.

"Or two."

The library was practically empty, and Susan, fueled by caffeine and determination to make the most of this last study day, found a spot at a table in a row of them lined up behind the stacks and got to work. Three hours later she sat back, took a sip from her cup, discovered it was empty, and looked around. There wasn't an empty seat in the house. Each and every chair was taken. Papers and books were laid out everywhere on the tables. Susan's neighbors had encroached on her personal space an inch at a time and she realized that her arms and legs were cramped. If she got up, how would she reserve her place? She glanced around. The man on her left was engrossed in a quantum physics text. The woman on her right looked familiar. What was her name? It started with a V. She leaned over and whispered in her ear.

"Vicki?"

"Hi." Midterms seemed to have taken a toll on this young woman. There were dark circles around her eyes and her hair gave no evidence whatsoever of having been shampooed recently. She didn't seem to realize who was talking to her.

"You probably don't remember me. I'm Susan Henshaw. I was Merry Kenny's lab partner."

"Oh, that's right. It was your backpack that killed her."

Well, that was an attention-getter. But most of their tablemates couldn't have cared less.

"Shh!!"

"Shut up!"

"Hey, lady, shut up!"

"Do you want some coffee?" Vicki asked.

"Good idea." Susan looked around. Students wandered about, anxious expressions on their faces, apparently looking for a spot to perch. "If we leave, we'll lose our seats." As she spoke, she realized it wasn't really a concern for her. She was prepared. For her, at least, study time was over.

Apparently, the same thing was true, if for different reasons, for Vicki. "Yeah, but I'm getting nothing done here. Let's go to the Student Union. I can get some breakfast. Then I think I'll go back to my apartment and get some sleep."

They gathered their stuff and left. Their seats were filled before they were out of the room.

"You know, I think I'm done studying," Susan said, thrilled to be saying the words out loud.

"You're kidding. I've got tons to do."

"Really? I thought you'd pulled an overnighter," Susan said, remembering a term from her school years. "You look a little tired."

"Tired! I'm exhausted. Completely wiped."

"Paper due?" Susan suggested as they pushed through the heavy doors. Cool air and brilliant sunshine greeted them. "Wow! What a gorgeous day!"

Vicki squinted and, grabbing sunglasses from her purse, smashed them down on her nose. "God, it's bright!"

Susan was taking reviving breaths of fresh air. "Gorgeous," she repeated.

Vicki didn't seem to be finding the brisk air reviving. "Coffee," she muttered, and turned down the path leading to the Student Union.

"You know," Susan began, struggling to keep up with the young woman, "sometimes the best thing to do is not study too much. Sometimes taking a break helps, then you come back to your work renewed, refreshed, and . . . and all that. I was really struggling last night, but I went to bed and got a good night's sleep and this morning I actually got my work done. It was amazing.

"You were talking about going home and getting a nap and maybe that's a good idea. A break from all your hard work, you know," she continued when Vicki didn't answer.

"I don't need a break," Vicki said. "Do I look like I need a break?" She turned and looked straight at Susan.

"You don't look well, you know. You look sort of . . . I don't know. Like you're getting the flu?"

"Or like I'm hung over?"

"Oh, I didn't realize. Well, a large cup of coffee is what you need and . . . and milk thistle."

Vicki opened her eyes wider than she had all morning and regarded Susan with new respect. "You know about milk thistle."

"Of course," Susan said, not admitting that she hadn't, in fact, even heard of its existence until a few weeks ago. Standing in line for more gingko biloba at the health food store, she had overheard a young, long-haired clerk recommend it as a cure for overindulgence at raves. From what Susan had heard about this particular form of entertainment, she figured milk thistle, if it worked, would go down in history as a miracle cure.

"Well, they don't sell it here. I guess I'll have to settle for granola and yogurt. After you." Vicki opened the door to the Student Union and Susan entered before her. They headed straight for the cafeteria line, Vicki ordering the healthful breakfast she had indicated and Susan splurging on French toast with bacon. After all, she had been working since dawn; she deserved a good meal.

"You think I'm an idiot to be partying right in the middle of midterms," Vicki said after they were seated at a table.

"It's not my business. Besides, who knows what works when it comes to studying?"

Vicki, apparently relieved by Susan's statement, settled down to eat her breakfast.

"I was wondering . . ." Susan began tentatively.

"I thought you weren't going to question me." Vicki was instantly on the defensive.

"About Merry. I wanted to ask you some more questions about Merry."

Vicki shrugged. "Oh. Fine."

"Did you know she was having an affair with my . . . with a professor who teaches creative writing?"

"Professor Hoyer?"

"Yes."

"Where did you get that idea? She knew him, sure. But she hated him. Really hated him."

TWENTY-FOUR

"I SAW THEM TOGETHER AT A VERY EXPENSIVE—AND romantic—French restaurant in Greenwich," Susan explained.

"That doesn't mean anything. Look, you and Merry live—lived—in different worlds. You can probably go to places like that restaurant whenever you want. But not many of Merry's dates could afford to take her there—if they even thought of asking her. Your generation may be proud of inventing women's lib, but it's my generation that's living with the results. Most of my dates expect me to pay for myself. A few want me to pay for them."

Susan wasn't interested in listening to complaints about her generation from a young woman who didn't have the sense to sleep well during midterms. "So you think Merry would have accepted a date from someone she didn't like just because he was willing to pay for a meal in an expensive restaurant?"

"Yeah. Maybe. I know she was always crabbing about not having enough money. Maybe Hoyer made her an offer she couldn't refuse."

"Was she taking a class from him? A writing class?"

"Not that I know about. She got her humanities requirements out of the way in her freshman and sophomore years. I'm sure of that."

"So you don't think that Merry was . . . ah, sleeping with him to get a good grade or anything like that."

"No way!"

"She was a psychology major?" Susan asked, remembering the books in Merry's pack.

"Sociology. She wanted to be a therapist, but she didn't

want to do a whole lot of graduate work or go to med school. She figured she'd get her master's and set up a private practice."

"Is that all it takes?"

Vicki shrugged. "I guess. Merry should know. She said her parents sent her to a different therapist every year when she was growing up."

"She must have had serious problems."

"Who knows? Parents can be such idiots. Not that . . . I mean . . ."

"Please don't apologize. I've probably done my share of idiot," Susan admitted, not adding that Vicki would, too, when she became a parent. She wondered if Brett could track down information about Merry's family. Surely they had been notified of their daughter's murder; it had happened more than a month ago. Perhaps they had gotten over the initial shock and sadness and would be willing to answer a few questions.

"I shouldn't have said that." Vicki sounded sincere. "Merry's parents are really neat people."

"You've met them?"

"Sure. Her father used to teach at the college. He's retired now, but Merry's freshman year he was still here. He and Merry's mom moved to some little town farther north, up near the state line."

Maybe she wouldn't have to bother Brett. "Do you know the name of the town?"

"I don't remember. I think it had a flower name. Daisy or delphinium or something."

Delphinium, Connecticut? It didn't seem likely, but Susan could check a map later.

"I meant to write them a note when Merry died, but I never got around to it," Vicki said sadly. "Oh, well, I suppose they'll understand how busy I've been. Studying and all," she added, an embarrassed expression on her face.

"Sure." One point for the parents' side, Susan figured. "If Merry wasn't dating Professor Hoyer, was she involved with anyone?"

"Merry wasn't one to stay at home. She dated a lot of guys.

But she really fell for one—a T.A.—teaching assistant. When I saw them together at parties and concerts and stuff, she looked real happy to be with him. I heard later that they'd broken up, but I think Merry was really hung up on that guy."

Susan looked up. "What guy?"

Vicki hesitated.

"Look," Susan said, "I appreciate the fact that you don't want to say anything that might get an innocent person in trouble, but Merry was murdered. And the person who murdered her didn't do it with a gun from a window far away. The person who murdered her knew her well enough to be let into her apartment—or even to have a key to her apartment—get close to her, and then strangle her. It was someone she knew. It might have been someone you know."

"No one I know would kill anyone . . ." Vicki started to protest. "But that's probably what Merry would have said before it happened, isn't it?"

Susan, ignoring the tale Jinx had related about Merry's statement to the contrary just last year, nodded her agreement.

Vicki pushed her unfinished breakfast away and rested her elbows on the table. She closed her eyes and dropped her head into her hands. "God, I wish I'd stayed home last night."

Susan resisted the urge to lecture. "Look, just because you tell me about this guy Merry was serious about doesn't mean he had anything to do with her death. But he might be a lead. He might know someone who had a reason to want her dead."

Vicki seemed to realize that there was a possibility she was going to get off the hook. "Yeah, that's right. They probably had friends in common who I haven't even heard of."

"Sure."

"Well, his name is Rick. Rick Dawson. He's a graduate student. I think he's getting a master's degree right now. But Merry said he was planning to go for his doctorate."

"Is that what Merry was planning to do?"

"No, she wanted to get a MSW—Master of Social Work."

"Oh. Did they meet in class?"

"Sort of. He was a teaching assistant in one of Merry's intro to something classes. We were living together then and I remember the day she met him. She couldn't stop talking about this hot teacher who was taking over her group in class."

"Apparently, he felt the same way about her."

"Guess so. They went out on their first date two weeks after they met."

"I guess this Rick was what we used to call a fast worker."

Vicki looked perplexed. "Yeah, I guess. Well, they were together that entire semester. In fact, I began to feel like I didn't have a roommate, Merry spent so much time at Rick's place."

"Just that semester?"

"Well, I don't know exactly. I moved into a different apartment with my boyfriend and didn't see Merry as much. When we ran into each other sometime that spring—I think it was just after spring break, but I'm not really sure—she said she and Rick had broken up. She made it sound like she didn't care, but I got the impression that she was pretty upset about it."

"So you think that breaking up was his idea?"

"Probably. She didn't want to talk about it, but you know what was strange?"

"No."

"I ran into Rick right after that. It was almost the same day, and I remember thinking it was strange. Oh, and you know, this all happened right after spring break because I went down to Ft. Lauderdale and had this really great tan and I remember Rick commented on it."

"Really?"

"Yeah. And we talked about vacations. He had gone up to New Hampshire to ski, but the snow had been lousy and he'd had a rotten time. He said he was glad to be back on campus."

Vicki hesitated and Susan had no trouble guessing that she was uncomfortable with what she was going to say next.

"That's when he asked me how Merry was—no, I'm wrong. That's not what he asked. He asked if she was still around campus."

"You mean he wanted to know if she was on vacation or something?"

"That's what I thought, but it turned out that he thought maybe she had left school, dropped out."

"Why?"

"I don't really know. I asked, because it seemed a little strange. After all, I knew Merry was still in school. I was taking a class with her."

"What class?"

"Social Psychology II."

"Did you take Intro to Social Psychology together, too?" Susan asked, remembering that the paper for this class had led Merry into doing original research in Jinx's support group.

"I wish. Merry not only met Rick in that class, but she did some sort of project that got her an A—without doing all that well on her tests. I studied and studied until I had Freud and Jung and the collective unconscious coming out of my ears. And I got a B. But that's Merry for you."

"What do you mean?"

"She always got the interesting guys and took the interesting classes."

"Maybe just a bit too interesting this time."

"Yeah, I guess." Vicki yawned and rubbed her eyes. "You know, I think I'd really better go home and get some sleep."

"Of course. I just have one more question. Do you know if this Rick is still on campus?"

"Oh, yeah, I'm sure of it. I saw him last night, in fact. He was with some girl wearing a plaid skirt. God, some people. She had no fashion sense at all."

It was obvious to Susan that Vicki was running out of steam. "You better get to bed," she suggested. "Do you want me to drive you somewhere?"

"Where's your car?"

"It's . . ." Susan was surprised by the question. "In the commuting students' lot."

"Oh. No, I don't think so. By the time I walk there, I could be halfway home." Vicki got up and stretched. "I'll be fine. Don't worry about me."

"I'm sure you can take care of yourself," Susan said, not that she had seen much evidence of this fact. "Thanks for all your help."

"Yeah. Right." And with a yawn so large it threatened to

knock her over, Vicki pushed herself up and headed in the direction of the main entrance to the Student Union. Another exit led more directly to the building that housed the sociology department. Susan slung her backpack over her shoulder and made her way toward it.

The campus was beautiful in the sunlight. A group of students were tossing Frisbees in a game that apparently had rules and included three dogs. A young blond couple, sitting on a stone wall, hair gleaming in the sunlight, were pretending to read heavy tomes. Bikers zipped over the paths, full packs on their backs. A homeless man, ragged almost beyond belief, was dozing in the sun.

Susan realized that it had been a while since she'd taken the time to enjoy being on campus. A massive Burmese mountain dog dashed by her, accompanied by a young woman on Rollerblades. Susan took a deep breath and made a promise to herself. She would start enjoying what she was doing.

And, she decided, she would help other people enjoy life a bit more, too. She rummaged in her purse and pulled a five-dollar bill from her wallet. She walked over to the homeless man lying in the sun and offered it to him.

"This is for you," she said, tucking the bill in a surprisingly clean hand.

The man looked up at her as though doubting her sanity. "Why?"

"You . . . look as though you need it," she explained, feeling embarrassed.

"They don't pay professors much, but I don't need to take money from complete strangers yet!" the man announced, leaping to his feet. "Here. Maybe you should give this to someone who really needs it!"

"You're a . . . I didn't know you were . . . I'm sorry." Susan resisted the temptation to go after the angry man and explain. Besides, what could she say that would make it better?

Blushing, she speeded up her pace. It was time to find out who had killed Merry and why—and then she would tell him or her exactly what she thought about the choice of murder weapon!

She climbed the steps to the building that the sociology department shared with the anthropology department. The door, which carried a sign declaring the building closed on Sunday, was open. She marched in.

She had come to expect an overflowing bulletin board or two inside the front door of almost all campus buildings and this place lived up to those expectations. Even better, she only had to move three notices (Free HIV screening at the Health Center, Organizing Meeting Monday Night of Students for a Vegan Lifestyle, and an obscene Xeroxed sketch of a professor and three goats) to find a directory. Susan removed the drawing and put it in her pocket as she scanned the list of room numbers. An R. Dawson had a room on the fifth floor of the building. Susan glanced at the Out of Order sign hanging on the elevator's doors and started up the stairs.

She wasn't quite sure what she was looking for. Certainly she didn't expect Rick Dawson to just happen to be sitting in his office awaiting her visit. Her pack got considerably heavier as she climbed and the temperature got warmer and warmer. She didn't pass anyone on the stairway, but she did hear the click of computer keys and on the third floor someone was playing a radio very loudly.

By the time she arrived on the fifth floor, her heart was beating quickly and she was out of breath. Time to start exercising again, she thought, pulling open the fire door and walking out into the long hallway.

What she saw at the end of it caused her to stop breathing heavily. In fact, for a moment she thought she was going to stop breathing completely.

Michael O'Reilly was there. And he was stringing bright yellow scene-of-the-crime tape across the doorway of . . . of room 513. Susan took one step backward. Maybe he wouldn't notice her.

But she must have made a noise and he stopped what he was doing and turned to look at her. "Mrs. Henshaw?"

"Yes? I . . . I just wanted to talk with one of the teaching assistants. It's not important."

"Is it Richard Dawson you're looking for?"

"Yes, but if he's busy, I can come back another time."

But Officer O'Reilly said exactly what she didn't want to hear. "He's only busy if you count being dead as an active state."

TWENTY-FIVE

"YOU'RE NOT GOING TO GET AWAY WITH IT THIS TIME. YOU know that, don't you?"

"With what?" Susan was trying to look around him and into the room. They were on the top floor of the building and she could see a dormer window on the far wall over Michael O'Reilly's broad shoulders.

"Murder."

Susan tried to keep her voice from quivering. "Who died?" she asked quietly.

"Guy who works in this office. Looks too young to be a professor. 'R. Dawson,' his door says. ID in his wallet says he's Richard."

"Rick. Everyone calls him Rick," Susan muttered, taking a step closer. "And he's not a professor. He's a teaching assistant. You know, a graduate student."

"So you did know him?"

"Not really. We've never met. At least, I don't think we've ever met." She would know, of course, if this guy would get out of her way and she could see. "His name didn't seem familiar when it was mentioned to me a while ago."

"Someone just happened to mention this Rick Dawson to you 'a while ago' and you dashed right up here to see him? That must have been some mention."

She couldn't figure any way out of this without explaining at least a bit of why she was there. "Rick dated Merry last year."

"Merry?"

"Meredith Kenny. The woman who was killed about a month ago."

"This guy dated Meredith Kenny?"

"Exactly."

"And you're . . . you're what? Dashing around campus looking up Meredith's ex-boyfriends for some particular reason?"

"I know it sounds a little unusual—"

"No. It sounds interesting. Like you just might have a whole lot more of a connection to that first murder than ownership of the weapon."

"I don't own any weapons!" Susan protested.

"Your backpack—" he started.

"I know about my backpack. What was used to kill Rick Dawson?" she asked, suddenly wondering about a pen she had lost last week. Surely no one had turned that into a murder weapon!

"Well, I suppose it will be in the papers soon enough. He was shot."

"I don't own a gun!"

"The person who killed him would most likely say the same thing."

"But I didn't kill him! I told you! I didn't even know him!"

"I didn't say you did. But I couldn't help but notice that you didn't explain why you came to see him. You changed the topic to weapons—"

"I did not! You did that! I wasn't even thinking of my backpack before you mentioned it."

"Perhaps you were too busy thinking about what was in that backpack."

There was a remarkably repulsive expression on his handsome face.

"Exactly what do you mean by that?" Susan asked, confused. What the hell was he talking about?

"You know, we did a thorough job of investigating the scene of the crime."

"So Merry was killed in her apartment."

He seemed to find her statement disconcerting. He ran his hands through his bright red hair and looked at her more closely. "Were you under the impression that it happened somewhere else?"

"No, but I didn't know for sure, of course."

"Is there any reason why you should?"

"It's just that usually . . ." She stopped, not wanting to talk with him about the murders she had investigated—and solved. "Well, you see, I am friends with the chief of police in the town I live in."

"I read the papers, Mrs. Henshaw. Have for years. So I know all about your so-called murder investigations, but things are different around here—more professional—and we don't encourage women with nothing better to do to poke their noses in where they aren't wanted. Do you understand what I'm trying to say?"

"I understand exactly what you are saying. You're telling me to mind my own business."

"Sounds like a good idea to me. Unless, of course, you want us to start looking into that letter you wrote."

Susan hadn't had a moment to write a letter for almost two months. "What are you talking about?"

"The letter we found in your pack. The suspicious one."

For a moment, she wondered if it was possible that he had planted something in her pack. Something suspicious that would incriminate her in Merry's murder. Brett had warned her that O'Reilly hated suburban women. But he hadn't said anything about something as serious as this; he hadn't even suggested that she had to worry about anything illegal!

"There wasn't a letter in my pack. I'm sure of it. Unless there was something old in my Filofax. And what business is it of yours what I wrote, anyway? That's private, and it had nothing at all to do with Merry. Besides . . ." Suddenly she remembered that strange paper Merry had written and apparently placed in one of her textbooks. Could he be talking about that? But it wasn't a letter. There was no salutation, no signature at the end. He couldn't possibly have mistaken that for a letter. But what had he thought about it? She looked at him curiously. "I have no idea what you're talking about," she stated firmly.

He looked at her for a moment. "You write threatening letters to your professors and then forget all about them?"

"I've never written a threatening letter to anyone in my entire life!" What sort of horrible person did he take her for? "I've never even thought about . . ." She stopped and reconsidered. "Well, maybe I have thought about it, but I've never done anything like that at all! I . . ." She snapped her mouth shut and stared at him. "My God. You found my idea sheet, didn't you?"

He smiled.

Damn, this man had the nastiest way of smiling she had ever seen! "If that's what you're talking about, I can only tell you that you are making a huge mistake."

"So apparently you now remember what I'm talking about? What jogged your memory, if I might ask?"

"I don't remember a threatening letter. I just figured out what you were talking about. There were three or four sheets of notebook paper with ideas in my pack. They were concepts for stories." She took a deep breath and realized she would have to explain further. "I'm taking a creative writing class and we have to turn in either a short story of six thousand words or more or the first three chapters of a novel by the end of the semester. It's a really hard assignment. I still haven't started my project, and I know that some of the students have already turned in entire novels."

"So you thought that, since you were having such a difficult time with the assignment, you would just kill the professor."

"Of course I wasn't thinking that! I was just coming up with ideas—brainstorming—and following one or two of them to the logical conclusions. And I started getting angry at the professor because, I suppose, I was angry at myself for not having some sort of brilliant idea. And, anyway, I followed that to its logical conclusion and I started thinking about—well, fantasizing really—about killing Professor Hoyer."

"Who?"

"Professor Hoyer. He teaches my creative writing class. . . ." She stopped talking and looked at the policeman. "You know that he was dating Merry, don't you? Has your investigation turned up that fact?"

Finally she seemed to be getting through to him. "Are you claiming that this professor you wanted to kill was the one who killed Meredith Kenny?" he asked.

Boy, had she been wrong. "No, not at all. That's not what I'm saying. What I'm saying is that . . . well, I'm saying two things. First, I'm saying that what you apparently think is a threatening letter from me to my professor is an idea I had for a short story. It is, if you were noticing things, at the end of a long list of ideas for stories. I don't remember exactly now, but the other ideas were something about living with a golden retriever, traveling with small children . . ." She realized how dull this sounded. "We were told to start with our own life and elaborate, turn it into fiction. And it was just a beginning list. School had just started and class had only met once or twice. That's the first thing. The point is that I had—I have— no intention of killing anyone."

"And point two?"

"Point two is that I'm trying to help your investigation. I'm passing on information. You should appreciate that. I believe it is every citizen's job to help the police."

"Now let me get this straight. You never wanted to kill a professor. You just wanted to write an interesting short story. And you thought your professor would appreciate you writing about murdering him?"

"No. Not at all. I was just in a bad mood. I knew that the ideas I had weren't any good and I began to fantasize about killing the professor. I wasn't going to turn it in. I'm not an idiot." She looked at him closely. "You don't believe me."

"What I think of you has nothing to do with my investigation. Let's skip that for a minute."

Susan wasn't really ready to stop defending herself. "I—"

"Let's get back to your claim that you are trying to help our official investigation in some way."

"I am—"

"Your idea of help is apparently telling me that Meredith was involved with both Professor Hoyer—your creative writing professor—and this Richard Dawson, who has just been murdered."

"I . . . I know it sounds a little strange," Susan said slowly.

"And, coincidentally, you tell me this only a few hours after Dawson is shot by, as we like to say, a person or persons unknown."

"A few hours?"

"Yeah. What did you think? That it had just happened and the body was whisked away by some sort of magic?"

Susan didn't want to admit that she had assumed Rick Dawson was still lying on the floor. But, she realized, that explained the fact that there was only one officer there now. The crime team must have done their research and moved on. "I hadn't given that much thought," she prevaricated.

"So what have you thought about? Maybe you've been standing here figuring out a logical reason why you just happen to appear at the office of a man you claim never to have met."

"That's not what I said. I said I didn't think I had met him. I just heard about him earlier today and . . ." She knew she should have kept her mouth shut.

"Why? And from whom?"

"Why what?" She didn't want to answer the last question.

"Let's start with the person who told you about Rick Dawson. Who?"

"Who told me?"

"You're catching on, if slowly."

"Another student. Named Vicki." Susan suddenly couldn't remember Vicki's last name, if she had ever known it.

"We know about Vicki. She and Meredith were roommates last year. Lived together for a few months in the apartment where Meredith died."

"Then you know as much as I do."

"What I don't know is why you were talking to her about this Dawson. Why his name would come up in conversation and why you would dash right over here to talk to him. On a Sunday. On a Sunday right in the middle of midterms."

"I've finished my studying," Susan stated flatly. "And what I do and when I do it is my business, not yours."

"You dink around in other people's business. You know what I'm going to say. When you're involved in a murder investigation, a whole lot of things become your business."

"But I'm not involved . . ." She stopped, realizing she had no choice but to " 'fess up." "Okay, I am asking some people a few questions. I've wondered if I could find out just a bit more about Merry and who might have murdered her."

"Why?"

"Excuse me?"

"Why don't you just stay out of this? It's not your business. You just go take your cute courses about things that have always interested you, courses that will lead nowhere, and stay out of police business."

"I . . ." His evaluation of her choice of classes was so close to the mark that she didn't know what to say—and then she did. And she said it angrily. "How the hell do you know what classes I'm taking? And what gives you the right to question me or to judge what I do with my life? You arrogant, egotistical, self-centered, ignorant—"

She still had a lot more adjectives to use when Brett Fortesque tapped her on the shoulder.

TWENTY-SIX

"SUSAN . . ."

"I know what you're going to say, Brett. You're going to tell me I'm treading on dangerous ground. You're going to remind me that the campus police department isn't the Hancock Police Department. You're going to say that you're worried about this O'Reilly, that he really has it in for suburban housewives. You're going to tell me to be careful investigating Merry's murder. And you're probably going to remind me that another person has been killed and that this could be dangerous."

"You got that right. Now what are you going to say to me?"

"I don't know."

"You're going to promise me that you'll be careful. If you're smart, you'll tell me that you aren't going to investigate anymore, that it's a gorgeous fall day and you're going to go for a long drive with Jed or take Clue for a walk in the woods. You're going to tell me that you are definitely not going to hang around campus asking more dangerous questions and antagonizing the local police."

They had been walking across campus during this conversation, and they both stopped, having arrived at Susan's car.

"A ride? A walk in the woods," she muttered, looking in her purse for her keys. "Those are both good ideas."

"Those are both excellent ideas. Believe me, Susan . . ."

"I'll do both."

". . . you will only make things worse if you continue as you have. . . . What did you say?"

"I said I was going to do both. Take a long drive with Jed and walk Clue in the woods. First the drive. Then the walk," she elaborated. "What do you think?"

"I think it's an excellent idea."

She found her key and clicked off the car alarm. Brett leaned over and opened the car door for her. Susan smiled. He was such a nice man. She really didn't want him to worry about her. "It will be nice to spend the afternoon with Jed and Clue."

"I'm sure they both feel the same way about being with you. And, Susan, I'll check with my connections over here. Maybe this second death will offer a clue that will clear up both murders."

"I hope so," she said sincerely.

"If I find out anything, I'll call."

Susan got in her car and opened the window so that they could talk. "Great. But we probably won't be home until late. I'd really like to go up to this little town near the state line. . . ."

"Great idea. Go north. The leaves will be at their peak."

"I hope so," she assured him, and sped off.

* * *

"The leaves will be at their peak," she repeated Brett's words to Jed an hour later.

"I hope so," Jed replied.

The Henshaws were in Susan's Cherokee. Jed was driving. Susan was riding. Clue was in the far back, watching the world pass by. "But even if they're not, maybe you'll get the information you're looking for," he continued. "And Clue doesn't care about leaf color. All she's waiting for is a nice, long walk. Right, Clue?"

The dog's tail thumped so hard, Susan wondered if perhaps it would knock her car out of alignment.

She had spent the drive home from the college wondering how to present Jed with her plan for the afternoon. She didn't want to lie, of course, but she was afraid his opinion wouldn't vary much from Brett's. She considered suggesting a drive in the country, guiding him toward the town where Merry's parents lived, and then, with some appropriate exclamations ("Oh, my goodness, look where we are! Do you mind if we stop and see if possibly Professor Kenny and his wife are at home?") just happen to drop in on them. But Jed wasn't stupid. In fact, he was too smart and had lived with her for too long to be deceived by any fake surprise or accidental arrivals. She decided honesty was the best policy and told him the truth. Just not all of it.

"I hope this professor and his wife are home. Or did you call them?"

"I . . . No, I guess I should have. But if they're not home, we'll still have had a nice drive," Susan said.

"It's nice of you to want to offer your condolences, but do you think it might bring back painful memories for them?" he asked.

"Well, we'll see. I think we turn left up here. The map . . . Look, there's the sign."

"Who would have thought there was a town named Iris in Connecticut?"

"Not me. Left again here." She leaned forward to see out the windshield better. "Oh, look, that sign says three miles to the Boettcher Wildlife Sanctuary. That might be just the place for you to walk Clue."

"You're not coming with us?"

"Well, I was thinking about that on the way here, Jed. It might be easier if I saw the Kennys alone."

"I think that's an excellent idea. I could drop you off and you could visit and I could take Clue out for a good run. If I got back in about an hour or an hour and a half, how would that be?"

"Sounds great." Susan realized her husband had been dreading the visit she had proposed and was more than happy to take off with the dog. "We passed a sign to an Iris Inn right after we turned off the highway. Maybe we could have dinner there. It took less time to get here than I thought it would, and if you wear Clue out, she'll sleep in the car while we eat."

"Okay. Where do these people live?"

"Actually, I don't know. I was thinking I would find a phone book and look them up."

"I thought . . . oh, there's a drugstore. It should be open. Do you want to stop?"

"Yes. Definitely." Iris was a lovely town and the drugstore's quaint exterior disguised its modern interior. There was a pay phone right inside the door. A collection of thin phone books was stacked underneath. Susan easily found Kenny. There was only one, she noted thankfully. She had planned to claim to be doing a report on the history of the college if she had to call ahead, but this made her task easier.

"Do you know where Daisy Court is?" she asked the woman behind the cash register.

"Sure. It's not far from here. You just keep going down this street. Turn on Pansy, keep going for three blocks, and you're right there. What number are looking for?"

"Twenty-three."

"Turn right. Should be on the left side of the road."

"Thank you."

"Welcome to Iris."

"This is such a friendly town."

"You've gotta be when you've got a stupid name like Iris." Susan left the drugstore chuckling.

"Did you get the information you were looking for?" Jed asked. He and Clue were crossing the street. Apparently, they had just visited the little town square. The squirrels were in hiding.

"Sure did."

"Then why don't I drop you off—"

"Maybe you'd better wait around and see if they're home."

"I thought you were going to call."

"No, I just got their address from the phone book. Maybe you could wait around for a minute or two and see if they're there." She repeated her suggestion.

"And if they're willing to answer questions about their dead daughter?"

"You knew why I wanted to come here!"

"It didn't take a Sherlock Holmes to figure it out, Susan."

"But it may take one to find the murderer. I have more questions than answers. And every lead in any direction just runs into a dead end."

"Or into a dead professor?"

"He was a teaching assist— Jed, how did you know about him?"

"I got a call from Brett. He was worried about you."

"He called you?"

"Yes."

"And you didn't tell me . . ." She realized what her husband had just told her. "Why? Why was he looking for me? Did he think I should know about Rick Dawson's death?"

"Yes. Apparently, he was concerned about something one of the campus cops said about you. He was going to go over to the campus. Did you run into him there?"

"Sure did. Right outside Dawson's office door."

"What? You knew about the second murder, too?"

"I don't know why everyone keeps insisting this is a second murder, as though it's connected with Merry's death in some way. Couldn't it just be a coincidence?"

"What do you think?"

"Not a chance. But I don't know what the connection is. I mean, Rick and Merry dated last year."

"When did you find that out?"

Susan related her conversation with Vicki. "So I was hoping to ask this guy a few questions, only he was dead."

"Did anyone know you were on your way there?"

"No. If you're thinking maybe he was killed so he couldn't talk to me, it's not possible. The body was already gone by the time I arrived. When you consider how long it takes the police to photograph the body and do everything they need to do, he was probably dead before I even ran into Vicki." They were still sitting in the car; the key was in the ignition, but Jed had not turned it. Susan glanced over at her husband. There was a serious expression on his face. "Jed? What's wrong?"

"You know what you just told me, don't you? You were probably on campus when he was killed."

"No, that's not true. He could have been killed last night— late—or even yesterday!"

"No, Brett said someone heard the shot this morning."

"Oh, well, then I guess you're right. I was there. But in the library, Jed."

"With a lot of people around you, right?"

"Yes, but they were paying attention to their own work. They might not have noticed me."

They exchanged looks.

"But, Jed, why would anyone think I would want to kill this guy? I don't think I've ever met him!"

"You don't think so?"

"The name isn't familiar, but I didn't get a chance to see the body. He could be someone I sat next to in the Student Union or in a class or anywhere!

"Look, why don't we talk about this later?" She changed the subject. "I don't want to arrive at Merry's parents' home too late. They're old. They might eat dinner early."

"Okay."

The directions to the Kennys' home had been correct, if flowery, and in just a few minutes the Henshaws drove up to a charming Tudor probably built in the late thirties when that style had been so popular. There were two people working in a perennial bed next to the flagstone walk.

"Well, looks like they're waiting for you. Do you want me to hang around until you find out if you're welcome?"

"That would look a little strange, don't you think? Tell you what, don't wait for me and don't pick me up here. We're only a little way from town. Why don't we meet at the Iris Inn? I saw it across the green from the drugstore. I can walk there from here in less than twenty minutes. That way you won't have to be embarrassed waiting here for me. Okay?"

"I . . ."

"In two hours. Okay?" And without waiting for an answer, she opened the door and got out, putting a wide smile on her face as the two people turned to see who their guest was.

She heard Jed drive off behind her, but she didn't turn to look. She was too busy resisting the strong urge to turn and run after the Cherokee. How could she have gotten herself into this situation? She didn't want to bother this nice-looking couple, working hard on a fall afternoon; she didn't want to remind them of their recent grief. Damn it, she didn't want to be there!

"Hi," she said as cheerfully as possible. "I'm Susan Henshaw. I'm looking for Professor Kenny and his wife."

"Well, this is your lucky day, young lady. You've found them."

A large black standard poodle with a utility trim emerged from a big pile of leaves and walked over to greet her.

"It's been a long time since anyone called me a young lady," Susan said awkwardly, letting the dog smell her hands.

"My husband spent many, many years teaching at a private college down near the coast. He tends to address people as though they are all his students." The woman who spoke looked like a gray-haired version of Merry. The moleskin overalls she wore didn't disguise her trim figure. She also had a gentle smile on her suntanned face.

"I . . . So I understand. I mean, I know that you were a professor and just retired last year. I'm actually a student at the college where you taught. I just started this semester, in fact."

"Good for you! And what are you taking?"

"Victorian women writers, Italian, astronomy, and creative writing."

"That's very interesting," Professor Kenny said, glancing over at his wife. "We've been working very hard all afternoon and were just talking about taking a break. Perhaps you would like to come in and join us? We frequently have tea at this time in the afternoon. A professorial affectation, I'm afraid. It offers me an opportunity to tell you about my Fulbright year at Oxford without sounding like I'm bragging."

"And you can tell us how you knew my daughter," Mrs. Kenny suggested, as they walked together up the walk to the deep burgundy–painted front door.

TWENTY-SEVEN

"How . . . ?" Susan started to ask the obvious question as she followed Mrs. Kenny into the house. The hallway was paneled with dark wood, but the air was warm, scented with cinnamon and the brilliant rusty chrysanthemums in brass pots that brightened the corners.

"Just an educated guess," she replied, pointing Susan toward an open doorway. "Don't worry. Neither my husband nor myself mind talking about her. For me, it almost brings Merry back for a few minutes. And the professor is . . . well, just a bit less involved than I am."

The room Susan was shown into could have been imported complete from a rural cottage in England. As she looked around, Mrs. Kenny bent down and lit an already laid fire in the large stone fireplace. There were comfortable-looking couches upholstered with chintz. A needlepoint rug covered much of the flagstone floor. Horse brasses and pastel watercolors hung on the walls. A drinks tray sat beneath the bay window, which overflowed with blooming plants. An oil painting of a child with pale skin, black hair, and a bright green sundress hung above the fireplace.

"Merry?" Susan asked, indicating the painting with a nod of her head.

"When she was eleven years old. A friend of my husband's, now an art professor at Yale, painted it."

"It's wonderful. She must have been charming. Oh, I'm sorry. I don't mean that she wasn't later. When she was older or . . . or anything."

"Please don't apologize. The fact is, she was a repulsive teenager. Three years after that painting was done, her hair was the color of the dress and her clothing the natural color of her hair."

"Yes, Merry was an awful teenager," her husband agreed. "Of course, a remarkable number of excellent students at the college always choose to live—or at least appeared to live—an alternative lifestyle. But Merry was so immature, and we worried about her decision-making abilities as well as her academic interests." He looked over at his wife and smiled. "I'm afraid that's one of the problems with having an academic in the family. We tend to be obsessed with education."

"You never wanted anything but the best for Merry. And she knew it," his wife said reassuringly.

"Perhaps. But it would have been nice if she had admitted it," he said, sitting down on the couch across from Susan.

"I think the fact that when she was finally ready to attend college, she chose the one you had dedicated your life to was an indication of that. And I've told him so many, many times," she added to Susan. "Now I'm going to get that tea I promised. Everything is pretty much ready in the kitchen, so I won't be a moment." She turned and hurried from the room.

Professor Kenny headed for the drinks tray. "We call it tea, but we do offer the hard stuff. Would you like something? I'm going to have a large scotch myself. Take the chill out of my old bones. My wife adores gardening. After years and years of putting off helping her, I find that retirement has eliminated many of my excuses."

"Don't you believe him, Mrs. Henshaw. My husband is currently writing his memoirs. I have a feeling they are going to provide him with ample excuses for not helping out around the house for years to come."

"I will, however, help you with that, and pour a bit of rum in your tea as well," he said, leaping up to relieve his wife of the heavy silver tray she carried. He placed the tray on the low coffee table between the couches, then returned to the window to pick up his drink and a bottle of Myers dark rum, which he waved in the air to make his offer more concrete.

"That would be lovely, dear. But just a taste." Mrs. Kenny sat down and poured light amber tea into thin porcelain cups and passed them around. After that, she offered an oblong tray of assorted tea breads. "There's pumpkin and raisin, fig and pecan, and zucchini and pineapple. It's the very last of the zucchini," she added.

"Thank God. Next year, please don't even think of planting it. You know what Dickens said about abundance. I hate to think what he would have said about zucchini."

"I think he makes up these literary references," the professor's wife confided to Susan, passing her a plate piled high with food.

Susan hadn't eaten since her greasy breakfast in the Student Union. "Thank you. Everything looks wonderful." Now that she was there, she didn't know how to begin.

But the professor began for her. "If you've just started classes this year, you must not have known our Merry very well. Or, at least, not for very long."

"No. We were lab partners in my astronomy class, but that's all. To be honest, I don't think we spent more than an hour or two together."

"I don't mean to be rude, Mrs. Henshaw, but if you knew her so little, exactly why are you here?"

There was no mistaking the chill in Mrs. Kenny's voice.

"Please don't think I have some sort of morbid interest in your daughter's murder."

"Then perhaps you should explain," the professor said.

"I'm investigating her murder."

"You're a policewoman? A detective?"

"No. Nothing like that. Just let me start at the beginning. It won't take very long to explain." Neither of them objected, so she continued. "In the first place, I may have been one of the last people to see Merry alive—except for whoever killed her. We were going to meet that afternoon—the afternoon she died—to go over our notes for the first viewing in astronomy.

And the last time I saw her, she accidentally picked up my bag and took it with her."

"Your bag? What sort of bag?"

"I should have said my backpack. It . . ." In for a penny, in for a pound. "It's what the killer used to strangle her."

"And so you had Merry's pack," Mrs. Kenny said slowly. "I remember, it was in her apartment, along with her other possessions." She started to tear up and her husband took over.

"It was very difficult for my wife to go through Merry's things. A daughter is supposed to have an independent life by the time she's Merry's age. And mothers really have no business looking through their possessions under any circumstances. It would have been kinder if the police had just given everything away to charity, but I suppose they can't do that legally."

"I'm sorry. There's little reason for me to be so upset. It's just that I thought things were going to be so different. Merry had a rocky adolescence, but she had grown up; she was finally interested in school, getting an education, doing something with her life."

"You have had many reasons to be proud of her these last few years," her husband said earnestly.

"Yes. I know that, of course. It was just difficult going through everything." A tear slipped down her wrinkled cheek, and Susan realized she couldn't possibly ask if there had been anything in Merry's belongings that might identify her killer.

"The police asked us to go through everything carefully. They thought perhaps something in Merry's belongings might lead to the murderer," the professor explained, as if he could read Susan's mind.

"And did you find anything?"

"No. Nothing." Merry's mother fumbled for a handkerchief and blew her nose before continuing. "But why are you trying to find out who killed her? Certainly the fact that your pack just happened to be handy . . . was used to . . ."

"Two reasons," Susan stated flatly, trying to move on to less painful subjects. "In the first place, the police got me involved, calling me in for questioning. And then, well, frankly, someone told me something that didn't make sense, something that puzzled me. You see, I've helped the police—the local police in my town—investigate murders in the past. I know that makes me sound like a character in a novel, but that's just the way it's worked out."

"So you have experience with this sort of thing and you found yourself personally involved. Is that it?" Professor Kenny asked.

Susan looked him straight in the eyes before she answered. "That, and the fact that the police misunderstood something I wrote for a class and now they think I'm connected with a second murder."

"A second murder . . ."

"Another coed?" asked Mrs. Kenny.

"No, a teacher this time. A teaching assistant," Susan explained, hoping the difference between this and Merry's death would somehow soften the blow.

"Who? Is there a connection between this second murder and my daughter's?"

"The man killed was named Rick Dawson. I understand he and Merry dated last year."

"Of course. In fact, she brought him home for Thanksgiving dinner. A very good-looking young man," she added approvingly.

"I believe he told us he was getting a master's in sociology," her husband remarked. "But that's not important now. You're telling us he's been killed also."

"Yes." Susan took a deep breath and continued. "He was murdered this morning. Shot."

"Shot. How terrible." Mrs. Kenny pursed her lips and looked over at her husband. "I believe I will have a drink, dear. Scotch. Straight up."

"And the police—and you, apparently—believe his death is connected to Merry's."

"It's possible. Can you tell me more about him? About their relationship?"

"You were taking a class from him?" the professor asked.

"No, we've never met. In fact, I was on my way over to

meet him this morning when I discovered that he had been murdered."

"Why?"

"Why what?"

"Why were you going to meet him? Why did you want to see him?"

"Oh, well, you see, I had just found out that he and Merry had dated. I was hoping to talk to him about her."

"Why? Why him? Certainly there were lots of other people who knew Merry."

"Yes, but while she was dating Rick Dawson, she was . . . she was involved in something a little strange."

The couple exchanged worried looks, and then Mrs. Kenny reached for her half-empty scotch glass.

"What do you mean by strange?" Susan got the impression that the professor was working very hard to keep any emotion from his voice.

"That's probably the wrong word. As I understand it, Merry was working on a term paper for her Introduction to Social Psychology course, and instead of doing a lot of research in the library, she did . . . what I suppose you would call fieldwork. The topic was something like how members benefit from support groups. She attended a support group set up to help women whose husbands had left them. And she claimed that she was in the same situation."

"Well, that's certainly dishonest, but are you suggesting that someone from the group discovered what she was doing and killed her for it—almost nine months later?"

"I . . ." Susan stared at the man with a surprised expression on her face. "You know, I never thought about the timing before. You're right. Why would someone kill her about that so much later?"

"I don't quite understand why you connected her death with that group in the first place," Merry's mother said.

"Because she claimed that her husband, the imaginary husband she had created to be a part of the group, was going to kill her. When I learned that, I spoke to a friend in my local police department and suggested that he check on this man.

Which is when I discovered that Merry wasn't married—and hadn't been as far as anyone could discover."

"So your working theory is that an imaginary husband killed my daughter some nine months after she lied to a group of women who were going through divorce," Mrs. Kenny said, obviously distressed.

"Put like that . . ." Susan pushed away her plate. Suddenly, she wasn't all that hungry. She looked at the couple and recognized the lines of sadness on their faces. "I'm afraid I've been stupid, jumping to conclusions and then bothering you with the foolish results. I'm very, very sorry." She stood.

"Yes, I'm afraid you've upset my wife for no reason—"

"Please, Ernest, I'm fine, and I think I'm glad Mrs. Henshaw is here. I think I have some things to say to her."

"Susan. Please call me Susan."

"And we're Ernest and Evangeline. Feel free to smile; most people do when they hear our names."

"I'm too embarrassed to smile," Susan admitted. "I don't know why I didn't realize that the time that had passed between last fall and this fall made it unlikely that I was going to find a motive for your daughter's murder where I was looking."

"I don't know if that's true. It seems to me that it's quite possible for something to happen in the past that causes someone to act in the present."

"I suppose you're right, of course," Susan said slowly.

"And if we can help by telling you about my daughter, we would be happy to," Evangeline said.

"Your daughter?"

"Yes, Merry was my daughter. I had her before the professor and I got married. She always claimed that was one of her problems. That she didn't know who her natural father was."

"And you didn't tell her?" Susan asked.

"No. I may, of course, have been wrong, but at the time, it really did make sense."

TWENTY-EIGHT

"I FELL IN LOVE WITH A PROFESSOR," EVANGELINE KENNY stated flatly.

Susan glanced over at Professor Kenny.

"Oh, not my husband. Not that time," Evangeline continued. "This was before Ernest and I met." She smiled at him and continued her story. "Anyway, I was young and foolish, and I fell in love and got pregnant before the end of my first semester of college."

"Did you marry that man?"

"No. Although he wasn't married and would have, I think, done what was considered the honorable thing back in those days. But by the time I realized I was going to have a baby, I had also realized that I was not in love with him.

"You understand that things were different then. Abortions were neither legal nor acceptable. I don't know what I would have done in the same situation in the 1990s, but I gave birth to Merry in a home for unwed mothers two weeks before the fall semester began. I had planned to give her up for adoption, but once I saw her . . . Well, that was impossible. I took a year off, went home to live with my confused, concerned, but always loving parents, and tried to get my life together. I wanted to get a job and raise my baby, but my parents convinced me that I would be a much better mother if I returned to school, got a degree, and then looked for work. They generously volunteered to take care of Merry if I took their advice.

"To make a very long story short, I decided they were right, transferred to a different school, and got busy. By signing up for the maximum number of courses allowed and

179

not taking any time off in the summer, I graduated with a degree in nursing less than two and a half years later."

"And you met your husband during that time?"

"No. Evangeline met me in the hospital where she was working a few years later. I had foolishly gotten caught up in my 'Robert Louis Stevenson, Unappreciated Genius' lecture and fallen off the podium in one of my classrooms, managing to look incredibly foolish and break both my leg and elbow in one fell swoop—or in one swooping fall, to be more accurate. Evangeline was my night nurse. She was a wonderful nurse."

"And he was a terrible patient."

"And since we had nothing at all in common, we decided to complicate our lives a bit by falling in love and getting married."

Susan smiled at the happiness shining on their faces at the memory.

"But we're supposed to be telling you about Merry," Evangeline said. "She was almost four years old when Ernest and I married. Years later a psychiatrist told me that was probably the worst age to make a dramatic change in her living situation."

"Over the years, different psychiatrists have told my wife that she did everything wrong. Of course, each one blamed our daughter's misery on a different event or action."

"My husband has little faith in the psychiatric community."

"After the garbage they have fed us, I would be a fool if anything else was true."

"You said Merry had a difficult adolescence, but many children do," Susan interjected.

"She had a difficult childhood, a difficult adolescence, and a difficult young adulthood," Mrs. Kenny said sadly.

"You might have noticed that we weren't surprised when you told us Merry had lied about her marital status. She lied about many things over the years—mostly to increase her own importance," the professor explained. "We thought she would grow out of it. But when she didn't, we panicked. We hired therapists. We consulted anyone who would tell us anything. Nothing worked."

"What do you mean, 'worked'?"

"Merry was self-destructive in the ways most kids are. Mixing with the wrong kids, cutting classes, drinking. But the older she got, the bigger the problems, and then, about three years ago, things settled down. She got serious about her future, used her native intelligence to get excellent scores on her SATs, and got into college."

"The college you taught at. Did that surprise you?"

"Yes and no. Yes, because it was Merry's idea and she pur sued it on her own. And no, because she got a huge tuition break there. She was paying her own way in life by that time and I don't think she could have swung it—with an off-campus apartment—anyplace else. And, of course, it's always possible that she just wanted to be where her father was."

"Her father? Who. . . ?"

"It's another long story," Evangeline Kenny said.

"But one I think you have to tell her," her husband said gently.

Susan sat quietly and waited for Evangeline to begin.

"I didn't stay in touch with Merry's father. In fact, he never knew I was pregnant. I left school and he went on with his life: got married, had children of his own. And then, unfortunately, he came to teach at the same place my husband was working."

"You're kidding!" Susan exclaimed. "How upsetting. Or was it?"

"Not at all, really. I was a different person when I got married. Ernest and I had raised Merry together. It had been so long ago . . . I know it sounds stupid now, but the fact is, I had almost forgotten there was a natural father involved."

"Until Augustus Hoyer was hired by the college," said the professor.

"Dr. Hoyer? You're not saying he's her father?"

"Yes. Augustus Hoyer. Better known as Gus. It's a big world. Who would have thought that Merry's biological father would end up teaching at the same college where her adoptive father taught?"

"It's an extraordinary coincidence," Susan agreed, remembering the incorrect conclusion she had drawn when she saw them together at the French restaurant in Greenwich.

"Well, Ernest and I talked it over. Since Gus didn't know I had been pregnant when I left school or, of course, that my daughter was his, we didn't think there was any reason to tell him about Merry."

"We discussed it, of course," the professor added. "We were both concerned about the morality of not letting a person know that he or she is a parent and such things. But, in the end, we didn't have much choice. You see, while Merry knew I wasn't her biological father, she had no idea who the man was."

"She must have asked you about him," Susan said to Evangeline.

"Over and over again. But I had made a decision early on. When I didn't tell Gus about Merry, I knew that I could tell no one. There's no father's name on her birth certificate. Even my parents understood that this was just one mystery they would have to accept. And they did. But . . ." She looked over at her husband. "But it was different with Ernest."

"Because you both taught at the same college?"

"That didn't have anything to do with it. Not at first. You see, Evangeline told me about the man who was the father of her child when we got married. I suppose she even told me his name, but, frankly, it didn't register."

"I don't understand."

"When I met Professor Hoyer, I didn't think 'Ah-ha, here's the biological father of my daughter.' "

"Ernest adopted Merry when we got married," Evangeline explained. "She really was his daughter."

"I was proud that you allowed me to become her father. And even after all that's happened, I'm still grateful that I had the opportunity to help raise her. It enriched my life in many ways."

What nice people, Susan thought.

He returned to his story. "As I was saying, when I met Professor Hoyer, I didn't think anything in particular. I'd been at the university for years and years at that point and he was just another new faculty member who would either be granted tenure in a few years and stay around or he wouldn't fit in, would not be offered tenure, and would leave."

"You're an English lit professor. You and Professor Hoyer were in the same department, weren't you?"

"Yes. Although, as I say, I was around more than a dozen years before he arrived."

"You must have been shocked when you met him."

"Heavens, even I didn't realize he was Merry's father at first. It was at the annual department Christmas party," Evangeline said. "After all, it had been over sixteen years since I had last seen him. He'd changed a lot. He was no longer that handsome young man with the reddish beard. He was that handsome middle-aged man with the receding hairline."

"When did you realize who he was—or is?"

"That's one of the problems. You see, I was walking across campus one day and glanced at Gus out the corner of my eye and for some reason I recognized him. Or thought I did. It was, as you can probably guess, a shock. I wasn't sure, of course. I mean, I had just the momentary recognition. I thought that it might have been my imagination. I had thought about Gus off and on over the years. Wondering if Merry's problems were inherited or if they had been caused by my insistence on keeping her father's identity a secret."

"Two opposing schools of thought encouraged by different therapists through the years," the professor added.

"What did you do?" Susan asked.

"Regressed to acting like a schoolgirl. I literally hung around Gus's office door trying to catch a glimpse of him, hoping to confirm my suspicion. Well, that's not true. I was hoping it would turn out that he was not who I thought he was. I didn't see any way that the reappearance of Gus Hoyer could be anything but a complication in my life."

"And when you saw him?"

"I knew he was Merry's father. Sometimes I think I knew it all along. When we met at the party, his name didn't ring a bell. I knew him as Augustus—he said Gus was a hick's name back when I first knew him. And I didn't catch his last name. But once I saw his name on the office door, I couldn't deny the truth." She looked over at her husband. "I should have told Ernest right then. But apparently every time I got around Gus Hoyer, I did something stupid, and this time the stupid thing was that I didn't tell Ernest right away."

"You thought you were protecting me, dear."

"That doesn't mean it wasn't stupid. We could . . . we should have been acting together from the beginning of it all."

"We didn't know anything was beginning, remember."

"What happened?" Susan asked, completely confused.

"Merry met him."

"How did that happen?"

"She was screwing up her junior year of high school and got arrested for shoplifting. The store owner agreed not to press charges as long as she paid him for the goods. We insisted that she get an after-school job at the local 7-Eleven and put her name on the baby-sitting list that the university maintains for professors. She was fired from the 7-Eleven for incompetence and we were thinking of locking her in her room for the rest of her life when she got a baby-sitting job that filled the same hours and even paid a bit more."

"For Gus Hoyer?" Susan guessed.

"Exactly."

"But she didn't know he was her father."

"No—"

"We don't think so," the professor interrupted. "We've been talking about this recently. We're not really sure when Merry identified Gus as her father."

"But it couldn't have had anything to do with the job. That had to have been a coincidence. And, in fact, Gus's wife was the one who hired Merry to take care of their two children when they got home from elementary school."

"She was working?"

"She's a writer and, apparently, writing when her children were at school didn't provide her with a long enough day to get her work done. I hope that doesn't sound judgmental. I know everyone is different and everyone works at their own pace. I just wish Nina Hoyer had decided to spend some quality time with her children after school was over. It would have saved many people a lot of pain."

"What happened?"

"We don't actually know. At the time, we didn't think anything out of the ordinary was happening. Merry seemed to like the children and the job. She even talked about going to the local community college and qualifying to work in a day-care center."

"And at that time, we had serious doubts about her even getting her high school diploma, so we were thrilled."

"One of us was thrilled," Evangeline said. "I was terrified that someone would find out about the past."

"And that happened?" Susan asked the same question as earlier.

"No. What happened was that the Hoyer children loved Merry, and Gus and his wife were thrilled with her work, and as a result of her after-school sitting, Merry was hired to go to Martha's Vineyard with the Hoyers on their summer vacation. And she went," explained the professor.

"By that time, I had begun to believe that my secret was safe. That Merry and Gus could even be together on vacation and nothing would happen. No one would find out anything," Evangeline said. "I was even happy that she was going to leave, do something productive with her vacation, and, in fact, give Ernest and myself a summer alone together."

"Then we started getting these strange postcards," the professor said.

"And we should have known something was going on. Merry was a notoriously poor correspondent. And we were probably last on the list of people she wanted to keep in touch with when she was away from home."

"What did the cards say?"

"That she was in love. In love. In love. That was the first two weeks. She waited until the third week to inform us that she was in love with her married employer."

"You must have been hysterical," Susan said.

"Oh, yes. We were."

"I told Ernest who Gus was right away, of course. And then we stopped sleeping and talked about what our options were for a few days. Then we did the only thing we could do. We flew up to the Vineyard, planning to tell Merry the truth about her heritage."

"And did you?"

"Well, we flew up there, but the scenario wasn't exactly what we thought. You see, Merry wasn't having an affair with her father. She had made it all up. To punish us for keeping her father's identity a secret for all these years."

"How horrible." The words were out of Susan's mouth before she could stop them.

"Yes. 'Horrible' is the only word to use."

TWENTY-NINE

SUSAN HAD BEEN LATE MEETING JED AT THE INN. SHE HAD stayed with the Kennys, listening to their story, reliving the sad and confusing life of their daughter until, glancing out the window, she saw that the sun had gone down. Professor Kenny had offered to drive her to the inn, where Jed was waiting, an offer she eagerly accepted. She didn't want to walk around an unknown town in the dark; she didn't want to be any later than necessary.

"And I got the feeling that he wanted a few minutes alone with me," she added. Now seated in the oppressively dark, "early American" pine-paneled inn bar, she was telling Jed about her afternoon as they studied the menu.

"And you were right?"

"Absolutely." She pursed her lips and flipped to another page of the menu. "Do you think a place with so many choices can possibly serve fresh food? Is everything going to be prepared ahead and microwaved?"

"I don't know and it's not important. Susan, tell me what he wanted to say to you!"

"Pork chops sound good, but they don't reheat well—"

"Susan!"

"Well, you know how I told you that Mrs. Kenny didn't believe that Gus Hoyer ever knew that Merry was his daughter? She's not even sure he knows now."

"Yes . . . Oh, I guess we'd better order," he said, as a historically inaccurately clad serving wench from (presumably) the mid-1700s appeared at his elbow, notepad and ballpoint pen in hand.

"I'll have a green salad with—"

"We have a lovely cracked mustardseed and honey dressing."

"Fine. And some French onion soup—"

"Crock or pot? The crock is bigger."

"Crock. And do rolls come with that?"

"Crackers."

"Then may I have some rolls and biscuits, too?"

"Rolls is rolls and biscuits is biscuits. You have to order one or the other."

"Biscuits. And I'll have a pot of tea. Earl Grey if you have it."

"And you?" She nodded to Jed.

"I'll have the fried shrimp dinner. Baked with butter. Salad with Thousand Island dressing and . . . What vegetables do you offer?"

"Harvard beets, creamed spinach, carrot pudding."

"I'll have the carrots. And a beer."

"Draft or bottle?'

"Bottled."

Their waitress reeled off a list of brands that rivaled the selection of food on the menu.

Jed made his choice. "So Professor Kenny told you that he thought his wife was wrong," he continued when they were on their own.

"Definitely. Apparently, Mrs. Kenny based her belief on the fact that the Hoyers never changed their attitude toward Merry. She was their favorite sitter the year after that summer. They even wanted her to help out the next summer, but Merry had to go to summer school to get her high school diploma. And then, when she went away to college, they claimed to be disappointed that she wouldn't be around to help with their kids. And . . ."

Susan had stopped to peer into the plastic basket which the waitress had plunked on the table between them. It contained two square biscuits and one foil-covered rectangle of "bread spread" sitting on a paper napkin. "And then when Merry went off to college—"

"She didn't go to where her father was teaching at that time?"

"Nope. She went to someplace in Ohio. But only for two weeks. She dropped all her courses, got a refund for half her tuition, took the money her parents had given her for books and incidentals, and went off to the West Coast with friends. She lived there for years without any regular contact with her parents."

"Oh."

"But Evangeline Kenny said that every time she ran into either Professor or Mrs. Hoyer or both of them together, they would inquire about Merry and express concern for her welfare."

"I admit that's a pretty good argument for . . . Oh, thank you," he added as the waitress placed their salads before them. Each imitation-wood bowl contained a generous helping of chopped-up iceberg lettuce topped with three thin rings of red onion, four dried-out slices of cucumber, two radishes trying their darndest to look like roses, and one unripe cherry tomato. The dressings were thick and looked suspiciously like they had been poured straight from bottles. "Doesn't look promising, does it?"

"Nope. They even left off the pair of black olives," Susan said, staring down into her salad. "Oh, well, I'm hungry. I didn't feel comfortable eating any of the homemade goodies the Kennys offered. It didn't seem polite to stuff my face while they recited incidents from Merry's life." She stabbed a chunk of lettuce and popped it in her mouth. "So, anyway, that's what she believes. But the professor isn't so sure."

"Why?"

"A few reasons. The first is that he doesn't agree completely with his wife. He agrees that the Hoyers, when they ran into them socially, were just the same. Happy to talk about Merry, concerned that she might not be making the best choices in her life."

"But . . . ?"

"But he says that he got the feeling that Gus Hoyer was avoiding him on campus."

"Really?"

"Of course, he concedes that this is possibly the result of his own concerns, his own worries."

"That he imagined the change in the other man's behavior."

"Exactly. And it's possible that's all there is. But that's not all he said. You see, Merry knew that Gus was her father. Since the Kennys didn't tell her, she must have found out another way."

"Such as?"

"Snooping through the Hoyers' possessions when she was sitting for their children. In fact, that's what Merry claimed years and years later when she had supposedly gotten her life together and was talking things over with her parents."

"How did she say she found out?"

"She says that it started innocently enough—that she was going through old photo albums that were on a bookshelf in the living room, that she wasn't snooping in drawers or anything like that. But the professor admitted that he didn't necessarily believe her."

"He thought she might have been searching in more private places?"

"Exactly. So she might have found other things."

"I don't understand."

"Because I'm explaining badly. The way Professor Kenny put it is that Merry was always a lot more interested in other people's lives than was necessary—or good—for her."

"She was a snoop."

"Got it in one. So while he admits that she certainly would have had no compunction about looking through old photo albums on a bookshelf, he says that she probably also went through anything she could find while the kids were in bed and their parents were out."

"But could she have found out that Gus Hoyer was her father from the photo albums?"

"She could have guessed from it. Apparently one of the albums was a record of the year Merry was conceived. There were more than a few photographs of Merry's mother and in one or two of them she and Gus Hoyer were embracing. You didn't have to have passed your algebra courses to figure out the dates. That and the fact that Mrs. Kenny had never mentioned attending that college made Merry pretty sure that she had discovered something."

"Sounds logical."

"But her father thinks that she may have discovered something else. Something that didn't have anything to do with her own life, perhaps something the Hoyers wanted to keep secret."

"Are you saying . . ." Jed stopped while the waitress removed their now almost empty bowls (Jed had left his onions, Susan her cucumber slices) and placed their main courses before them. ". . . that Merry was blackmailing the Hoyers?"

"Her father thinks that she might have found out something that made the professor more than a little uncomfortable."

"Which would explain why the Hoyers together acted as though they cared and were concerned about Merry, but when Gus was alone, he tried to avoid Ernest Kenny and didn't speak about Merry."

"Exactly."

"Interesting, but does anyone have any idea at all what Merry might have found out?"

"No. But I think we might be able to find out by asking Gus Hoyer, don't you?"

"Why in heaven's name would he tell you? After all, suppose Merry discovered his deep dark secret. She's dead now, so why would he tell anyone else?"

"Because I just might be forced to go to the police with this information."

"You're going to threaten him? Susan, are you nuts? He might be the murderer, for heaven's sake!"

"I suppose that's possible—" She stopped in the middle of her sentence, a confused expression on her face.

"What's wrong?"

"Just wondering what sort of cheese is in this soup. It sure doesn't have much flavor. . . ."

"Susan!"

"I'm sorry. I . . ." She looked over at his almost empty plate. "How is your shrimp?"

"Terrible. Greasy and overcooked. But that's not important." He stuck his fork into his butter-smeared potato. "What's important is that you may have found Merry's murderer. If she had been blackmailing Gus Hoyer and he finally couldn't take it anymore . . ."

"Do you think she would do that to a man she had recently come to recognize as her father?"

"You don't?"

"I don't know. Her own parents didn't have a remarkably high opinion of her. And she might have felt some sort of misplaced anger at the man who left her mother pregnant, even though he didn't know it at the time."

"So Professor Kenny thinks Gus Hoyer might have killed his daughter."

"No. Besides, that's not possible. Professor Hoyer was in his office when Merry was killed. Being outside that office was my alibi, remember?"

"Oh, right. So what is he worried about?"

"Well, I think what's worrying him is that he thinks his wife might have done it!"

"I . . . Are you sure?"

"Yes. He finally came right out and said it."

"Just like that?"

"Just like that. But not exactly like that. He claims it must have been an accident."

"Could you strangle someone accidentally?" Jed asked, pushing his potato skin to the side of his plate and putting down his fork.

"Maybe. If you were angry enough."

"It does sound like Merry offered her parents a fair amount of provocation, but still . . ."

"I know. That's part of the reason I think it might just be

possible. I mean, suppose Merry had been . . . ah, wearing my backpack and her mother, outraged about something she either did or said, just used one of the straps. . . ."

"To strangle her?"

"It's possible."

"I suppose. And that's what the professor thinks happened?"

"That's what he's afraid may have happened."

"And he actually came right out and said it?"

"Yes, but not until he hemmed and hawed and talked about almost everything else. We were sitting in front of this building when he finally just came out and said it."

"Poor guy. He must be desperate. Did you get the feeling that he thought it was a real possibility?"

"Yes. But he was sure hoping that someone was going to come up with a reason why it couldn't have happened."

"Does anyone know where his wife was that afternoon?"

"Taking a walk in the woods. The very nature center you were in this afternoon, in fact."

"Then she doesn't have much of an alibi. That place is wonderful, but it's also a maze of paths. Someone could be in there for hours and no one would know it."

"That's what Professor Kenny said."

"So what do you think?"

"I think it's time to head home. I have my last midterms in the next two days, and after they're over, I'm going to have to get busy and solve this murder."

THIRTY

ONE OF THE BIGGEST CHANGES TO CAMPUSES SINCE SUSAN had attended college back in the late sixties was the addition of extensive security systems. On the Monday of the second week of midterms, many of the international orange call-for-help boxes had posters hanging below them announcing Rick Dawson's murder and questioning the effectiveness of the campus police. Susan wasn't surprised that the shooting was being talked about more than exams were.

"First that student is strangled, now a teacher gets shot. If this keeps up, my parents are going to wonder why they refused to pay my tuition at NYU," a young woman was saying to her friend as they stood in front of Susan in the cafeteria line at the Student Union.

"What I want to know is why the killer didn't choose a professor from one of my classes—they would have had to cancel the midterm if the professor was shot, wouldn't they?"

"Who knows? But the guy who was killed was just an instructor. I don't think anyone cares much about them."

"Yeah. They spend a lot of time grading papers, though. Maybe the person who killed him was trying for a better grade."

"Yeah. God, can't this line move a bit faster? I'm gonna be late for my next class."

Susan glanced down at her watch and realized that she, too, was in danger of being late. And Cordelia Brilliant had warned that the doors to the classroom would close promptly at the beginning of class and absolutely no one would be allowed in late.

She decided to do without the caffeine and hurried off to her exam.

Professor Brilliant was wearing black: boots, dress, shawl, scarf tied around her long gray ponytail. She was prepared for the saddest of occasions. Susan just hoped her failure in this class wasn't one of them. She slid into an empty seat near the front of the room, pulled her pen and notebook from her backpack, and, putting what she hoped was an intelligent, alert expression on her face, waited for the test to begin.

"This is a blue-book test. Please put away all notebooks. If you've kept up with your reading and listening in class, you shouldn't have any problems." As she spoke, Professor Brilliant walked up and down the aisles, passing out the square little azure notebooks. On top of each she carefully placed a sheet of paper, printed side down. The clock on the wall clicked the hour; she closed the door and returned her attention to the class. "You have forty minutes to take the exam. You may begin now." There was a general shuffling of papers as the students got their first look at the test. "Oh, and I need to see Ms. Henshaw right after class," the professor added. "Good luck, everyone."

Susan didn't know which was worse. There was only one question on the test—no choices, no second chances. And the professor wanted to see her after class. She took a deep breath, picked up her pen, and pushing the second problem out of her mind, got to work.

Time might fly when you're having fun, but sometimes the same thing happens when you're terrified. Susan had just put down her pen and picked up the blue book to reread her work when Cordelia Brilliant's voice interrupted her train of thought. "Time. Please close your books and pass them to your left. If you're sitting on the left side of the room, please bring me your pile on your way out the door."

Susan did as she was instructed, put away her pen, and stood. Her lower back ached and her neck creaked as she twisted her head from side to side. The younger students didn't seem to be having any of these problems as most of them almost leaped to their feet as soon as their tests were out of their hands.

"Please don't forget that I need to see you, Ms. Henshaw."

Susan dropped back into her seat, a stab of pain alerting her to the mistake she'd just made. "Damn."

Students quickly filed from the room, one or two glancing back over their shoulders with what Susan imagined was a look of pity. Was it possible that she was going to fail this class without even having the opportunity to learn the results of the midterm? Professor Brilliant was busy with a young woman, known to be the best in the class. The people they were discussing—truly minor women writers?—were completely unknown to Susan. She moved nervously, trying to find a more comfortable position. There wasn't one. The pain in her back was horrible.

"Is something wrong, Ms. Henshaw?"

Susan grimaced. "I think I've thrown out my back."

"Oh, you poor thing. I know exactly how that is. I have back problems myself. The only thing that helps me is yoga—and some heavy-duty muscle relaxants."

"Yoga. Isn't that offered on campus?"

"As one way for the more artistically inclined to fulfill their gym requirement, yes. But I go to the local Y. I'm afraid I don't have a healthy enough ego to wear leotards in a group of twenty-year-olds."

Despite the pain, Susan felt a smile forming on her face.

"You look relieved. . . ."

"I think maybe my back is getting a bit better," Susan lied.

"Well, those classes are as much a prevention as a cure. You really should look into them."

"I will." After all, if she was going to fail this class, she'd have some extra time on her hands.

"Ms. Henshaw . . . Susan, I wanted to talk with you about something rather personal." Professor Brilliant was flipping through the blue books nervously. She opened one and then another as though searching for something. "I . . . Doesn't anyone listen in class?" she interrupted herself angrily, making a large mark with a red pencil across the page she had just read. The handwriting in the blue book, Susan was relieved to note, was much more artistic than her own. "Sorry. I take teaching very seriously."

"You're a wonderful teacher," Susan said sincerely. "You really are. I love what we're reading in class and your lectures make the Victorian period come to life. I . . . I'm not just saying that because you're holding my midterm in your hand," she added, suddenly embarrassed.

"I'm sure you're not. . . . Yes, Mr. Bernstein, may I help you?"

They were interrupted by a student anxious to discuss his answer to the essay question. Professor Brilliant put him off gently, and when they were alone again, she suggested a more private place for them to speak.

"I'm afraid anyplace on campus is going to be like this. Students who have been avoiding their professors like the plague come out of the woodwork demanding conferences—

or long conversations—during midterms week. I wonder . . ." She stopped. "Look, I don't want to impose. I know you're in the middle of your first midterms in years. After listening to the women in that support group, I do understand a bit better now how difficult it is to be a returning student."

"Don't worry. I'm doing fine. I mean, I think I'm doing fine. If you want to talk . . . or something, I'd be happy to."

"Would you be able to come to my apartment? I live only a few blocks from campus."

"Now?"

"If you're busy . . ."

"No, not at all. I'm free the rest of the afternoon. I have my Italian midterm tomorrow, but I've studied and studied."

"Who's your teacher?"

"Paolo—"

"You mean you have the campus heartthrob? He's a charmer, isn't he?"

"Yes. I just wish I was doing better in his course."

"I wouldn't worry about that. You know how it is with languages. Suddenly you acquire an ear and then you're talking like a native."

Susan suspected that what was true for this woman wouldn't necessarily be true for her. "Well, I hope so." She picked up her backpack but held it in her hands. "I suppose I'd better figure out a better way to carry my books if my back is going to start acting up."

"Do you mind walking? It really is only a few blocks, but with your back . . ."

"No, it feels much better now that I'm standing. And it's beautiful outside."

Cordelia Brilliant surprised Susan by starting to talk, not about whatever was worrying her but about the test. "You were surprised I didn't offer a choice." It was a statement, not a question.

"Yes, I was."

"I decided to try something new. Of course, I won't know how successful I've been until I read the answers."

"How successful you've been?"

"Whether I've managed to get across the ideas I think are the most important."

They walked along and Susan didn't answer for a while. It wasn't until they were out of the building and crossing the campus together that she said, "I never thought of it like that, as testing the teacher as well as the students."

"Most students don't. The gulf between professor and student is wide and sometimes impossible to surmount. Why, look at us. We're close to the same age and we probably have more in common than not."

The walk across campus and then the few blocks to Cordelia Brilliant's home was, as promised, not very long. But it was long enough for Susan to realize that Cordelia was trying to seduce her!

Oh, not sexually, but certainly the professor was attempting to get Susan to like her. And by the time she was waiting for Cordelia—and who would have thought even an hour ago that she would be on a first-name basis with this woman—to unlock the door of her apartment, she understood what the expression "dying of curiosity" meant.

Cordelia's apartment was in an old prewar brick building, one of a row of identical structures that lined a few streets near the college. If she had thought about them at all, Susan would have imagined them full of students. But the hike up the wide dark stairway to the fourth floor, where Cordelia lived, displayed none of the bicycles, posters, and brightly colored flotsam and jetsam of student life.

"Welcome to my garret," Cordelia said, swinging open the door of her apartment.

Susan blinked. The entire wall on the opposite side of the large studio was glass, and early afternoon sun filled the apartment. "It's wonderful!" she enthused, taking a few steps into the room. "Really, really wonderful!" She loved her home, an elegant family place with lots of large, airy rooms filled with memories of happy times. But if she had ever lived alone, this is where she would have wanted to live. The walls of brick and pristine white stucco were hung with original watercolors. A massive white flokati rug lay in the center of the shiny wood floor. Upholstered couches and comfortable chairs were arranged in conversation circles. Against one wall stood a daybed, covered with a blue spread and lots and lots of handmade pillows. A small kitchen area stood on one side of the room. Twin doorways led, presumably, to a closet and a bath. And everywhere, like a dusting of snow on a winter day, there were books, brightly colored paperbacks and hefty dark tomes from the library. On shelves, stacked on the floor, on the bed and a few of the chairs.

"Thank you. I love it, too. I've lived here for almost twenty years. I'm going to hate to leave it."

"Leave it? Why would you ever leave this place? It's perfect!"

Cordelia unwrapped her scarf and her cape and hung them in an antique wardrobe. "May I take your coat?"

"Why would you ever leave this place?" Susan asked again, handing her navy pea jacket over and dropping her backpack on the floor out of the way.

"The building was sold recently. A few of the buildings on this street have been, in fact. The new owner plans to convert them into condos. After renting for all these years, I haven't exactly built up the sort of nest egg necessary to buy a luxury condominium. In a few years this building will be full of students whose parents think buying a condo in this town is a good investment. Their kids can live there while they attend college and then, at the end of four or five years, it can be sold at a profit to the next set of rich parents."

"What will you do?"

"Find someplace inexpensive to live until I retire. It won't be like this, of course."

"But—"

"You know, I haven't given you time for lunch. I'm not much of a cook, but I can open a can of soup and make some tea."

"That would be nice. Would you like me to help?"

"I can add the can of water all right, but I suppose you can stir."

Susan was immediately put back in her place and Cordelia seemed to realize it.

"I'm sorry. I was just feeling a bit defensive. You probably have a freezer full of homemade soups and stews."

"Well, I did when the semester started," Susan admitted. "But how did you know?"

"Have you noticed that there are two groups of women in the returning students' support group?"

"No."

"Women who are happily married and have just discovered their empty nest and women who, for one reason or another, are suddenly living on their own. The women in the first group all seem to have spent the month before school started filling their freezers."

"Guilty."

"Lucky. I can't tell you how cheering a freezer of food would be right now." Cordelia seemed to be paying more attention to the can of Campbell's chicken noodle soup than was necessary. Susan stood by the sink full of dirty coffee mugs and teacups and waited for what was next. "Of course, I didn't ask you here to talk about food or about the sale of my apartment building."

"I didn't think so."

"I can't believe I'm saying this, but I asked you here to talk about murder."

"Merry's murder?"

"Merry? Oh, you mean Meredith Kenny. No, the murder I'm talking about is Rick Dawson's. You see, I ran into Rick occasionally this fall. This isn't a terribly large campus, after all. And he was . . . well, in a panic. And then Merry was killed and I saw him once again."

"He'd changed?"

"Yes. He was almost relaxed. As though he hadn't a problem in the world."

"So I guess he had no idea that someone wanted to kill him," Susan said.

THIRTY-ONE

"**Y**OU'RE SURPRISED."

"Yes. I've been assuming the two murders were connected. Because they dated, you know," Susan explained.

"Oh, yes, I know. And I'm not arguing that they're not connected. I'm just talking about Rick's death."

There was a long silence while Susan waited for the professor to continue. Finally she had to say something. "I think the soup on the bottom of the pan may be burning."

"Oh, how foolish of me!" Cordelia picked up the saucepan and stared down into it. "Do you think it's ruined?"

Susan shrugged. "Why don't we pour it into bowls and taste it? I'm starving."

"Great. Oh, I forgot the tea. There's some diet soda in the fridge. And wine, I'm sure."

"I'll have whatever you're having."

"I'm going to have a glass of California merlot," Cordelia said.

"Sounds wonderful."

The soup was scorched, but Cordelia either didn't mind or didn't notice. They were scraping up the last of the gummy noodles when Susan decided it was time to speak. "I don't want to rush you and I do have the afternoon free, but . . ."

"But of course. I'm very sorry. I asked you to come here. I feed you a horrid lunch and then can't seem to find the words to say what I want to say. I'm just so upset about all of this."

"Why don't you tell me why you thought I could help you."

"The campus police have been asking questions about you. Did you know that?"

"I . . . No, I didn't. When?"

"Back when Merry was killed. And then today In fact, there was an officer in my office asking about you right before the test today. An Irish-American. I got the impression that he doesn't think very highly of you, frankly."

"If his name is Michael O'Reilly, I think you could say that he hates me."

"Any particular reason?"

"Apparently, I'm sort of the archetype of woman who once broke up with him or something like that. Frankly, I think he's nuts. He knows I didn't kill Merry. And I just happened to be going to see Rick Dawson right after he was murdered. . . ."

"You were? You talked to Rick yesterday?"

"No. I went to see him after he was killed, but I didn't know, of course. I wouldn't have wanted to see him if I'd known he was dead."

"You knew Rick?"

"No, I don't think I've ever met him, in fact."

"Then why were you on your way to see him in his office yesterday morning?"

"I . . ."

"Were you in a class with him?"

"No. I wanted to talk to him about Merry. I had just found out that the two of them dated last year."

"But that's been over for quite a while," Cordelia persisted.

"How well did you know him?" Susan asked slowly.

"Too well."

Susan was silent, waiting for more.

"Look around here." Cordelia surprised her by changing the topic. "Everything I own is here."

"This place is wonderful. . . ." Then Susan realized what the other woman was saying. "Everything?"

"Well, not quite everything. I do own a 1993 Toyota Camry and a bicycle that I store in the basement in the winter. But this is it. I don't have a house. I don't have a family. And while I have wonderful friends, it's not exactly the same thing. When I was younger, it was enough. I made enough to live on and what I had left over at the end of each year I spent on travel and books."

"That sounds lovely. Wasn't it?"

Cordelia smiled. "In fact, it was. And it was the life I chose. The life I wanted. But recently—in the past few years—I've started to wonder if it's been enough. I'm a full professor at an excellent school, but I would have gotten where I am faster and more easily if I had been a man. And as for my future, I will have very little retirement income and, I'm seriously afraid, inadequate medical insurance. I am not looking forward to an easy old age," she summed up.

"No, I guess not. But I don't understand. What does this have to do with Rick Dawson? Or Merry Kenny?"

"I'm making excuses for some sort of midlife crisis, I guess. That or a mental breakdown. I've thought about it and thought about it and there's just no other explanation for getting involved with Rick Dawson. None."

"You were romantically involved with him?"

"We had an affair. A stupid affair. Based on sex. I can't possibly imagine what else we might have had in common. There was, I'm afraid, nothing romantic about it."

It was obvious to Susan that Cordelia was embarrassed by her admission and angry at herself as well. "I don't see why you shouldn't have gotten involved with a younger man. Men have been getting involved with younger women for years and years."

"I must admit I am one of those women who thought things would be different when we managed to pry a bit of power and prestige from the male sex. In my case, at least, that hasn't been true."

"I don't mean to sound stupid, but what was wrong with having an affair with Rick Dawson? Besides his age."

"Everything. He was an awful person. He valued almost nothing that I do. His intellectual base was shaky, to say the very least. He cared more about his mental and financial comfort than anything else. He actually told me that he was planning to become a professor because he wanted the credentials to get grants and increase his private practice. He was hoping to arrange his life so that he had as little contact with students as possible—and that he had no intention of submitting to the intellectual rigors of doing original research."

Susan was confused. "Why did you become involved with him?"

"I was stupid. I was ripe to be seduced, I guess."

Susan was silent for a moment.

"I know what you're thinking," Cordelia said. "You're wondering why me. Why he would choose me."

"I . . ." Susan frowned. "I don't want to insult you, but I guess that's exactly what I was thinking. Not that you're not a woman who many men would want . . ." (Heavens, here she was, talking to her English lit professor, and she couldn't seem to manage a cohesive sentence!) "But if Rick Dawson was as shallow as you say . . ."

"He was, and that's exactly why he was interested in me. You see, I'm a member of the committee that approves faculty appointments. I could have stopped Rick from continuing his job as a teaching assistant. It's the first step to getting on the tenure track when he finally becomes a full professor. He wanted to get my vote and I was stupid—and vulnerable—enough to be blind to his ambitions. Not exactly a theme unknown to me, considering my field of expertise, frankly. I felt like a fool when I discovered what had happened. And I feel like a fool telling you about it now."

"But you thought I should know."

"Yes."

"Because you think it might have something to do with his murder."

"Yes."

"Then you don't think the second murder was connected to the first."

"Oh, you misunderstand me. I think, in fact, that Rick's death was definitely connected to Merry's death. What I think is that Rick killed Merry—"

"What? You think . . . Why do you think that?" It was one possibility she hadn't even considered.

"Because he once told me that she kept secrets about people, and by the way he said it, I got the impression that she knew something about him that he would rather have kept private."

"Private from everybody?"

"I guess so. But especially private from me and the other committee members."

"Why?"

"The institutions of higher learning are no longer ivory towers, separate from the world that surrounds them. We are part and parcel of the fray and, I'm afraid, very vulnerable."

"I don't understand."

"Because I'm explaining badly. To put it bluntly, the college is paranoid about being sued."

"Why? By who? Whom?"

A bit of Cordelia's sense of humor returned for a moment. "I wonder if I would have spent so much of my life listening to people correct their grammar if I hadn't been an English professor?"

"Probably not. So who is going to sue the college? Students who don't think they got the education they deserved?"

"Now that's a unique idea. In my experience, most students are trying very hard to get as little education as possible.

"No, it's the parents the college worries about. 'In loco parentis' is a difficult concept—and not bound by many legal precepts. Someone's little darling has an affair with a professor and gets in over her—or his—head and then runs home to Mommy and Daddy. And the first thing Mommy and Daddy do, after drying their poor innocent's tears, is call a lawyer. When I started working, the term used in our contract was 'moral turpitude'—a professor or instructor could be fired for moral turpitude. And the joke was that that meant you weren't to have sex with the freshmen. But times have changed and while there's a lot more sexual activity in some ways, there's also a more encompassing concept of sexual harassment and inappropriate sexual behavior."

"Are you talking about yourself? You and Rick?"

"No. I'm talking about Rick and every female who walked through his door after someone in the sociology department was stupid enough to give him a private office."

"Merry?"

"Including Merry. I'm sure about that. He told me about the affair while it was going on."

THIRTY-TWO

"WELL, LADIES, WE'VE MADE IT HALFWAY THROUGH THE semester."

"More than halfway, actually. There are only six weeks until the first final exam."

"Six weeks! I may shoot myself right this very minute."

Another meeting of the returning students' support group had begun. Susan leaned back in the uncomfortable folding chair and thought about how she had met Jinx just seven weeks ago at the first meeting. And now there she was, waiting for her new friend to join her so that they could go to their creative writing student-teacher conferences together after group. They had both turned in first drafts of their final writing projects. They were both worried. And as Jinx had said on the phone the night before, when she suggested this scenario, misery does love company.

"So what did you get? What did he think of your idea?" Jinx asked as she slipped into the seat beside Susan. The midterm grades had been passed out during her Italian class earlier that day.

"B-. And I think it was a gift. Paolo didn't make as many corrections as he could have on the essay part of the exam and he said I got some extra credit for creativity."

"What did you do that was so creative?"

"Nothing. That's just it."

"Oh, well, apparently you did just fine. A little extra studying and you'll ace your final."

"Don't mention finals!" Susan wailed more loudly than she had planned. "I don't even know if I passed my astronomy midterm yet!"

"Well, I think Ms. Henshaw has probably introduced, rather dramatically, the topic I was planning to pursue today. Of course, those of you who are here apparently did make it through the first midterms you've taken in a while." Cordelia Brilliant had entered the room and the meeting was about to begin.

The group chuckled, but Susan wondered if she heard a death rattle in there someplace.

"Doesn't he ever get off the phone? I swear, every time I come here, he's talking to that wife of his." Jinx plopped on the desk outside Professor Hoyer's open door.

Susan was leaning against the wall nearby. "I thought you would be especially appreciative of a husband who was devoted to his wife."

"Yeah, especially those two, after all they've been through. . . ."

"What do you mean?"

"I shouldn't say anything," Jinx said, lowering her voice.

Susan suddenly realized what was going on. "She was in that support group for women whose husbands had left them! Right?"

"Yes. And she's one of the ones who took him back."

Gus Hoyer, hanging up, looked up from his desk. "Ms. Jensen? I'm glad you're here. I must tell you I found your novel fascinating. Absolutely fascinating!"

"Ms. Henshaw? Ms. Susan Henshaw?" Dr. Madeline Forbes-Robertson waved a sheet of paper in the air. Susan hoped the woman wasn't handing back their midterms in any particular order, since she was the last student in the class to receive hers. "Congratulations, Ms. Henshaw." The paper on Susan's desk had a large B+ scrawled across its top. "Frankly, you did much better than I was expecting you to do."

"Uh, thank you." That was a compliment, wasn't it?

"If you keep this up, you may actually pass the class."

"Minor Victorian women writers. Minor Victorian women writers. Minor women writers in Victorian England." Dr.

Cordelia Brilliant paced back and forth in front of the classroom, blue books in her hands. "I am returning your midterms and suggest that those of you who received less than a C+ should make an appointment to see me in my office. To the rest of you I offer my congratulations and hope you continue to pay attention in class and do your reading."

Susan's book was on top of the pile. Cordelia dropped it on her desk without acknowledging any relationship between them. Susan took a deep breath and opened the book. B+! She suspected that Jed, working on Madison Avenue, could hear her loud sigh of relief.

PART III

FINAL EXAMS

THIRTY-THREE

THE DOORBELL RANG AND SUSAN, STIFF FROM SPENDING TOO much time hunched over Jed's desk, struggled up to answer it.

"Kathleen! I'm so glad to see . . . Is that snow?" Susan interrupted herself, peering over Kathleen's shoulder.

"Just a few flakes. The weather report said that it was going to hold off until tonight."

"I hope so. My last final is this afternoon. And I can't wait until it's over."

"You deserve a celebration. I was going to ask you and Jed over for dinner, but I thought you might be too tired. So I brought this."

It was an example of how exhausted Susan was that she hadn't noticed the dark blue casserole her friend held. "Kath, how nice of you. Bring it into the kitchen. I need another cup of coffee."

"It's a cassoulet. I know it's one of your specialties, but we learned to make this in class and I . . . I really think it's wonderful." She paused. "I wanted to bring you something to show you how proud I am of you. This couldn't have been an easy few months. Well, I know it hasn't been. Jed's been keeping Jerry informed about how hard you've worked. I'm impressed. And more than a bit jealous."

Susan, whose head had been full of Italian irregular verbs, looked at her friend and smiled. "That's one of the worst things about being a mother. When you're taking care of your kids full-time, you're sure the world is passing you by, and when you're busy with other things, you're overwhelmed with guilt. Don't worry. Your nest will be empty sooner than you think and you'll be able to do whatever you want."

"All I want to do is never go to a soccer game again."

"You mean Alex is involved in one of the junior leagues? Kath! Why didn't you tell me—" Susan snapped her mouth shut. Kathleen hadn't told her because Susan had been so self-involved that she probably wouldn't have listened. "Any games left?"

"The last one of the season is on Saturday at eleven."

"Great. Jed and I will come, too. I'd love to see Alex play."

"He'll be thrilled that you're there."

"Kath . . ." Susan didn't know how to begin.

"If you're going to apologize for ignoring old friends for the past few months, please don't."

"I was. And I should."

"Susan, you not only went back to college, you got involved in solving two murders."

"And we can only hope I do better in my classes than I did solving those murders. I couldn't get a handle on either one of them, for some reason."

"Well, you didn't have the local police department to rely on. Maybe you just didn't have enough information."

"You know, that's what I thought, too. But I think it was exactly the opposite. I think it was sort of like the way I was studying for my astronomy quizzes at the beginning of the semester."

"What do you mean?"

"Too much information. I think maybe I just haven't managed to sort out what is important. You see, in the beginning of my astronomy class, I tried to study all the material in the book and everything that Dr. Forbes-Robertson wrote on the board and whatever information we picked up in the weekly star watches, and as a result I flunked the first few weekly quizzes. It wasn't until someone told me that all I needed to pay attention to was the information on the class synopsis that I began to do well on the tests," Susan explained.

"Too much information," Kathleen said slowly.

"Yup. I think I've been concentrating too much on Merry and her background and not enough on what was going on in her life at the time of her death."

"Such as?"

"School."

"You mean the classes she was taking?"

"Hmm . . . and the work she was doing for them," Susan said, passing Kathleen a mug of coffee, then taking the time to put the casserole in the refrigerator before sitting down at the table with her.

"How could you possibly find that out?"

"I don't know. If this had happened in Hancock, Brett would know and he'd tell me."

"You would talk him into telling you."

Susan grinned "Exactly."

"Who else would know?"

"Well, Merry must have registered for all her classes just like everyone else. I suppose the registrar's office is as good a place as any to start. I wonder if they're open this afternoon?"

"Even if they are, how are you going to talk them into giving you the information you need?"

"First I pass my Italian final and then I worry about that," Susan said, glancing at the copper clock hanging on her kitchen wall. "Wish me luck!"

"I do, but you won't need it. You'll be just fine. First you impress that sexy Italian professor, then you'll knock them dead at the registrar's office."

Susan could only hope there was a grain of truth in Kathleen's predictions.

Jinx was waiting outside the door of the classroom as Susan left her Italian final. "How did it go?"

"Incredible. I really think I may have done well. I felt like I knew most of the words on the test. It was almost like it had been written for me."

"You're kidding!"

"No, it was all about food and shopping and going to art museums in Florence."

"Ah, Signora Susan, how did you enjoy your first Italian final exam?"

"It was much better than I thought it would be!" Susan answered her professor without thinking.

"Ah, I tell you and I tell you. A beautiful woman is always a success in Italy. You will be fine. *Bene!*" He slipped into his soft leather coat and walked off down the hall, a bevy of young female students in his wake.

"That's Paolo?"

"That's Paolo."

"I think I'm going to take Italian next semester," Jinx announced.

Susan laughed and then, her expression becoming more serious, changed the topic. "If you're not busy, would you like to go to the registrar's office with me?"

"Sure. I had my last test this morning. I just came over to see if you wanted to get some coffee somewhere. But a stop at the registrar's office is just fine with me. Why are you going? Trying to get your grades early?"

"No. I'm still trying to figure out who killed Merry and Rick Dawson."

"And what does the registrar have to do with that?"

"I wanted to find out what classes Merry was signed up for this semester."

Jinx was instantly alert. "You think they had something to do with her death?"

"Yes. Nothing else had changed in her life except her classes. And . . ." She suddenly remembered something. "And there was that incredibly romantic essay that I found in my pack. It might be interesting to discover which class that was for."

"Good thinking. So how are you going to convince the registrar to tell you about Merry's schedule?"

"I guess I'll figure that out when we get there."

But there was nothing to figure out because no one was there. The sign on the desk by the door said: NO GRADES AVAILABLE FOR ONE WEEK. PLEASE DO NOT ASK in bold print. Underneath someone had written "Sorry, Staff meeting. Be back by two o'clock" in red pencil.

"What are you going to do now?" Jinx asked. "If we knew someone who was a first-class computer hacker, we might be able to get into Merry's file."

"That's right," Susan said, staring at the computer on the desk. "I was imagining everything being kept in file cabinets, but probably everything we want is in the computer." She walked over to the desk.

"What are you going to do?" Jinx sounded worried.

"I wonder what would happen if I just typed in 'Merry Kenny.' "

"Susan . . ." Jinx looked over her shoulder. "Do you think you should do that?"

"I know I shouldn't, but let's give it a try. Would you just stand there and let me know if anyone is coming?"

"Sure. Why not? I've always wanted to be a lookout."

Susan was already sitting at the computer, her fingers flying.

"Hey, you really know how to use that thing, don't you?"

"Not really. Hey, I think I may . . . I'll try it with Susan Henshaw first. Got it! Now let's see. Merry Kenny . . ."

"Meredith. Merry was a nickname, right?"

"Right. Damn!"

"What happened?" Jinx turned back to Susan, alarmed by her expletive.

"Just a typing error . . . I think . . ."

"Hey, are you the woman who can give me my grades? I gotta have 'em. My parents are gonna flip if I failed anything this semester." The young man Susan had watched entertaining a bevy of female students in the Student Union the first week of classes was standing behind Jinx, a worried expression marring his good-looking face.

"Uh, no. We don't work here," Jinx said.

"Then what—"

"We're repairing the equipment," Susan interrupted to explain. "You know how these things are always breaking down."

"Women repairing computers?"

"Can you think of some reason only men can do it?" Susan asked.

"No, of course not. I was just surprised. I don't suppose you could go into that thing and get out my grades?" The look he flashed them was full of charm.

"No way."

"It's a federal offense," Jinx added. "You don't want us to get arrested, do you?"

"You shouldn't even be asking," Susan told him, hoping he would just go away and let her find . . . "Got it!" she exclaimed as Merry's class schedule flashed on the screen.

"You fixed it?"

"Yes. Now if I can just figure out how to print it . . ." Susan looked up. "He left?"

"Sure did. What did you find?" There was a grinding sound and then the printer sprang to life, papers rolling from its front. "How many classes was she signed up for?"

"Oh, shit! It's printing everyone's schedule!" Susan grabbed the top sheet and stood.

"Everyone in the college?"

"I sure hope not. But I'm not going to stay around to find out. Let's get out of here," Susan said urgently.

They hurried away, leaving the building by the first exit they passed.

"Where are we going?"

"Student Union."

There were no seats in the cafeteria, so Susan and Jinx leaned against the bulletin board in the lobby. Notices of offers to share rides home for the holidays fluttered in the chill breeze as doors opened and closed, and just for a moment, Susan considered the coming holidays.

But just for a moment. She was too busy trying to figure out the relevance of Merry's class schedule to have time for visions of mistletoe.

THIRTY-FOUR

"I DON'T SEE A DAMN THING," SUSAN SAID. "WHAT ABOUT you?"

The two women read through the list together: Astronomy, Social Psychology III, Social Systems and Their Effect on Individuals, the Anthropology of the Northwest Indigenous Population, and Yoga.

"Nope."

"Wait a second." Susan grabbed the paper and stared at it for a few moments. "This doesn't make sense. Or am I missing something?"

"What? I don't know what you mean."

"Remember those pages about a meeting that I found in my pack?"

"The ones that were there when the police returned it to you. Yes. What about it?"

"Which of these classes would she have written it for?"

"I don't know. It doesn't exactly fit any of these descriptions, does it?"

"No . . ."

"But why was it in your pack in the first place?" Jinx asked. "I mean, nothing else that belonged to Merry was."

Susan looked at Jinx, her mouth falling open. "Do me a favor and say that again."

"What? That the only thing Merry put in your backpack was the letter. Well, not that she put it in your pack . . . Did she?"

"She must have. And you know what? I'll bet she didn't do it accidentally. I'll bet she wanted it in there. And that she knew perfectly well that it was my pack it was going in."

"Why?"

"Because she put those papers in one pack and her astronomy books and notes in another."

"But why would she do that? Why would anyone do that?"

Susan sighed. "Damned if I know. But I'll bet if we found that out, we'd be a whole lot closer to finding the murderer."

"So what are we going to do now?"

"I don't know about you, but I think I'd better head home. Jed was working late tonight and I left early this morning. Someone's got to walk the dog." Susan suddenly realized that Jinx had never been in her house. "Would you like to come over?"

"I'd love to, but I still have to go over my final rewrite of my story for creative writing."

"Jinx! That was due last Friday!"

"I got an extension."

"Professor Hoyer said there would be no extensions!"

"I know. I'm not supposed to tell anyone about it." Jinx smiled happily. "He really liked what I wrote and he had a few suggestions. I want to make those changes and others. I really thought it would be finished before this, but I keep rewriting the murder scene."

"Well, good luck."

"Thanks. I'm meeting him in his office late tomorrow afternoon to go over my work. See you." Jinx waved, and Susan started out of the building. "Oh, and I dropped a surprise off at your house!" Jinx called out. "I sure hope you like it!"

There are lots of reasons to own a dog. You get a lot of exercise. There are many opportunities to become friends with other dog owners. There's always a good excuse to replace the living room carpeting. But the very best reason is the expression on your pet's face when you come home after a discouraging day.

Susan tossed her pack on the chair in the foyer and squatted down on the floor to greet her dog. "Hi, sweetie, guess what? I'm done with classes!"

The enthusiasm with which Clue greeted this statement was evident in the beating of her tail against the wall.

"How about we go for a long walk?"

The golden was out the door before the words were completely out of Susan's mouth. Fortunately, there was a pile of newspaper near the door waiting to go into the recycling bin. She grabbed the top section, stuffed it in her pocket, and followed Clue.

It was a cold day with just a hint of snow in the air. Her dog was sweet and affectionate. Her exams were over. Her short story was turned in. She could start getting ready for her favorite season.

If only she knew who had murdered Merry and Rick. Susan followed her dog down the street, thinking less and less of school and the murder and more and more of Christmas and her family. Chad would be home in a few days; she'd better get busy baking so he wouldn't be able to claim deprivation. In a few weeks, Chrissy and her new husband would arrive to spend the holiday with the Henshaws. But Chrissy's work schedule and her husband's class schedule would limit the couple's visit to a few nights. Since they would be accompanied by two young bull mastiffs, perhaps it was for the best.

Clue had stopped for a few moments, and Susan spent the time considering whether the newlyweds would be happier sleeping in Chrissy's old room or the much neater and more spacious guest room. By the time she realized that this was a decision Chrissy could make, Clue was finished and she bent down to pick up the resulting mess.

"What a good dog . . ." she started automatically, and then stopped, staring down at the paper in her hand. "What the . . . ?" She was silent for a moment, reading the banner headline.

Susan had been so busy since school started that her normal reading matter had been ignored. There was a pile of *New Yorker*s, *New York*s, *Elle*s, and *Vogue*s on the kitchen counter that she was planning to get to as soon as the holidays were over. She had given up any pretense of reading either the local paper or the daily *New York Times* after midterms. And she'd never been particularly interested in the college's student newspaper, although she had picked it up on occasion. And there it was: the issue published the week Rick Dawson died. With his photograph covering most of the front page.

"I've seen this man before, Clue. He . . . I think he was in my astronomy lab right before my pack and Merry's were switched. I'm sure he was!" Susan folded up the paper and put it in the pocket of her sheepskin jacket. "I remember thinking how good-looking he was.

"This is important, Clue!" She sat down on the stone wall near the sidewalk and thought about what she'd just learned.

By the time Brett drove by, her feet were freezing, but she had a working theory.

"Susan? Is that you? Are you all right?" he called, pulling his police cruiser over to the curb and rolling down the window.

Clue strained against her end of the leash and Susan hopped down. "Brett! I was just wondering if I should give you a call. I think I know who killed Merry Kenny!"

"I want to hear all about it. Do you want to get in or shall I get out?"

"I'd get in, but it's been weeks since Clue was groomed or even bathed. I'm afraid we'll get your car awfully dirty."

"Don't worry about it. We'll put her in the backseat and the next person we arrest can just complain about the dirt.

"Tell me what you've learned," he added as Susan pulled the car door closed behind her and, tearing off her gloves, warmed her hands in front of the hot air vents.

"It's this photo," Susan explained, pulling the newspaper from her pocket and unfolding it for Brett. "This is Rick Dawson."

"So?"

"I've never seen him. Well, I did once. That's the point."

"This newspaper is more than six weeks old."

"Yes, but I just saw it for the first time about half an hour ago."

"So?" he repeated.

"I saw him before he died." She shook her head. "That's not the point. I saw him right before Merry died."

She had his full attention. "Where?"

"In the astronomy lab. Where our backpacks were switched. I've been sitting here thinking and thinking—and now I may know what happened. Would you mind listening to my conclusions?"

"I would love it! Please."

"Okay. Well, to start with, we both know that Merry was a pretty awful person. She seems to have thrived on keeping her parents on edge for years. And, supposedly when she had finally gotten her life together and gone back to school, she got involved with her professors romantically and proceeded to make the lives of those around her uncomfortable, to say the least. She was involved with Rick Dawson last year and I'd bet anything he broke up with her."

"Why?"

"Because she went after him. Oh, you mean, why did he break up with her? Probably because he found out that she could be dangerous to his plans. And then, of course, when he broke up with her, she did exactly the thing he had been worrying about. Am I making any sense?"

"Not yet. But go on. It may come together as you explain."

"You see, I think Merry was angry at Rick Dawson, so angry that she set out to get her revenge. She signed up for a class this fall in which he was the teaching assistant. I didn't know that until I read his obituary in the *Clarion*."

"The *Clarion*?"

"That's the name of the student newspaper. The final paragraph of the article about him lists the classes he was teaching. Merry was taking one of them and I would bet, if we check into it, that one of the requirements of the class was to turn in some sort of psychological profile."

"So?"

"Well, there was a something like a short story in my backpack when it was returned to me by the police. It was about a romantic meeting between a man and a woman."

"And you think she wrote it about Rick Dawson?"

"Yes. And I think she did it for revenge. But, you see, he came into the lab at the end of my astronomy class and she panicked—whether she would have decided not to give it to him or to turn it in or what, we'll never know now. But what we do know is that when Merry saw him, she stuffed the paper away—in the wrong pack, as it turned out. In fact, it was probably her panic that caused her to put it in the wrong pack."

"And you think he followed her to her apartment and killed her?"

"Yes. Because he had a key to her apartment and she didn't. And, apparently, no one else let her in that day. I had her pack, remember, and her key was in it."

"You think he killed her because she was going to make this paper public?"

"Yes. And if the information on those pages was assumed to be true and became public knowledge, he might have lost his job at the college and his reputation would have been ruined. He would never have gotten a job at another school. At least not a good school. And, you know," she added, remembering her discussion with Merry's father about the cause of her death, "Rick might not have meant to kill her. It's entirely possible that he was trying to get the pack off her back and in the struggle she was strangled accidentally."

Brett was quiet for a moment after she stopped talking. "Even if you're right, we'll never know it, will we?"

"Not unless Rick Dawson told someone that he did it before he died," Susan admitted. "Do you think I'm right? Could the story go like that?"

"It's possible, but I sure would like to prove it. Who do you think killed Rick Dawson? Do you think his murder was related to Merry's?"

"Probably. But I have no idea how." She frowned. "I sure hope I did better in my classes than in figuring out the murderers."

"Sounds to me like maybe you figured out half the story just fine," Brett reassured her, turning the corner to the block where the Henshaws lived.

"Oh, fine. Fifty percent. That's still a failure," Susan said, getting out of the car and turning to open the back door to release Clue.

"Don't worry about it," Brett called out, starting to back out of the driveway. "Maybe they'll grade on a curve and you'll end up with the only A in the class."

Susan smiled. "Fat chance," she muttered under her breath.

* * *

There was a rectangular package wrapped in brown paper lying behind an urn of dead flowers. Susan bent down to pick it up, thinking it was time to get rid of the flowers as she did so.

"Hey, look at this! It's from Jinx. She said she was going to drop something off here. I'll bet it's the manuscript of her novel, Clue!" Susan picked it up, tucked it under her arm, and followed her dog into the house. She was proud of her own short story and thankful that she would never have to write one again. But Jinx's enthusiasm for the novel she was writing had grown throughout the semester and Susan's curiosity had grown as well. She was dying to read it—especially the murder scene. She'd make a pot of tea—the real stuff, not something good for her—light a fire in the fireplace in the living room, and read. After all, she had time again, time to do whatever she wanted.

When Jed came home from work, Susan was still on the couch reading. She looked up long enough to accept his offer to pick up something for dinner and, a while later, when she had eaten the meal he provided, had gone on reading. At eleven, Jed said good night, took Clue for a walk, and went upstairs to bed.

At one-thirty-seven in the morning, Susan read the last page of the manuscript, sighed loudly, and got up and poured herself a large snifter of cognac. Clue, who had been lying on the other end of the couch, Susan's cold feet tucked underneath her warm fur, stirred and then went back to sleep.

"I know who did it," she announced quietly. "I know who did it. I know why. But I sure don't know how to prove it."

She wandered off to bed. She would sleep late in the morning. She could do anything she wanted to do. Including driving up north to a small town called Iris.

She had called the Kennys from her cell phone and Evangeline had answered. The professor's wife had agreed to her visit. Susan heard the reluctance in her voice and had understood. She hated doing what she had to do.

"My husband is out for the day." Evangeline Kenny had greeted Susan at her door with the news. "And I can't say I'm sorry. I think . . . I would prefer . . . I don't see why we can't keep this between us."

Susan did, but this wasn't the time to argue. "I appreciate your seeing me" was all she said.

"I didn't have any choice, did I? Come on in."

The house hadn't changed much in the last month or so. If anything, the mums in the hallway were larger and brighter, but the weight of what Susan had to do colored her feelings and today she found the dark paneling depressing and even sad.

"I've been doing a bit of holiday baking," Evangeline said. "Maybe we could talk in the kitchen?"

"Of course." She followed her hostess down the hall and into a delicious-smelling room.

"Tea?"

"No, I'm fine. But get some for yourself," Susan added, thinking it would give the other woman something to do.

"I'm fine. Have a seat."

"Thanks. I don't know how to make this easier," Susan started immediately. "You took something from Merry's apartment, didn't you?"

"I guess that Officer O'Reilly told you that."

"No. He doesn't tell me anything," Susan admitted ruefully. "But the top drawer of her desk was empty. I didn't think anything of it at the time, but . . . Well, I recently read something that caused me to realize how unusual that was. The rest of the place was stuffed—books, clothes, even cosmetics in the bathroom, and food in the refrigerator. You only took the things that you were looking for, didn't you?"

"I didn't go down there to look for anything. My first impulse, in fact, was to tell the police to just give everything to charity. But then I started thinking more about Merry. She . . . Well, you must realize by now that she had a side that wasn't especially nice. I didn't go there to protect anyone other than Merry."

The timer rang and Evangeline got up to remove a loaf of

bread from the oven. Her back to Susan, she kept on talking. "Do you have children, Mrs. Henshaw?"

"Susan. And yes. A boy and a girl. They're both pretty much grown now though."

"I hope they are both leading the lives you wished them to have. Merry . . . Well, Merry rarely chose the path I would have chosen for her. And after she was killed, I decided one of the last things I could do for her was clean up, get rid of anything that might hurt . . . well, let's be honest, anything that might hurt someone else."

"I—"

"I knew the police had gone through her possessions thoroughly. I knew that any clues to her murderer would have been preserved. I just . . . I just wanted to make everything better somehow."

"I understand." Susan stood and put her arm around Evangeline Kenny's shaking shoulders. "I really do. And I'm not here to hurt anyone, but you do know that you can't protect a murderer. You can't just let him get away with killing someone."

"I know. I've thought and I've thought about it. You see, I know he wouldn't kill anyone else. Merry provoked him. Like she always did. That must be why he killed her. He was her father, after all. . . . He—"

"What? Mrs. Kenny. Evangeline. I'm not talking about your daughter's murderer. I'm talking about Rick Dawson's murderer. I'm talking about Gus Hoyer."

"Gus. Augustus . . . I thought . . ."

And to Susan's great surprise, Evangeline Kenny put her head down on her kitchen counter and cried and cried.

THIRTY-FIVE

SCHOOL WAS OVER. THE HOLIDAYS WERE APPROACHING. IT
was a time for getting together with old and new friends. And
the Henshaws were doing that very thing. A fire was lit in the
fireplace and four couples were gathered around it, talking
over the last few months.

"You see," Susan explained to the group assembled in her
living room, "Evangeline Kenny thought her husband had
killed Merry. She took Merry's papers from the desk in some
sort of mistaken attempt to protect him."

"Did you know that?" Jed asked, getting up and pouring
more wine in his guests' glasses.

"Nope." Susan shook her head. "When I went up to Iris
that day, I realized that the professor thought that his wife
might have been involved in Merry's death, but it didn't feel
right to me, so I didn't think much of it."

" 'It didn't feel right to me!' Rubbish. That's why I think
suburban housewives should stay out of murder investigations! The only thing worse is soothsayers and fortune-tellers!
Why . . ." Michael O'Reilly would have continued along these
lines for a while if the woman sitting next to him on the Henshaws' couch hadn't put a restraining hand on his arm.

"Susan did solve these murders, Mike. And I think you
might just think twice before you criticize middle-aged suburban housewives and what they can or can't do. You were
pretty happy with one just last night." Jinx Jensen reached up
and fluffed his hair, a fond expression on her face.

Susan grinned as Michael O'Reilly displayed an unexpected ability to blush. He put his hand on Jinx's black

velvet–clad knee and squeezed. "You're right. I'm wrong and I'll admit it."

"Go on. I'm still confused," Jinx urged, reaching for her glass of merlot.

"You remember when we went through the things in Merry's apartment?"

Jinx nodded.

"Well, the top drawer of her desk was empty—and it was the only thing empty in that room. I thought about that and thought about it some more. Logically, Merry would keep what she was working on in that space—close at hand. So she had probably taken the profile about Rick Dawson from there or at least a part of it. Remember, some of the pages were missing.

"But when I started thinking over her life, I realized two things were happening as the semester started. She was trying to get some sort of revenge on Rick. And she was in an expensive French restaurant with her biological father. Merry was meeting Gus Hoyer for the first time in years. And maybe, once she knew what his reaction to being her father was, she planned on blackmailing him."

"We didn't know that." Michael O'Reilly interrupted her explanation. "We did suspect that you were keeping things from us. When you keep clues from the police, they can't do their jobs effectively. Why do you think I kept following you around all over campus?"

"To get to know Jinx better?" Susan suggested playfully.

"That, too," he admitted to the laughter of everyone else in the room.

"Well, if you hadn't been following Susan all over campus, Brett would certainly have been sleeping better." Erika, who was leaning in the crook of Brett's arm on the couch across the room, spoke up.

Susan was surprised. "You worried about me so much that you lost sleep?"

"Did you think that I just happened to be driving around your block late at night and early in the morning?" Brett asked.

"I . . . I was so involved with what I was doing that I didn't think about it," Susan admitted. "You . . . you were trying to protect me?"

"Well, it wasn't the first time I worried about a murderer deciding you were just a bit too close on his or her trail for comfort and deciding a second murder wasn't all that bad an idea. But this was the only time I worried because a fellow police officer seemed just a bit too interested in your life. Of course, I guess I just wasn't familiar with Michael O'Reilly's method of courting."

"I admit I got more involved in this case than perhaps I should have. . . ."

"Just a bit!" Jinx said, laughing. "You convinced Lillian Wesley that I was some sort of monster for just asking a few questions. I still don't know what you said to her."

"I was just trying to find out more about you," he protested. "After all, I didn't want to discover that the woman I was falling for was a murderer!"

There was more laughter, and Susan, taking advantage of the break, suggested that her guests head into the dining room. "I have a few last touches to add in the kitchen and then we can start our meal," she explained.

"I'll help," Kathleen offered, and grabbing two platters with the remains of a smoked salmon fillet, butter, brown bread, and beluga caviar, she followed Susan from the room.

"Tell me what happened without interruption," Kathleen asked, as the kitchen door swung closed behind them.

"Just let me turn up the flame on the beef," Susan said, heading straight to the stove.

"Okay. It's not all that complicated a story. Rick—"

"—killed Merry to keep her from blackmailing him. He was worried about his future, his career. Right?"

"Right. And Gus Hoyer killed Rick."

"But why?"

"Out of anger. Out of revenge. Out of some sort of misplaced paternal feelings. He killed Rick because Rick killed the young woman he had only recently come to know as his daughter."

"Susan, how did Professor Hoyer know Rick Dawson was the killer?"

"It was in Jinx's novel."

"Jinx is a novelist?"

"Not yet. But if a publisher is looking for a violent mystery novel with lots of sex, she's got it made. As long as she isn't afraid of getting sued."

"Huh?"

"Jinx turned her true-life divorce into a fictional murder mystery."

"So?"

"See, our assignment was to start with something from our real lives and turn it into fiction. I knew that Jinx was writing a mystery novel about her ex-husband. In fact, I knew that he was the victim. What I didn't know is that the suspects were all members of her divorced women's support group."

"You're going to tell a bit more of the story, aren't you?"

"The story isn't important except for the fact that all the women in the group were somehow connected to a college in some way. A few were students, but most of them were the wives of professors."

"So?"

"So when Merry sat in the group telling outright lies about an ex-husband that she didn't even have, there was an important person listening. Gus Hoyer's wife."

"Who knew Merry as a teenager."

"And who had been concerned about Merry from that time."

"And . . ."

"And that was all in the novel—very, very thinly disguised as fiction. Merry wasn't married in the novel—any more than she was in real life—and while Gus Hoyer's wife might have told him all about it when they got back together, it probably wasn't until Merry was killed that Professor Hoyer decided the ex-lover might be Merry's killer. The stories Merry told to the group were pretty much reported word for word in Jinx's novel."

"But . . ."

"See, Merry told Gus Hoyer that she was his daughter—probably that night I saw them together in the restaurant in Greenwich—and his wife had told him about this horrible man Merry was involved with. But Merry never told anyone in the group who the man was—because he was fictional, of course. But Gus Hoyer had no way of knowing that. So here was Professor Hoyer, presented with a new daughter who is then killed within the week. I think he probably started to look for the identity of the killer right away."

"And how did he find him?"

"The same way I did. First he figured out the key thing . . ."

"But how?"

"I was in his office the day that Merry was killed—in fact, possibly when Merry was being killed. And he may have recognized the pack I was carrying, which I accidentally dumped on the floor. So he could see the contents—and the keychain. He put two and two together the same way I did and realized that the person Merry had been involved with may have had a key to her apartment. Of course, he didn't know it was Rick then."

"Keep going."

"Part of the problem is that Jinx isn't a very good fiction writer. She might be able to get a job as a journalist though," Susan mused.

"Susan, tell me how Professor Hoyer knew Rick was the killer from Jinx's book!"

"Jinx changed the names of everyone in the book. But she used their real descriptions; she told me that months ago. And she also told me that Merry had described this mean ex-husband; good-looking, young, blond . . . Rick Dawson. Cordelia Brilliant told me that Rick and Merry were an item on campus. All Gus Hoyer had to do was put two and two together. Rick Dawson killed his daughter. In a rage, he killed Rick."

"Horrible."

"Yes. Horrible. I'm just glad it's all over."

The two friends were quiet for a moment. "Gus Hoyer almost got away with it, didn't he?" Kathleen said.

"What's worse is that Gus Hoyer almost killed a second time. He was meeting with Jinx, supposedly to discuss her novel, but he really wanted to find out if she knew what her story actually revealed. And kill her if she did. When I realized what was going on, I called Brett, who called Mike O'Reilly. Usually the police don't show up for a student-teacher conference. Apparently, Gus Hoyer saw that he was trapped and admitted what he had done." Susan paused to pick up the large pot from the stove and move it closer to the serving dish on the counter. "I understand his lawyer has been going from one psychology professor to another trying to get expert witnesses who will claim that he was psychotic at the time of the murder."

"So . . . What's that?" Clue was barking hysterically.

"Probably those squirrels are in the plants out front again. Clue is really going nuts."

"Sounds like they got into the house," Kathleen said. "That noise is coming from the hallway." The kitchen door opened, letting even more noise into the room—as well as a handsome young man wearing a Cornell soccer-team parka.

Susan spun around and almost dropped the main course on the floor.

Her son was home! And he looked wonderful!

"Chad! I didn't think you were going to be here until next week. I . . . Your hair is so long and you . . . you look taller. Is it possible? Could you be taller? Oh, Chad, it's so good to see you!" And she forgot that maternal enthusiasm embarrassed her son to death and threw her arms around the beaming young man standing in her kitchen doorway.

It was after midnight when the last guests left. Susan and Jed waved to the Gordons as they drove out of the driveway.

"Where's Clue?" Jed asked.

"Chad was tossing a ball to her in the backyard."

"In the dark?"

"Yup. Do you think maybe he's missed us?" Susan asked.

"I don't know about us, but I think you can rest assured that he prefers your food to anything Cornell has to offer. For a while there I was worried that our guests were going to starve." Jed put his arm around his wife's shoulders. "How about going to bed? It's been a long week."

"Okay, but . . . but I want to turn on the dishwasher before I come up."

"Fine." Jed smiled and ruffled his wife's hair. "Just don't talk to him too late. He'll be home for almost a month, hon."

"I won't." She hurried off to the kitchen.

Chad was seated at the table, a cup of hot chocolate in one hand, the last slice of chocolate mousse cake in the other. Clue, ever alert for a chance crumb landing on the floor, sat at attention nearby. But Chad wasn't eating. He was staring at a piece of paper on the table before him. Susan realized it was her grade sheet.

"I can't believe it. I really can't believe it." He looked up at his mother. "I come home to tell my mom and dad that I have a B average for my first semester at Cornell, and would you look at this? My mom's grades are even better than mine!"

A large grin appeared on his face. "Way to go, Ma!"